D0982738

LAWLESS TOWN

Center Point
Large Print

**This Large Print Book carries the
Seal of Approval of N.A.V.H.**

LAWLESS TOWN

A Western Duo

Lewis B. Patten

CENTER POINT LARGE PRINT
THORNDIKE, MAINE

This Circle ⓥ Western is published by
Center Point Large Print in 2015 in co-operation with
Golden West Literary Agency.

First Edition
April, 2015

"Death of a Gunfighter" first appeared in
Best Western (12/55). Copyright © 1955 by Stadium
Publishing Corporation. Copyright © renewed 1983
by Catherine C. Patten. Copyright © 2015 by
Frances A. Henry for restored material.

Printed in the United States of America on permanent paper.
Set in 16-point Times New Roman type.

ISBN: 978-1-62899-526-8 (hardcover)
ISBN: 978-1-62899-531-2 (paperback)

Library of Congress Cataloging-in-Publication Data

Patten, Lewis B.
[Short stories. Selections]
Lawless town : a western duo / Lewis B. Patten. — Center Point Large
Print edition, First edition.
pages cm
Summary: "In two western stories, a reluctant gunfighter and a former
buffalo hider must stand alone against lawless men to make their chosen
towns safe"—Provided by publisher.
ISBN 978-1-62899-526-8 (hardcover : alk. paper)
ISBN 978-1-62899-531-2 (pbk. : alk. paper)
1. Large type books. I. Patten, Lewis B. Death of a gunfighter.
II. Patten, Lewis B. Lawless town. III. Title.
PS3566.A79A6 2015
813'.54—dc23
2014049682

LAWLESS
TOWN

Table of Contents

DEATH OF A GUNFIGHTER

I

At Montezuma, the middle-aged woman passenger left amid the considerable confusion of her welcome, and the driver lit the lamps on either side of the stage. Street and the other man stayed in the coach, which was in itself rather odd for it had been a long, hot day with not too many stops for stretching the legs and moving around. They watched each other carefully in the wanly flickering glow of the two oil lamps, neither speaking.

Street was a tall, lean man nearing thirty. His body possessed that hard-packed solidness that denies any excess of flesh. His dark-bronzed face had the same spare look as his body and was clean-shaven save for the sweeping, tawny cavalry mustache that decorated his upper lip. He wore a townsman's gray broadcloth suit, and while it fit and looked well upon him, he somehow carried it uncomfortably. His watching eyes betrayed a mixture of caution and cynical bitterness.

A relief driver came out of the darkness, put his face against the open window, and asked with bored cheerfulness: "Ready, gents?"

Street nodded briefly, vaguely irritated by the impulse that made him want to avert his face.

Street's fellow passenger said shortly: "Whenever you are."

The driver withdrew. In the cool night, in the thin air of this desert town, each small sound stood alone, plain and very clear. There was the metallic clink of harness rings, the scuffle of hoofs on the dusty street, a voice distantly shouting, and the tinny sound of a saloon piano. The coach tilted as the driver pulled his weight aboard. Then loudly and dwarfing all other sound came the driver's shout and the crack of his whip as he laid it out over the heads of his team. The coach lurched and rolled ahead.

Street settled back. He found a cigar in the pocket of his vest, bit off the end, and lit it. In the match's bright flare he caught the speculative and studying eyes of the other upon him, and knew a rising exasperation—more than exasperation, too, a stirring of dormant anger, because the ancient pattern was again being repeated.

Montezuma's buildings ran briefly past, lights flickering warmly in their windows, and then it was wholly dark save for the two oil lamps. The coach slowed noticeably as it began its ascent out of this deep cañon and onto the high desert plain above.

For the twentieth time in the last couple of days, Ben Rawlins, Street's fellow passenger, dragged the dog-eared copy of *Leslie's Weekly* from his pocket and studied it. Street waited with patient aggravation for his soft-repeated comment—"Damn if you don't look like this guy."—but tonight it didn't come. Instead, Rawlins dragged out of the stub of a pencil and began to scratch idly on the paper, occasionally looking at Street as he did. After that he put the pencil and paper away, shifted around uncomfortably, and tilted his hat down over his eyes against the flicker of the oil lamps.

Both puzzled and relieved, Street puffed his cigar and stared unseeingly out of the window, forgetting Rawlins in the rush of his thoughts. Two years it had been, two endless years. And now they were over. He would see Verona again. He would hold her warmth in his hungry arms. The hand that held his cigar was trembling; all the assurance, all the steady self-possession were abruptly gone from his face. In their place was an odd mixture of fear and anticipation. He finished his cigar and tossed the stub out the window.

By now the coach was rolling along at a fair clip, having negotiated the last hairpin in the ascending road and come out onto the relatively level plain above. Street turned and put his feet up on the opposite seat. He searched for and found a place where he could rest his head without undue discomfort. He tilted his hat down over his forehead but beneath its wide brim he could still see Rawlins. Street stared at the man for a moment, warily weighing the danger he

13

presented, then closed his eyes. Thinking of tomorrow and of Verona, he experienced again that unsettled nervousness that was so unlike him. He smiled wryly to himself. Walt Street, the man without nerves. Well, he had nerves tonight, and it wasn't altogether because of tomorrow, either. It was because of instinct as well, instinct that told him the past two years, their striving and loneliness, were in jeopardy tonight from the man who rode with him. Because Rawlins thought he had recognized a resemblance between the old daguerreotype of Street in *Leslie's Weekly* and the man across from him.

Feeling Rawlins's steady gaze, Street opened his eyes, ruefully amused at the abrupt way Rawlins closed his. *Hell,* he thought, *if it came to that, this Rawlins could be mistaken for Street, too.* He had the same build, if less solid, the same coloring, and the daguerreotype was fortunately a poor likeness, and old. The coach lurched and swayed interminably through the night's still darkness. Into the windows came the sharp smells of the high desert—sage, dust—the smell of horse sweat. Off somewhere to the right a pack of coyotes yammered noisily.

Street dozed. The hard lines of his face relaxed and at last, asleep, he looked only tired. Certainly he did not look dangerous. Rawlins watched him in unmoving silence for a long time. Uneasily he fingered the copy of *Leslie's Weekly* in his

14

pocket, his face a study of indecision. Gradually, how-ever, that disappeared. His eyes took on a widely frightened look and his lips firmed out with determination. Stealthily his hand crept under his coat, withdrew a small pocket revolver. Holding the gun against his coat to muffle the click, he carefully drew back the hammer. Then sharply, loudly he said: "Street!"

An instant before, Street had been asleep, his eyes closed, his breathing steady and quiet. Now he was suddenly awake, his eyes open and clear, watching the man across from him without expression.

Rawlins blurted: "Hang it, you are Street."

"You're sure now, are you?" Street was smiling sourly.

"You're blamed right I'm sure."

"Mind telling me how you got so sure?"

"The way you came awake when I said your name."

"What are you going to do about it?" There was a dangerously still patience in Street's voice.

"Take you in to the sheriff at the next town. By Judas, that's what I'm going to do." Rawlins was scared.

Street said soothingly: "You're forgetting something. I'm not wanted by the law."

"There's a bounty on your head, and I could use it."

Street murmured: "A private matter. Jagger

offered a thousand dollars more than two years ago to the man who killed me. The law is not concerned in it."

Rawlins appeared to be thinking that over. He was tight-drawn, frightened, doubly dangerous because he was so frightened. Street didn't like the look that came into his eyes, the pupils pinpointing. He didn't like the whitening and the tightening around Rawlins's mouth. He'd seen that look before. Hang Frank Leslie and his lousy *Weekly*! With a convulsive jerk, Street flung himself off the seat, rolling, lashing out as he did with a wildly swinging arm. He felt his wrist connect with Rawlins's hand, felt the burn of powder, and then the report was ringing in his ears, deafening in the close confines of the coach. The bullet seared across the long muscles of his shoulder, leaving a numbness but no pain.

Street was unthinking now, an animal fighting for its life. He came scrambling up from the floor, hampered and cursing the close quarters in a softly muttering voice. He threw his weight against Rawlins, who had half risen and was thumbing back the hammer of the gun for a second shot. Rawlins's legs caved and he lurched back against the coach door. It gave with a splintering crash. Street, rising against the man with all the drive of his powerful legs, was unable to catch himself and helplessly followed Rawlins through the door. He cleared the coach wheel by a scant margin and struck the ground on his face and shoulder, skidded an instant, and then began to roll.

The coach went on, its driver's shouts only a background to the sounds of struggle on the ground. Street's dirt-filled eyes found Rawlins and he lunged forward, thoroughly angry now. His body struck the revolver, forcing it upward. His outflung hands groped and one of them closed like a vise over Rawlins's right wrist. He twisted viciously. His other hand had struck Rawlins's cheek bone, flinging the man's head aside. The gun discharged for a second time. An awkward, senseless fight, in which there was neither grace nor skill, ending as senselessly and without pattern as it had begun. Rawlins went limp and fell away, pulling Street down into the dust with him.

Street came clear, knowing with shocking clarity that Rawlins was dead. For an instant he stared down at the man. Growing within him was a wild, outraged anger that this thing could have happened. Two years of striving and danger were wrecked. When it was known who he was . . .

Automatically he stooped, doing this as much by instinct as by conscious thought. He fished his own wallet from his pocket and quickly exchanged it for the one in Rawlins's pocket. He started to straighten, then remembered the copy of *Leslie's Weekly*. He found that in Rawlins's side coat pocket and quickly stuffed it into his own. Then he stood up and faced toward the stage, which had turned around and was now returning.

The driver hauled his team to a halt and climbed down. "What the devil's going on here?"

Street said irritably: "What's it look like? This damned fool tried to kill me."

"Is he hurt?"

"He's dead."

"Oh, Jesus, did you have to do that?" The driver kneeled beside the still form and struck a match.

"What would you have done? Let him kill you? Besides, I never even had my hand on the gun. He shot himself."

The driver fished Street's wallet from the dead man's pocket. He straightened. "Who was he?"

Street took the *Weekly* from his pocket. "He could be this Walt Street. He looks something like the picture."

He struck a match, held it over the paper. The picture of Street stared up at him, decorated with a penciled cavalry mustache. So that was what had made Rawlins so sure. He let the match burn his fingers and dropped it. But the driver had seen the penciled mustache and had thrown a quick glance at Street. He said: "You even look a little like Street yourself."

Street made himself laugh. "We were talking about that. I said he looked like the picture and he said . . . 'Hell, you do, too.' He drew the mustache to prove it. But he must have got scared. Because he pulled down on me while I was asleep."

The driver whistled. "You're lucky, man!" He whistled again. "Lordy! Imagine that. Walt Street riding my coach and I didn't even know it. You're due to collect that bounty, friend."

"Yeah." Street's tone dismissed the subject. He growled: "Well, hell, are we going to stand here jawing all night?"

The driver stared at him. "You're a cool one, ain't you? I'd be shaking like a leaf, if I just killed a man."

Street muttered: "Who says I'm not? I just don't want to stand here, looking at him all night." He managed to make his laugh shaky. "Let's put him in the coach. I'll ride the box with you the rest of the way."

Together they lifted the dead man and put him in the coach. The driver found a piece of wire and wired the door shut. Street mounted the high seat beside him and the coach lurched ahead.

Out into the high brush it went, turning, the driver cursing and popping his whip. Then back on the road and ahead toward Escalante and the waiting Verona.

Now a new worry entered Street's mind. Verona would give him away. He shrugged that off. No. She'd not cry out his name. She was as interested as he was in keeping his identity a secret. She was not even using his name, but her own, Verona Ormsby.

The stage driver chattered excitedly over the noise of the thundering coach. He speculated and guessed at the reasons for Street's presence on his coach. He said: "Mebbe he was going to rob the bank at Escalante."

Street said dourly: "He ain't an outlaw."

"Hell! All them gunmen're outlaws. What's the difference? You kill a man or you rob a bank. Which is the worst?"

Street shrugged, silent. You could never explain. You couldn't ever make people believe the killings were unavoidable, even sometimes justified. You couldn't make them understand how the thing got started, a man stealing a horse out of your father's pasture. You yell at him to stop, but he doesn't stop. You fire, and the man falls. Only later do you discover that he is Lee Myers, the famous gunman. So overnight you're famous yourself. Being a kid and having no defense against the deteriorating effects of fame, you begin to pack a gun and to practice with it. Your old man takes a buggy whip to you, trying to make you stop, and you run away from home. Now you're on your own. You're Walt Street, the kid who killed Lee Myers. And along comes another tough kid who wants to be the kid who killed the kid who killed Lee Myers.

Street laughed softly, bitterly and wholly

without humor. You're twice a killer now and learning to be tough and hard. The years and the towns flow past in a seemingly unbroken stream. And then you fall in love. Verona Ormsby. Verona Ormsby Street. A girl in one of the towns you pass through, a girl with copper hair, green, laughing eyes with tiny flecks of brown in them, a girl to make your blood run hot. Maybe she's taken with the fame you pack in your holster. Maybe there's a yearning for excitement and adventure in her. Anyway, she marries you. Her parents try to run you out of town without her, but you take her anyway—on a fast horse. She loves you and you love her. But love can't live on the run. It can't live with fear, and distrust, and cold camps in the open and dreary hotel rooms. It can't live when you come home to her with that look in your eyes that says you have killed again.

So one day you come home and she's gone. There's a note, a tragic, half incoherent note. *Walt, put the gun away for two years. I'll wait, Walt. I'll wait and then we can start again.* Angry at first, you are, wildly, violently angry. Then hurt. Then lonely. And at last you admit that she was right. So you leave the country. You put the gun away and you ride. You change your appearance by growing a mustache. You get an honest job and save your money. When the two years are over, you visit the town where you first found her. Maybe you've succeeded. Maybe

you've made a man of yourself, because her father, so bitter before, now tells you where to find her. Escalante, Colorado. You come to her with clean hands, your heart blazing with the flame of your need for her.

Street's face contorted in the darkness. His eyes were dead, still, bitter. Because of an article in *Leslie's Weekly* and an old daguerreotype—because of that bounty Jagger put on him for killing Jagger's brother—because of these things it all went sour. Tonight he'd killed in self-defense. He hadn't even really killed. But would Verona believe that? When he came into town on a crest of this notoriety, would Verona believe he had changed? He knew she wouldn't.

II

Through most of the night the stage brawled along across the seemingly endless reaches of desert, but when dawn's gray streaked the eastern sky, it silhouetted the towering rims of the Cougar Plateau. The stage driver, having talked himself out during the night, now drove with relaxed and bored concentration.

Gray crept across the desert floor and at last the clouds over the Cougar Plateau's high rims turned pink. The sun came up, laying a clean, clear magic of light across the land, giving color to the desert flowers, to the purple haze of distance to north and south. Dawn's chill evaporated with the warm rays. Street straightened from his relaxed position, fished for a cigar, and asked: "How long now?"

"Hour. Mebbe a little more." The driver was cryptic and Street grinned at him.

The driver was a small, oldish man and now his face was coated with a light film of dust. Around his eyes, where the wind had fetched moisture, it had streaked and turned to mud. He had not shaved for several days and the stubble on his face was mostly gray. His eyes were blue and friendly, framed with crow's-feet from his constant squinting against sun and dust.

They came into a wide cañon formed by a split in the plateau, and after another ten minutes reached a bridge crossing a tumbling, roaring whitewater stream. Shouting over the noise of the water, Street said: "Thirsty. Dirty. Mind stopping for a minute?"

The driver shook his head and pulled up. Street got down stiffly, yawned, and walked off to the bank of the stream. He dropped to his belly and drank, holding his body off the ground with his hands. Then, squatting, he removed his hat and splashed the icy water over his face, scrubbing vigorously. He got up, ran his fingers through his hair, and replaced his hat. Face dripping, he returned to the coach, refreshed.

The driver, standing beside the coach, was eyeing him oddly. "Took you fer a townsman," he said. "Though you drink like you've drunk that way before."

Street grinned. "Getting down, you mean? Best way, ain't it?"

The driver shrugged, and climbed aboard. Street followed and the coach rolled on.

The horses were tired, having traveled steadily since the last change at midnight, but they knew this run as well as the driver. Knowing it was near its end, they quickened pace. The cañon gradually narrowed and the walls of the plateau grew steeper. Then, as they rounded a bend, Street saw the scattering of buildings that was Escalante ahead. And like the blow of a fist in his belly the fear hit him. It was not fear of anything physical, nor even fear of the repercussions that might arise from the killing last night. It was fear of meeting Verona. It was fear that she would not believe he had changed.

He caught the driver watching him. The man said sympathetically: "Feeling peaked, son? Wouldn't blame you if you was. Something to ride into a strange town like this, a dead man behind. Something to step down offen a coach and say . . . 'Walt Street in back there. Dead. I killed him.'"

"I didn't kill him. It was an accident." Street's voice was strange.

"Accident, hell! Suppose you wasn't so quick on your feet. Suppose you wasn't now? Would it be him laying back there? No, sir. It'd be you. You killed him all right."

Street's hands clenched. His face was twisted, white. His eyes were wild and he yelled savagely: "Shut up, damn you! Shut up!"

The stage driver started violently. He shrank away from Street as far as the narrow seat would allow. He opened his mouth, but he didn't say anything. He swallowed as though his throat were dry. Finally he got out a shaky: "Hell, no need to take on so. What'd I say wrong?"

Street fought himself for control. He made his voice calm. "You didn't say anything wrong. It's me. I'm sorry. Guess I'm more upset than I realized over last night. I guess I don't like to talk about it."

The driver relaxed. He shifted back to where he had sat before. He said: "Know how you feel. Sure I do. Ain't every day a man does what you had to do. Reckon I'd feel the same way."

But Street did not really hear him. They were rolling through the outskirts of Escalante now, through a scattering of squalid shacks. A child yelled and a pack of them came running to line the road and wave. The driver waved back, grinning perhaps a little proudly. He was an idol to these children, and he played the part. But Street's eyes were on the main part of the town

25

ahead. Which house did Verona occupy? Would he see her on the street as they rolled in? Or would he have to wait until later?

Escalante was not a large town. Its business section contained but two streets, Main and Cougar, running parallel and a block apart. Along Main were the hotels, the better saloons, and the retail stores. Along Cougar were the livery stables, a lumberyard, a feed store, and two of the more disreputable saloons. Also on Cougar was the stage depot and freight yards.

By the wide verandah of the Escalante Hotel the driver turned, swinging wide amid a cloud of dust. A handful of townspeople stared without much interest, but Street saw no women among them. Down the block they went, swinging wide again into Cougar. A horseman spurred to avoid them, grinning and raising a hand to the driver. They came into the yard of the stage depot, stopping before a side door.

Hostlers came to unhitch the team. The driver called down to a man who came out the depot door: "Get Ralph Coe! Got a dead man in the coach."

That widened the other's eyes, removed from him his air of agreeable boredom. He yelled out into the slab-fenced yard: "Alf! Come 'ere!"

Street climbed down, his body stiff and aching now. Where Rawlins's bullet had burned his shoulder, it was beginning to feel sore and stiff.

Apparently the slight wound had bled a little for Street could feel his shirt sticking to it.

A boy of perhaps eleven came running from the back of the yard. He was tow-headed, tousled as though he had not bothered to comb his hair yet this morning. But he had a cheerful, freckled face. The man who had called him said: "Fetch the sheriff, Alf. Tell him we got a dead man in the coach."

The boy's eyes widened. He hesitated, looked at Street. Street grinned at him and the boy grinned back. Then he was off like a streak.

The horses were led away and a couple of men began to unpack the baggage and freight from the boot. And Street was forced to another decision. Should he claim his own luggage, or that of Rawlins? Mentally he inventoried the possessions in his own luggage, cataloging their value and replaceability. There was a picture of Verona, which he would hate to lose. There was his gun, holster, and cartridge belt, which, he decided, he would be better off without. Aside from those two things, he carried only clothes, razor, and the odds and ends a man finds essential when traveling. Already he had given up what money he had managed to put aside, trading that for whatever identification might be in Rawlins's wallet. His expression turned rueful as he stepped forward. Rawlins had probably been stony broke or he wouldn't have tried so desperately for that $1,000 bounty last night. Ignoring his own luggage, Street picked up the battered suitcase that had belonged to Rawlins.

The boy, Alf, came trotting back, followed by a tall, gaunt man in his late sixties. The man opened the coach door and peered inside. Closing it, he turned. His face was deeply seamed, his eyes neutral to friendly. He wore a long, drooping mustache, the ends of which were stained with tobacco. He tipped back his disreputable broad-brimmed hat, revealing hair that was thinning and snow-white. He was as dark as an Indian, his dark skin and white hair creating a rather striking contrast. His shoulders were rounded with age, but his step was firm enough, as was his voice. He looked at the driver, then at Street beside him. He said: "Seen you somewheres, ain't I?"

Street said: "I doubt it. I'm Ben Rawlins."

The sheriff nodded. "That's it, then. You look like Will some."

This was puzzling to Street, but he held his silence. The sheriff, Ralph Coe, asked: "What's this now? Who killed that one and who is he?"

The driver got out a breathless, excited: "He's Walt Street, that's who he is, Sheriff. This here fella had a scuffle with him. Gun went off."

If the sheriff was surprised, it didn't show. He stared with dry amusement at the excited driver. He said: "All right, Perry. Send the body to the feed store. I'll have Doc look at it soon as he gets back to town." He looked at Street. "You'll be around a while. I expect you've come to take over Will's place. Want to talk to you, though, 'fore you go out there."

Puzzled, Street nodded. He picked up the suitcase and headed for the hotel, a tall, dusty man with a shadow of weariness lying over his features, a tear in the shoulder of his gray broadcloth coat. As he came into Main, his eyes roved up and down the street, lingering with restrained excitement for an instant on each female figure they touched. His face settled a little and he turned to climb the steps. Perhaps it was better this way. Perhaps it was better to let Verona get the news and see her after the first shock had passed. Give her a chance to decide what she would do. But he was hungry for the sight of her, hungry to feel her warmth in his arms.

He signed the hotel register and climbed the stairs to the second floor. He found his room, went in, and closed the door behind him. Then he fished out Rawlins's wallet, emptied it on the bed, and stared down at its contents. $23—Street had been carrying nearly $600—a bad trade. There were a few business cards, all bearing Rawlins's name. It appeared he had been a watch salesman. There was a folded and crumpled letter that Street unfolded and read. Headed Escalante, Colorado almost a month ago, it advised that Will Rawlins was now deceased and that so far as

29

could be determined Ben Rawlins was his only kin and as such entitled to inherit his worldly goods. It did not list the worldly goods, but hoped that Ben Rawlins would be able to come at once.

Street muttered: "The blamed place had better be worth six hundred." He put the suitcase up on the bed, untied the strap that was knotted around it, and let fall open. Dirty shirts and underwear, an extra suit, fortunately clean, a single clean shirt. Street thought bleakly: *What can you offer Verona now? Something better than you did before? No job. No money. No name. Just a lousy shack out in the hills somewhere.* He slammed the suitcase shut with a sour residue of anger, crammed the contents of the wallet back into it, then stuffed the wallet into his pocket.

His shoulder was hurting so he shucked out of his coat, vest, and shirt. Peeled to the skin, he backed against the cracked mirror and peered at the bullet welt, angry red against the white, smooth muscles of his shoulder. Lucky. It had barely broken the skin. He poured water into the wash pan, and then began to wash. He remembered the shaving things in the suitcase, got them, and began to shave.

Before he was finished, he heard steps in the hall, and an assertive knocking on his door. Without turning, he called—"Come in!"—but he kept his eyes on the mirror in which he could see the door.

The door opened and a man came in, a man Street had not seen before. He closed the door behind him, put his shoulder against it, and insolently surveyed Street's back. He was a short man, stocky and swarthy of skin. His hair was black and crisp, curly and uncut for a long time. His chin and hollow cheeks were covered with a two days' stubble of black beard. A man of monstrous self-assurance, this, a man who mocked the world and all who were in it. He smiled, showing teeth that were white and firm. "You're Ben Rawlins, I take it." His voice repeated the casual insolence of his eyes.

Street nodded without turning. He had missed no small detail about this man that could tell him more of the man's character. Nor had he missed the peculiarly efficient-looking gun at the man's thigh, butt forward on the left side. Cross-draw man. Probably damned fast. A bully, too, from the look in his eyes. One who insisted on respect tinged with servility. Street's failure to turn had been deliberate and it kindled a spark of anger in the ebony eyes of the stranger.

Street said, irritated immeasurably by the man's manner: "What do you want?" He ran the razor down his long jaw.

"Hang it, turn around when you talk to me."

Street's eyebrows lifted. Anger that had smoldered in him all night now bubbled to the surface. He started to whirl but caught himself in time. His mind cautioned: *Don't take his bait. You're Ben Rawlins not Walt Street.*

He turned slowly, concealing a part of his anger but letting just enough show. He said: "Just who the hell are you and what do you want?"

"Bauer. Max Bauer. Ramrod for Gunhammer."

Bauer was dressed in an untidy black suit. A carelessly knotted black string tie held the collar of his shirt together but the second button was gone and the gap in his shirt exposed a thick mat of black hair on his chest. Lower, there were stains on the shirt, probably from food or a spilled drink.

Street experienced that odd, instant dislike that occasionally comes to a man on his first meeting with another. It almost amounted to hatred, so strong was its impact. Street said: "So you're Max Bauer, ramrod of Gunhammer. That still doesn't tell me what you want."

"Why, we're neighbors. I called to pay my respects."

A spare grin split Street's face. He said: "All right. Pay 'em and then let me finish shaving."

He was rewarded by a violent, unstable flash of anger in Bauer's eyes. But he had to admire the man's iron control of himself. Bauer's hands clenched with effort. His smile was a mere split of his narrow lips, a showing of his flawlessly white teeth. He murmured: "I came to say something and I'll say it. Gunhammer is offering you five hundred for Will's outfit. Twenty a head for the cattle, cows, calves, horses. Think it over." With a final, baleful glare at Street, he turned, yanked open the door, and went out, slamming it viciously behind him.

Street heard his clipped steps retreating along the corridor. Thoughtfully he returned to his shaving. He'd made an enemy of that one without half trying. Bauer must have lots of enemies in this country or else it was populated with gutless men. $500. And $20 a head for his stock. Not bad, but a deal he could never take, because a sale of land required a signature, and because if Street ever signed a deed he would be a forger, a criminal. Well, what the devil, he didn't want to sell anyway. He finished shaving and dried his face, wondering at the odd uneasiness that possessed him. Rationalizing, he discovered it was caused by a belief that this Bauer would not give up easily. Gunhammer wanted the Rawlins spread, and Bauer had the look of a man who got what he wanted. Hang it, couldn't a man ever live in peace? Must trouble forever dog his unwilling heels?

III

There was a heavy, oppressive weariness in Street now that the week-long stage journey was over. His body ached from the ceaseless pounding of the coach's thinly upholstered seats. His eyes fought to close and a leadenness was in his mind. Yet there could be no sleep for him, and this he knew well. He wanted no rest until he had seen Verona. He shrugged into the clean shirt, then slipped on the dead man's clean trousers and coat, absently transferring the copy of *Leslie's Weekly* from his own coat to this one. He pulled on his boots and ran his discarded and soiled shirt over them to remove their dust.

The lobby was cool, tile-floored, and lined with black leather-covered sofas and chairs. The verandah held the usual sprinkling of loafers, smoking, talking, eyeing each woman who walked the dusty street. Street fished for a cigar and recalled at once that he had left his vest in the room. He walked back into the lobby and stepped to the counter. He started to order cigars, remembered the $23 in his pocket, and bought a sack of tobacco and papers instead. He paused again on the verandah and shaped a cigarette. With it lit and dangling from his lips, he stepped down to the walk and rounded the corner, heading for Cougar Street.

Ahead of him walked a woman, altogether unmistakable. Oh good Lord! Verona! Involuntarily Street broke into a run. He stopped abruptly. After two years, let their meeting at least have dignity. Let him meet her as a man who has fought himself and won, not as a disheveled, breathless one who has pursued her nearly a block. His eyes devoured her. Verona still had that straight, proud walk, her head high, blazing copper in the sun. Her figure was perhaps a little fuller, he thought, but he liked that. She had been too thin those last days of their life together.

She walked between two men, one of them clearly identifiable as Sheriff Ralph Coe. The other, shorter than Coe but half a head taller than Verona, Street had never seen before, but the man was young, that was obvious. He appeared to be, at this distance of nearly a block, quite handsome. Street felt a stir of jealous fear. Suppose Verona had not waited? Suppose she had divorced him already, and married someone else? The thought was intolerable, so Street suppressed it. But he found that in spite of himself he was hurrying.

Ahead, the trio rounded the corner and disappeared. Street strode along at a pace just short of a run. He came around the corner just in time to see the three enter a tall, weather-beaten building on whose side was painted in black, block letters: OVERMEYER FEED COMPANY. Below that, in smaller letters, was the word:

UNDERTAKER. It was quite common in towns too small to support a full-time undertaker for someone in another business to combine undertaking with it. Apparently such was the case here.

There was a wagon dock at the side of the building, covered by a board awning. A few bales of hay sat on the dock, along with several burlap sacks of grain. Street climbed the two steps from street to walk and paused before the door. Unconsciously he wiped the palms of his hands on his trouser legs. Then his lips firmed out and he stepped inside.

The front office smelled of hay and grain, a thoroughly familiar smell, and was empty. From the open door of an adjoining room, Street could hear voices, could hear the full, mature cadences of Verona's voice. His boots seemed to make a thunder on the bare board floor of the room as he crossed. He paused in the doorway of the adjoining room and stared inside.

Verona stood with her back to him, dabbing at her eyes with a scrap of handkerchief. On a long, oak table laid the corpse, a sheet over him. Coe stood at the corpse's head, his hand holding the sheet away from the face so that Verona could see. This became suddenly clear to Street, and he knew a trapped feeling. Coe had rummaged through his luggage and had found Verona's picture. He had brought her here for the purpose of identifying the body. But Street seemed unable to concentrate on this new complication. His eyes drank in the beauty of the woman. How old was she now? Twenty-three or -four, he guessed. He remembered her twenty-first birthday. They had spent that one together. In Abilene. He'd bought her a brooch, a cameo brooch from a saloonkeeper who had made a loan on it. And he'd managed to get her a bunch of violets, begged from a kindly gray-haired woman out at the edge of town. Coming up the street to the hotel, he'd been jumped by a scout for a trail herd who had stubbornly forced a fight. Street had run from that one, ducking into a building entrance, and running out the back door. It had been one of the few fights he'd run from, and he'd only done it for Verona. But he'd lost both brooch and violets and had come to her empty-handed. Perhaps she had made up her mind to leave him that day. Thinking of it now, he guessed she had.

Coe turned and saw Street in the doorway. His eyes held Street's and his head made an almost imperceptible negative shake. He said: "There's no doubt, then, Verona? It's him?"

"Yes. That's my husband, Mister Coe." Her face twisted. She dabbed at her eyes with the handkerchief and turned. Her eyes touched Street's. A shock that was almost physical ran through him. This shock held him utterly motionless for the barest instant. He saw Verona's eyes widen, saw her face go quickly pale. Her full, red lips parted, and her breathing hastened.

Coe stepped into the breach. "Verona, this is Ben Rawlins. The man Street tried to kill last night."

Street had started forward. Now, suddenly, he caught himself. The time was not yet. Verona's eyes held no welcome for him. Instead, they showed him a flash of pure hatred. Actress? Lord, she was that all right. She wanted the name of Walt Street buried with the body of Rawlins on the oaken table.

Verona's voice was low, filled with venom. She hissed: "He's a liar! He killed Walt for the bounty."

As though she would attack Walt Street, she came gliding forward, her face a study of hate. Was this acting, too? Walt Street stepped backward involuntarily. Coe jumped forward and caught Verona's arm. His wise old eyes held a certain puzzlement mingling with the warning he flashed at Street. He said swiftly: "Get out of here. I'll see you later."

"Sure. Sure." Street backed out the door and crossed the bare front office. He walked around the side of the building and leaned against the wagon dock. He fished the sack of tobacco from his pocket and built a cigarette, his hands trembling. He licked the paper thoughtfully, put it between his lips, and then forgot to light it.

Was this the homecoming he had built in his mind for the past two years? He scowled with bleak despair. Verona had not been acting except as she failed to expose him, except as she accepted him as Rawlins. The hatred in her eyes could not have been feigned. Then, she thought, he had not changed. He had come to her after two years, again with blood on his hands, and she hated him for that. She'd waited for the two years to end just as he had, and her wild disappointment in him turned to hatred.

Street felt a stir of pity for this woman who had been his wife, who, he hoped, was still his wife. The years had not been easy for her. She had built her hopes as he had built his and today her hopes were cruelly shattered by the belief that Street was still a killer. No wonder the hate in her eyes looked so real.

He saw her come into view, closely followed by Coe and the other man. Coe glanced toward the dock, hesitated, spoke to the two, and then halted. Verona and her male companion went on. Street studied her companion, jealousy tingeing his study with dislike. The man was not as tall as Street, but he probably weighed as much. Without being stocky, there was still a blocky solidity about his body. Dark-haired, dark-eyed, he moved with an odd grace unusual in men used to the saddle.

Coe came slouching toward Street, his old eyes

sleepily alert. He stopped before Street, silent for an instant, and then he said: "Don't be too hard on her, Rawlins. Don't be too hard. Seems she quit this Street two years ago, hoping he'd change his ways. She heard from her father last week saying Street had come looking for her. She thought he'd changed." Coe shrugged wearily. "Guess a man doesn't change much. Guess Street hadn't. It was likely quite a blow to her."

Street felt the strangest urge to confide in this seemingly gentle old man. He restrained it with an inward smile. Probably the quality that made men want to confide in him was one of the sheriff's most valuable assets. Besides, Street had not missed the puzzlement in Coe's eyes back there in the room with Verona. Coe had sensed that something did not ring true in the meeting between Street and Verona. He had sensed that and in his gentle, tenacious way he'd keep worrying at it with his mind until he puzzled it out. Well, suppose he did? The truth had to come out sooner or later. Street had no intention of letting things ride indefinitely this way. He only wanted Rawlins's identity long enough to convince Verona he had done what she asked. He had changed. He had put aside the gun. He had to convince her that the killing last night was as unavoidable as winter's snow, as the change of seasons. But to do that, he had to see her.

Coe said: "Been to see Hayden yet?"

It was hard for Street to take his thoughts from Verona. He looked at Coe blankly for a moment. Hayden? Then he remembered. The name signed to the letter he had found in Rawlins's wallet. He shook his head.

Coe said: "He wants to see you right away. Something's come up, he said."

Street shrugged. "Where will I find him?" There was an almost total lack of interest in his voice.

Coe studied him. "Down toward the end of Cougar. His office is that little yellow building next to the lumberyard."

Street straightened, threw his unlit cigarette away.

Coe said: "Verona upset you, didn't she?"

"She's a beautiful woman. It's upsetting to see that much hate for yourself in any woman's eyes."

"I suppose it is." Something about Coe's manner held Street still.

Coe hesitated and finally said: "I ought to warn you. This place of Will's . . . Gunhammer wants it bad."

"Why?"

"It lies between Gunhammer and Chain. Gunhammer's owned by the Lacey tribe . . . Bruce, Glenn, Nick, and the old man, Brandt. It was Bruce you saw with Verona just now."

Street waited.

Coe went on: "Don't quote me. But Gunhammer's

getting too small for the Lacey bunch. The boys are men now and they want something of their own. Particularly Bruce. Gunhammer's big, but it ain't big enough to split four ways. On the other hand, Chain's got more graze than they can stock. So Gunhammer's figuring to move in. Your place straddles the only decent trail between 'em."

Street murmured: "I got an offer a while ago."

Coe's eyebrows raised questioningly.

Street said: "Five hundred. I turned it down."

There was careful approval mingled with doubt in Coe's ancient eyes. He said: "Used to be a watch salesman, didn't you? That's what Will said."

Street nodded, suddenly cautious. If he were going to maintain this masquerade, he would have to appear more timid. He asked: "Tell me something? Will Gunhammer get tough about it?"

"Might. Probably will."

"And where do you stand?"

Coe looked away. He didn't answer at once. When he did, Street thought he detected a note of shame in his voice. "Twenty years ago I'd have told you not to worry. But I've got an invalid wife in a sanitarium over in Denver. It takes money to keep her there. So whether I like it or not, I've got to advise you to be careful. I'd even go so far as to advise you to sell."

Street grinned sourly. "At least you're honest."

Coe's expression was bleak. "It's all I can give . . . honest advice."

Street said dryly—"Thanks."—and turned away. Without looking back he walked down Cougar toward the large frame building with the lumber piled behind it. He passed it and came to a smaller frame building on whose window was the sign: JEROME HAYDEN, ATTORNEY-AT-LAW.

The morning sun was warm and Street's forehead was damp. He could feel the clamminess in his armpits, but that had no connection with the heat. He always perspired under severe nervous strain. He opened the door and went in.

The place was musty, cool, and filled with cigar smoke. Behind a roll-top desk sat a man, the fattest man Street had ever seen. His face was pink, almost completely round, and wholly without wrinkles. His eyes, close-set, were bland and inquiring.

"Mister Hayden? Coe said you were anxious to see me."

Hayden got up, reminding Street of an elephant he had seen once rising from a prone position. Hayden's suit was like a tent, wrinkled and untidy. His large, full-lipped mouth split in something that was undoubtedly meant to be a smile, exposing enormous, gold-filled teeth. Street felt somewhat overwhelmed. Hayden said: "You're Ben Rawlins, then. I did want to see you. Got a deal for you on that ranch of Will's."

Street asked: "You're the administrator?"

Hayden nodded ponderously. "About this deal . . ."

"I've already heard it."

"The Laceys need the place. They've offered a fair price."

"I'll see the place before I sell it. Maybe I'll like it. How do I know?"

Hayden's piggish eyes narrowed. A warning crept into his voice. "I'd sell. I'd advise you to sell. Take my word that it's a fair price."

Street murmured: "I still want to see it. If I decide to sell, I'll let you know." He stared at Hayden hard. Hayden started to protest further, but he must have seen something in Street's eyes that killed his protest. He mumbled weakly: "You're making a mistake."

Street shrugged. "Maybe. The offer doesn't expire at midnight, does it?"

Hayden did not reply. Street turned and went out the door. He supposed there were some formalities connected with the transfer of property, but he was in no mood for them today. He wanted to find Verona, convince her she was wrong about him, take her and get out of Escalante forever. Besides, he didn't relish signing the name of Ben Rawlins to anything.

He'd lived out his life without tangling with the law and he didn't want to start now.

He angled across the dusty street, scuffing the dust thoughtfully. He realized that there was a core of resentment and irritation in all his thoughts, realized as well that so long as it remained he had no business talking to Verona. Convincing Verona would take all the persuasion and tact of which he was capable. And, besides, she needed time to cool off from their encounter this morning.

So it was rest, then, and food afterward. Tonight, he would seek out Verona. The mere thought of it made his stomach feel hollow. He was briefly chagrined at the weakness this need for Verona could cause in him. Frowning a little, he strode into the hotel, crossed the lobby, and climbed the stairs to his room. Weariness was an opiate in his thoughts and body. He pulled off his boots, lay down on the bed, and was instantly asleep.

IV

The room was dark when Street awoke. For a moment he lay still, staring into the blackness, letting his mind renew all the happenings of the past twenty-four hours. Then quickly he swung his legs over, sat up, and stooped to pull on his boots. He found a match in his shirt pocket and thumbed it alight. Locating the lamp in its feeble glow, he crossed the room and lit it. He stared at himself in the mirror beside the lamp. His hair, as tawny as his mustache, was rumpled from sleep. His eyes, pale gray, stared back at him with somber lack of expression. His lips, below the mustache, were long and firm. Absently he scrubbed a hand over his strong jaws, deciding that twice a day was too often to shave.

He poured the basin full and splashed his face. He dampened his hair and dried off vigorously. He ran the broken comb through his hair. He wished he had a clean shirt, but he didn't. He re-tied his string tie, pulled at his coat to straighten it, picked up his hat, and went out into the hall.

Ravenous, the smell of frying steak drew him into a restaurant before he had gone half a block. He ordered steak and fried potatoes, ate swiftly and with single-minded concentration. Finished, he called the waitress over, paid his bill, and asked: "Could you tell me where to find Miss Verona Ormsby?"

The girl looked around uneasily, frightened, and Street said: "It's all right. I'm a friend."

"Well . . . she lives in the two-story white house up at the upper end of Main."

"Thanks." Street got up and went out, hurrying in spite of himself. A boy who had been staring through the window now transferred his attention to Street. It was the tow-headed kid that had run for the doctor this morning. Alf, the stage line agent had called him. Street grinned down. "Hello, Alf."

The boy ducked his head, not replying. He raised it again almost immediately. His washed-out blue eyes studied Street unblinkingly.

Embarrassed, Street tousled the boy's hair, then continued walking toward the upper end of Main. There were a few horsemen on the street, a couple of buggies, and half a dozen people on foot.

He stopped before the two-story white house, noting that it was the last one on the street. Next to it was a wire-fenced pasture and beyond that in the distance the ponderous rims of the Cougar Plateau. A breeze came down from the Plateau, cool and fresh, reminding Street that the season was yet early and that undoubtedly snow still lingered in the high country. Excitement was high in him as he stared at the lit windows of the house, yet he lingered, trying to down his doubt, trying to kill the fear that had made of his stomach a hard-knotted ball. Then with sudden decision, he reached for the gate.

A voice came softly from the darkness, "Wait a minute, Rawlins." It was a voice dimly recognized, associating itself with a figure that stepped out of the darkness inside the gate. Street waited, premonition tightening his muscles. There had been menace in that voice, and no attempt to cloak it with pleasantry. The gate swung open and Max Bauer came out. He said: "Miss Ormsby doesn't want to see you."

Street said: "I'll hear her say that, if you don't mind."

"You heard me say it."

In the dim light Street could see that Bauer was grinning with obvious anticipation. He felt suddenly just as he'd felt one night a good many years ago as he stepped into a rigged fight in a little town called Blackhawk over east in the Colorado Rockies, for his eyes caught the shadows of two more men inside the picket fence. Time to back down and move away. Don't go to Verona with your face beaten to a pulp. Don't get involved in a fight at her very door or she won't ever listen to what you have to say. Street swallowed his mounting rage. He made his voice even and soft. "All right. Let it go. I'll see her some other time."

He hated himself. He was eating crow. Ever a proud man, it galled and rankled. He started to turn, stopped quickly as he heard the soft laugh of the man called Bauer. The laugh told him more plainly than words could have done that Bauer was not going to let him go. Bauer had set himself for a fight and meant to have it.

Bauer said: "You won't see her some other

time. You won't see anything at all for a while. But when you can see, send for Hayden and a deed to your outfit."

Street had expected a little more talk. Or a sneak punch as he turned away. He was surprised, then, at the whistling blow that came directly out of the darkness. He flung his head aside and it grazed across his high cheek bone. The blow had come from Bauer, and Street felt a stir of surprise. He had not believed a man could move so fast. He had no time to dwell on his surprise, however. Hardly had it registered, when a second punch landed flushly on his jaw. He felt himself going backward, falling. His legs pedaled frantically for balance, but the edge of the walk dumped him down in the street's soft dust.

He had waited two years and it came to this. He had dreamed a thousand dreams of Verona, and the dreams were dead. A terrible rage soared through his brain. He could see the other two coming through the gate and he knew at once they meant to be thorough. He couldn't win, even if he soundly whipped all three. For he would be marked and beaten, and after that what slim chance remained of convincing Verona he had changed would be gone. For a second time in his life he ran, his face hot with the humiliation of it. He scrambled up out of the dust, dodged Bauer's kick, and sprinted down Main.

But fate, it seemed, had other plans. Street

collided violently with a small figure in the darkness, and sprawled again. He heard a shrill boy's yelp as he went down, and then they were on him, holding him, raining kicks and blows into his helpless body. That damned kid! Alf. He must have followed all the way from the restaurant. Street had no time to wonder why. He gathered his strength and expended it in a single explosive effort, and broke away.

Running was now out of the question. Marked already, he'd give them what fight he could. He struggled to his feet. Breath heaved gustily in and out of his starving lungs. He caught a roundhouse swing in the belly and it doubled him over. An uppercut straightened him up. Off balance he took a fist in his eye and he knew that one at least would swell shut.

He got his balance and lifted a knee brutally. A man yelled with pain and fell away. Street swung his right and felt it sink into something soft, into Bauer. The man grunted softly, but seemed to be slowed not at all. He was fast as a panther, and just as deadly. Street followed that right with a left, a savage hooking left that slammed into Bauer's ear. Bauer fell aside from that one, and Street followed him, throwing punches with rhythmic speed. Bauer, hurt, countered in desperation with a punch that landed flush on Street's nose.

The blow brought tears to his eyes and momentarily blinded him. Something awfully hard crashed down on his head from behind. Light flashed briefly before his eyes. He went to his knees. In this position, he caught the force of Bauer's knee full in the face. The iron-hard object cracked the back of his head for a second time, and still he would not go down. Bauer stood before him, slugging viciously and each of the man's blows landed accurately on Street's unprotected face.

Street heard a scream, a yell, and his eyes caught the light of a swinging lantern. Still fighting, or trying to, he struggled to his feet. Spraddle-legged, tottering, he peered around, seeking Bauer's hated face. Blood streamed from his nose. His face was numb and pulpy. Something warm trickled down the back of his head. Bauer's helper had slashed with the pistol barrel instead of delivering a solid blow. Perhaps only this had kept the blows from shattering Street's skull. Street's ribs were a solid wall of pain. Hands caught at him, but he flung them aside. He staggered down the street, heading for the hotel.

He heard Coe's voice, imperatively saying: "Son, you need some help."

"The hell!" He stopped, fighting the awful nausea and dizziness that threatened to overcome him, and then fell forward, stiff as a tottering pine. He had the brief sensation of falling, and then he wanted only blackness and peace and a cessation of pain.

The scream Street heard came from a girl. She was tall for a girl with a slim boyish figure. She ran forward as Street fell and kneeled in the dust beside him. Her smooth face showed nothing but pity as she stared down into his bloody, battered face. Coe stopped at her side, holding the lantern, and she looked up at him with boundless indig-nation. "What did he do to deserve this? When is this country going to put a stop to Gunhammer's brutality?"

Coe's ancient, seamed face flushed. Perhaps to avoid an answer to so direct a question, he spoke to a man at the edge of the gathering crowd. "Carry him to the hotel. Get someone to help you."

The girl watched him, her face revealing both disappointment and disgust. Coe, still avoiding her eyes, caught young Alf Browder by a thin shoulder and said: "Fetch the doctor, son."

When he could no longer decently avoid it, he returned his gaze to the girl. Her eyes awaited his answer. He said: "Rose, when the man comes to, if he wants to swear an assault warrant, I'll serve it. Does that satisfy you?"

She asked with a certain contempt: "Does it satisfy you, Mister Coe?"

She stood up, to be out of the way as the two men lifted Street's limp body. She faced Coe, a study of indignation, hands on hips, dark eyes flashing. She repeated: "Does it satisfy the sheriff's office?"

He made a patient, helpless gesture. "Rose, what would you have me do? The man's beat up. It happens all the time. Am I supposed to charge someone with attempted murder every time there's a fight?"

"Suppose this one dies?"

"He won't. If he does, I'll have Bauer in the lockup within twelve hours."

Rose Healy snorted in a most unlady-like way. "And he'll be out in another twelve on a self-defense plea."

Coe shrugged wearily.

Rose stamped a small foot angrily. She studied Coe's face for an instant, and then her shoulders settled in defeat. Turning, she ran after the two men who were carrying Street.

Catching up, she asked: "What are you going to do, just dump him in his room and leave him?"

The man carrying Street's head and shoulders answered: "Coe sent the Browder kid after Doc."

Rose subsided, helplessly angry still. She held the hotel door while they carried Street inside, and followed up the stairs behind them.

Doc came shuffling into the room before they hardly had time to straighten Street out on the bed. Doc was a small, totally bald man. He wore pince-nez glasses that gave him a studious, intellectual look. But Doc was an awful soak,

Rose knew. She peered into his eyes now, seeking signs of drunkenness. The reek of his breath was almost overpowering, but his eyes were clear for once.

The two men who had carried Street in now left, breathing heavily. Doc went over to the wash basin and poured it full. While he washed his hands, he studied Rose. Her expression was one of purely unselfish concern for the hurt man on the bed, and Doc made a gently mocking smile. "Another of your strays, Rose?"

Her eyes flashed. She stared at him angrily for an instant. Then, like the sun breaking through the clouds, her smile broke through the somberness of her face. She said ruefully: "I suppose so. But, Doc, it just isn't fair. This man has done nothing to Gunhammer."

He replied dryly: "Except inheriting Will Rawlins's place." He dried his hands and looked over toward the man on the bed, then back at Rose. He stared at her thoughtfully a moment with some hope in his eyes but finally shook his head. "Hell, no. You haven't even thought of it yet."

"What are you talking about? What haven't I thought about yet?"

"You haven't even realized that this man stands between you and Gunhammer. You haven't even thought of using him."

Rose felt a vast impatience. "Of course I

haven't thought of it. Get over there, Doc, and patch him up. He could die while you stand here gabbing."

"Yes, ma'am." Doc grinned but he opened his bag and went to work.

V

The doctor worked steadily for a full thirty minutes. When he finished, there was the reek of alcohol in the room. The gaping slashes in Street's head were sewed up. Street's face was clean, the cuts salved. Doc wiped off his hands.

Rose sat in the room's single chair, her face white. Doc said: "He'll live. He's got a bad concussion and it may be morning or after before he comes to. He's got to rest until he's well."

"Can he be moved?"

Doc grinned mockingly. "Rose, I remember riding clear out to Chain once to splint a robin's broken wing. You haven't changed, have you?"

She flushed. She had always felt guilty about that. But there was a consuming compassion in her for all hurt things, which time had not dimmed. She murmured: "I wouldn't do it now. I wouldn't make you come that far for a robin." She made an impish grimace. "But I'd want to."

Doc's face lost its mockery and became kindly. "All right, Rose. Take him home with you if you want. Cushion his head good. It won't hurt him no more than lying here without any care."

"You're sure, Doc? I wouldn't want to hurt him worse."

"He's a hard-headed brute. I've got to come out and see old Sean anyhow tomorrow. I'll look at this one while I'm there."

Rose smiled again. Her face, containing neither patience nor humor in repose, changed entirely when she smiled. She was a girl meant to smile often, but her smiles had been few the past couple of years. There had been Sean's illness, coupled with the constant pressure of Gunhammer against Chain. There had been the burden of running Chain, the worry of losing it. There had been her unhappy love affair with Nick Lacey, terminating when she discovered he wished not to marry her but Chain.

She said, as Doc went out: "Seguro's in the bar. Ask him to get the buckboard and fill the back with blankets. Tell him to come up when it's ready and bring someone else to help."

"All right, Rose." Doc paused in the doorway for an instant, hesitating. Seeming to make up his mind about something, he finally said: "Rose, don't get burned again. You don't know a single blamed thing about him."

Rose closed the door firmly in his face, appreciating the motive behind his warning, yet angered all the same.

She sat down and stared across the room at the stranger's face. Her mind admonished: *Be honest, Rose. Nick did hurt you. But this one won't. Because when he's well, he'll sell to Gunhammer and go away.*

The thought made her vaguely unhappy, blue. It is doubtful if anyone else could have seen what Street was like, looking as Rose had only at his beaten, battered face. Yet in Rose was the odd ability to look beyond the distortion of a creature's wounds. And she had found something in Street she liked. It could have been the way he stood, glaring around him as he tried to find his enemies, the ones who had beaten him and gone away. It might have been the way he refused all help, falling on his face for lack of it. Or it may have been only his helplessness.

Yet like all the other creatures she had helped, he would heal and go away, forgetting the care and the nurse who gave it. No. Perhaps this one would stay. If Gunhammer had not already killed his spirit.

Ralph Coe returned to his office on Cougar, opened the unlocked door, and went inside. He crossed the darkened room, avoiding furniture with an uncanny precision born of complete familiarity with each object in the room. He struck a match, raised the lamp chimney, and touched the flame to its wick. Then, he sank down into his creaking swivel chair and raised his scuffed boots to the desk.

He cuffed his hat back on his forehead and sighed heavily. Today had taken a heavy toll of his self-respect and he knew if he had any left at all when this was over, he'd be a lucky man. The years rested heavily on his shoulders tonight. He should have retired ten years ago, and he almost had. But then Mercy had been stricken with her illness. The first year had eaten up all the savings of a lifetime. Elections came along and Coe had seen no alternative but to run again. The voters liked him. They proved that again and again. He was old, but he was active. Perhaps they felt that he could deputize strength, but that only he had the experience and know-how a good lawman needs.

He looked back at his life briefly, proud of it all except for the past few years. Proud of it until the Lacey boys grew into men and began to ride the country with their rough-shod ways. Proud of it until Nick Lacey brought Max Bauer back from Denver to ramrod Gunhammer. He had known then, knuckling under to old Brandt Lacey, that Gunhammer could lose him an election any time he failed to please them. And what would he do if they did? How would he get the money he had to send over to that sanitarium in Denver if he didn't have the sheriff's pay coming in each month?

Well, maybe it wouldn't be so bad. Gunhammer had probably broken this Rawlins's spirit tonight. When he recovered, he'd sell. Coe felt bad about Rose Healy. But he knew Gunhammer would leave her enough of Chain to live fairly comfortably. And she'd get married sooner or later. Too bad she hadn't married Nick Lacey when he was courting her. Then all this trouble might have been avoided. Anger stirred this old man for an instant, then went away. Shame came and he fought it fiercely. A man did what he had to do. This was what Ralph Coe had to do. Maybe he didn't like it. Maybe his pride fought it. But there was no single, other way out for him.

Scowling, he heard a step outside the door and looked up. Max Bauer came in, grinning. One of Max's lips were puffed, one of his eyes was swollen and slightly blue.

His manner was mocking as he said: "Sheriff, you weren't thinking of swearing out any warrants, were you?"

Coe's face flushed. Trust this evil one to seek out a man's weaknesses, his sore spots, then deliberately rub salt into them. Bauer was a man whose greatest pleasure was inflicting pain, whether it be physical or pain of the mind and soul. He knew Coe's sore spot was his relinquished self-respect and tonight he had come deliberately to grind what was left of it into the dirt. Coe took a grip on the arms of his swivel chair and said: "No. I wasn't thinking of swearing out any. Rawlins might when he comes to."

Bauer laughed, tossing his shaggy head and showing his even white teeth. Coe thought: *The teeth are Bauer's vanity. Too bad Rawlins couldn't have knocked them out.* He said: "Max, don't go too far. Don't go so far the Laceys won't back you."

Bauer's smile was wicked. "Threatening me, Coe?"

Coe shook his head wearily. "No. I'm not threatening you. I know better than that." He stared up at Bauer, suddenly tired of this cruel fencing. He said: "Max, get it over with and get out, will you?"

He could not help the pleasure he felt, seeing the flash of anger in Bauer's eyes. Bauer growled: "You're the second one who's told me to get out today. Watch your step, you old fool, or you'll be hunting a job next election."

Coe swallowed. He looked at Max's boots and his voice was very low. "All right, Max."

This was apparently what Bauer wanted—the sheriff's complete surrender. He laughed softly, his mood bright. Then without another word he turned and went out, slamming the door behind him with deliberate viciousness. Coe discovered that his hands were trembling. His head felt light, almost as though it were separated from his body.

He sat very still for a while, and finally fished a

sack of tobacco from his pocket and began to build a cigarette. His hands were steady now, and he made himself a promise that might never be kept. But he made it anyway. *Max, if ever Mercy doesn't need me, if ever the time comes when I don't have to have this job . . . why, Max, I'm going to kill you. I'm going to rid the country of you once and for all.* And having promised himself this, a measure of his manhood began to return.

VI

At midnight a curtained buggy drove into Escalante off the Cougar Creek road. It was followed by two horsemen, one of whom trotted ahead as it approached the two-story house of Verona Ormsby. This one dismounted and tied the buggy horse. The other swung down beside the buggy and waited with a sort of deference for its occupant to alight. An old man got out of the buggy, snarled irritably at the dismounted horseman, and then stalked stiffly toward the house. Apparently someone inside had been expecting visitors, for the door flung open at the first sound of his boots on the porch. The other two, having tied their mounts, followed him silently inside. This was the Lacey tribe, old Brandt with Nick and Glenn following him in. Bruce, the handsome one, was the man who met them at the door.

The old man shucked out of his coat, tossed his hat on a chair. Then he went directly to the fireplace, backed against it, and spread his horny, gnarled hands to its meager warmth. He glared irascibly at his three sons, letting his gaze rest finally on Bruce. He said: "Now. What the hell's been happening in town today? Why do you have to drag me 'way down here in the middle of the night?" He completely ignored Verona, seated on a brocade sofa over against the wall, a slight she resented violently.

Bruce was a classic-featured, dark-skinned man of perhaps twenty-five. His eyes were dark, holding a devil of merriment that Verona knew was not merriment at all but a kind of wastrel refusal to take anything seriously. Bruce said: "That damned Rawlins came in on the stage this morning. Seems he had a tussle with a gunfighter on the stage and accidentally killed him. I guess he was feeling pretty big about it because he wouldn't listen to either Bauer or Hayden."

Old Brandt's face flushed with anger. His voice raised irritably: "Damn! It looks like I'm going to have to do this myself."

Nick broke in calmly: "Don't get yourself worked up. It's all taken care of. For some reason Rawlins tried to come here tonight. Maybe he wanted to square himself with Verona, but . . ."

The old man interrupted savagely: "Don't tell

me not to get worked up! And what in tarnation's Verona got to do with it?"

There was a silence in the room, broken by Bruce's nervous cough. The old man's eyes sought him out and pinned him fiercely in place. "Well. What's she got to do with it?" There was a world of contempt in the way he said *she*.

Bruce colored. His smoothly olive face glistened with a beading of sweat. He said: "The gunfighter was Verona's husband."

Old Brandt shot a glance at Verona that made her shrivel. Then he turned back to Nick. "Go on."

Nick, the strongest of the tribe and a squarish man of thirty, said: "Max was laying for Rawlins. He guessed he was coming here and got ahead of him with two of the crew. They worked him over out in front of the house. Damned near killed him."

Again there was the briefest of silences, broken this time by Verona's sharply indrawn breath. Brandt glared at her again. "So what did that accomplish?" he asked of Nick.

"Why, the man will sell when he's well enough. Isn't that what we've been working for?"

Brandt's voice became very quiet but it was laden with contempt. "Yes. That's what we've been working for. It's what we've been working toward for damned near two years. And have we got it yet? Hell no. Because the bunch of you are bunglers. Because you refuse to use your stupid brains." He paused for breath, and then went on. His audience was taking this with varying degrees of false humility. Bruce's eyes held merry mockery, carefully veiled. Nick was angry. Glenn, the hypocritical one, was nodding sober agreement. Verona was white and trembling with her dislike and humiliation. Brandt said, patiently as though talking to children: "We need to own that Rawlins spread. It's deeded land. If we take it, in comes the U.S. marshal and we can't handle him like we do Coe. So what happens? Will Rawlins tries to hold us up for it. Ten thousand he asks for it. And you get him killed. Does that help? Hell no. Because you didn't take the trouble to find out whether or not he had any heirs. It turned out that he did. You know how you could have handled that? Sent a man back East to where this Rawlins lived, bought him out, if he'd sell. If he wouldn't, kill him and forge a deed."

Gradually the force in him and the logic of his argument subdued the resentment in his sons. Their expressions became faintly sheepish. Bruce asked: "What do we do now?"

Brandt shrugged. "Wait till the man recovers. Let Max approach him then. Let Max threaten him a little. See what happens."

"What if that don't work?"

Brandt smiled patiently. "The time is past for working with brains and logic. If he won't sell, work him over again. And again. Until he does sell."

He seemed to dismiss the subject from his mind. He left the fireplace and got his hat and coat. He stopped and looked down at Verona, asking disgustedly: "What the hell does Bruce want with you anyway?"

Giving her no chance to reply, he stalked out the door. Verona sprang up from the sofa, her green eyes blazing, her face chalky with rage. She turned her rage on the hapless Bruce. "Who does he think he is, coming in here like that, insulting me? Don't ever let him in here again, or I'll kill him!"

Bruce slipped the Schofield .45 from its holster and handed it to her, grinning. "Want me to call him back?"

She threw the gun at him with all her strength. He ducked it easily and it smashed a vase on the table. His grin widened.

Bruce's mockery did not abate. But a certain spark grew in his eyes that had not been there before. He said: "Better go, boys. She's a heller when she gets this way."

They got their hats and hurried out. A moment later, Verona heard the drum of their horses' hoofs retreating down the street. She looked at Bruce, hating him, wondering how she could ever have loved him at all. She said: "You, too. Get out of here."

The spark was plain in his eyes now, and the mockery was dying before it. He murmured: "Sure you want me to?"

"Yes. Yes. Go on home. I want to think."

The spark died in his eyes. He grinned again, mocking. "Grieving for your husband, darling?"

She sat down and buried her face in her hands, unspeaking. She could not combat Bruce. She ought to know better than to try. He could show her either passion or mockery, but nothing else. Whatever went on inside his head, in his secret thoughts, he never revealed, even to her. She realized suddenly that he was like a complete stranger to her.

He took a step toward her, his expression briefly serious, hesitated, then turned away. He got his hat and jacket from the tree beside the door and put them on. She did not glance up, so he opened the door and went out, closing it softly behind him.

Only then did Verona raise her head. She listened to the faint sounds Bruce made, getting his horse from the stable at the rear of the house, saddling, and riding away. Verona got up, crossed to the table, and began to gather up the pieces of the broken vase. Her hands trembled and she frowned at them. It had been a trying day. But at least her secret was safe. Not one of the Laceys had guessed her husband had been the killer, not the killed. *What do I do now?* she asked herself bleakly, and found no immediate answer.

She carried the broken vase to the kitchen and threw it away. She returned to the living room and picked up the Schofield .45. She held it thoughtfully for a moment, vaguely wishing she had the courage to turn it upon herself. Realizing that she had not, she opened a drawer and slipped it inside.

She had made such a terrible mess of things. Such a mess and now there was no way out. Walt had suffered terribly because of her, and he must suffer more before this was finished. "Oh, I'm no good. I'm just no damned good," she whispered violently. Why hadn't she waited for Walt? Why hadn't she believed? She shrugged. Had Walt justified her belief? No. She admitted he hadn't. Where he had been the past two years she had no idea. But he had not changed. He was still a brawler, a killer. He had killed on the stage half a day out of Escalante. He would kill again now. Walt would never take such a beating as he had received tonight. He would bathe the country in blood. Her hatred of him had been a violent thing this afternoon. Tonight her hatred was for herself, not for Walt Street. He had become no better in the two years he had been gone. But Verona had changed for the worse.

She walked across the room and stared into the leaping flames in the fireplace. She had acquired security, something that seemed inordinately important immediately after she had deserted Walt. He had offered her no security at all. He had not even been able to buy her a trinket for her birthday. An extravagantly beautiful woman was Verona, standing there. Her skin was like milk, flawless and having transparent appearance. Her eyes were green, framed by long, delicate lashes. Her lips were full and red, her body perfect in the green satin dress. But her expres-sion was petulant, showing neither happiness nor contentment.

Nervously she crossed the room, re-crossed it. For a few moments she paced back and forth like a trapped lioness. Perhaps now Bruce would want to marry her. And if he did, what would she tell him? How would she put him off? Bruce believed her husband was dead. She thought: *I can put him off for a while. I can say it wouldn't be decent so soon after Walt's death.* The irony of that did not fail to touch her. Who was she to talk of decency, living openly with Bruce, taking this house he had given her and all the other things? She knew she was accepted in Escalante only because the full power of Gunhammer insisted upon it. She knew what the town really thought of her. She wondered piteously, aloud: "What can I do? Oh, what can I do?" She had a thought then of which she was instantly ashamed. *Perhaps they'll kill Walt. . . .*

She threw herself face downward upon the sofa. Her hands were claws digging at the brocade upholstery. She whispered hoarsely: "Now I've reached the bottom. Now I even want Walt dead so that I can get out of this mess I'm in." But she didn't really want Walt dead, and she hadn't reached the bottom. Walt was perhaps the one good thing that had happened to her in her life. The love they shared between them. She'd been too weak to appreciate it, to cling to it. And now she must pay for her weakness.

VII

On most nights, young Alf Browder went home immediately after his work at the stage depot was finished. Usually he fixed himself some supper and then lay down on the bed for a nap. At 11:30, he would rise and go out into the night again. At midnight he would be waiting before the hotel for his mother to come out. She protested endlessly at this, but to no avail. "Alf, you don't have to come for me every night. You need your sleep. You work hard over at the stage depot."

But the boy had a certain grown-up self-importance about this and stubbornly refused. He did not like his mother walking home alone at midnight. Some nights, particularly Saturdays and Gunhammer's pay-day nights, the streets were loaded with drunks. And Mrs. Browder was a pretty woman despite her thirty-five years and the menial work she did at the hotel. What the boy would have done if a drunken and insistent cowpuncher ever had accosted the pair was problematical. Yet perhaps it was the boy's very presence that discouraged such advances by making known the fact that here was a respectable woman despite the hour.

Tonight, however, the boy missed both his supper and his nap. He had experienced a terrific excitement this morning when the stage had come in with the body of Walt Street inside, with Street's killer calmly riding the box with Jim Perry, the driver, and admiration that amounted to hero worship had been born in the boy. It was not the first time he had formed an attachment like this one. He had formed one for the sheriff at one period in his life. He had felt a short-lived hero worship for Max Bauer, abruptly terminated by Bauer himself when he callously and irritably cuffed Alf out of his way and cursed him.

Alf had spent practically all of today thinking of the stranger, unconsciously imitating his gestures and his way of walking. Tonight his need to see more of the man was like a thirst. So, instead of going home, Alf headed for the hotel. He slipped inside and timidly queried the clerk regarding the stranger's presence in the hotel. Informed that the stranger was in his room, the boy took up his vigil in a corner of the long verandah. Later, he saw Street come out. He followed at a discreet distance, his eyes drinking in every detail of the stranger's dress, his erect and alert bearing. Without realizing that he did so, Alf straightened his own shoulders and threw back his head. He admired tremendously the stranger's tawny, sweeping mustache, and the lean lines of his face and jaw. He thought: *That's how I want to look when I get big.*

While Street was eating, the boy peered at him through the dirty window. Afterward, his heart stood briefly still when Street spoke to him and tousled his hair. Alf blamed himself for Street's vicious beating, since it was he over whom Street had fallen as he tried to run. And the shining star of hero worship had dimmed somewhat, for a hero did not run. Not even when so savage a beating was a certainty. Yet in Alf, hero worship went hand-in-hand with loyalty, at least until loyalty was no longer possible. So he told himself emphatically: *He must've had a reason for runnin'. A good reason. It wasn't because he was afraid. A man like him ain't afraid, I can tell you that. So he must've had a reason.*

Alf was breathless by the time he returned from fetching the sheriff. He was almost exhausted after being sent for Doc. Excitement held him rooted there as the crowd began to disperse. He listened to the talk, his face flushed. Coe stood in the middle of the street, his lantern casting a weird circle of light. In this light, Alf saw Jim Perry, the stage driver, stoop and pick up a paper from the street. Perry moved over to the sheriff and Alf edged closer to listen.

Perry said: "Sheriff, look at this. It's the paper Rawlins was carrying when he tusseled with Street last night."

"What of it?"

"Why it's got an article in it about Street. And a picture." He unfolded the paper and both he and the sheriff peered at the picture. Coe said: "Hell! Looks about as much like Rawlins as it does Street. Especially with that mustache drawn on it."

"Yeah. But look what it says. This Rawlins has got a thousand dollars coming to him for killing Street. Everybody's heard about that bounty but this proves it. A guy over in New Mexico named Frank Jagger has offered to pay a thousand to whoever kills this Street. Seems Street killed his brother, two or three years ago."

Coe said: "The offer's probably expired by now." He gave a last, searching glance at the scene around him, then turned and headed toward his office, leaving Perry standing alone holding the half-open paper.

Alf wished he could see that paper, and the picture. Maybe if he stuck with Perry a while, the man would throw it away. Perry hesitated an instant, then folded the paper. Carrying it in his hand, he headed toward the telegraph office down at the lower end of Main. There was a single lamp burning in the telegrapher's office as there always was. The telegrapher sat at his desk, a green eye-shade banded around his forehead.

Perry went in and Alf edged close to the partly open door to listen. Perry wasted little time in pleasantries, before he launched into a story of all that had happened. He finished with: "This Rawlins is a nice guy. He got a bad time out of Gunhammer tonight and I thought maybe I could do something to make him feel better. A thou-sand ought to make a man feel better, hadn't it?"

The telegrapher's dry voice said: "I'd think it would. You want to send a telegram to this Frank Jagger?"

"Yeah." Alf could hear the crackle of paper. "Let's see if the address is here. Yeah. Las Vegas, New Mexico. What's it going to cost, Russ?"

But Alf was gone. For he had suddenly remembered that he was supposed to meet his mother at the hotel. It must be midnight, or past. She would be waiting, worrying about him. He'd ask Perry for the newspaper tomorrow. Maybe he wouldn't get it, but he'd ask. As he ran, he felt a rising exhilaration. *A thousand dollars! Lordy, that ought to make the stranger feel good!*

From Escalante, the road climbed gradually as it followed the winding course of Cougar Creek. Twelve miles out, the road forked. The right fork continued to follow Cougar Creek while the left led to Gunhammer and Chain, along a trickle appropriately called Dry Creek. The land was arid here, a wide flat valley lying between the towering rims and covered with scrub sage and tall greasewood. But after seven or eight miles you rounded a turn in the road and got a genuine surprise. For before you lay the broad acres of Gunhammer, fifteen hundred acres in hay, emerald green at this time of the year and dotted with unused haystacks looking like nothing so much as fat brown loaves of bread. Gunhammer's buildings were like a small town dominated by the house, an enormous one-story log building that had been added to in haphazard manner through the years as Gunhammer and the Lacey family grew, until now it was a maze of wings, conflicting roof lines, and stone chimneys.

The road went past the house half a mile from it and continued upcountry, crossing Gunhammer's hay field and entering a narrower part of the valley that was choked with willows and brush. Now you discovered why Dry Creek was dry. For here was Gunhammer's dam and head gate and here the bulk of Dry Creek flowed into Gunhammer's ditches. The brush continued for half a mile and then the road came out into another meadow with a one-room log shack in its middle. This was the Rawlins spread.

Some freak of rock formation had narrowed the space between the rims to less than a mile here, and they rose a sheer five hundred feet above the valley floor. Except in midsummer, the sun never reached the Rawlins fields until late morning, and it disappeared a couple of hours later behind the rims. A run-down bachelor's spread, probably as much like a boar's nest inside as it was out. Worn-out machinery littered the yard. Fences sagged, corrals were a maze of scattered, rotting poles, the door of the house stood open. The road went on, entering another brush thicket, then climbing in a series of switchbacks cut from solid rock until it came out on a bench that seemed to lay level and flat for a hundred miles.

Actually the distance across this bench was fifteen miles, and actually it was neither level nor flat. But it was lush with grass, belly-deep on a horse. Dry Creek, gathered into a single stream at the cañon's entrance, made countless narrow streams as it fanned out upcountry toward its many sources in the high country. This was Chain and it was not hard to understand why Gunhammer coveted it so enviously. Less pretentious than Gunhammer, Chain was just as solidly built, just as tidy and well-kept. And it was in this log house at Chain that Street awoke.

At first he simply stared blankly at the ceiling. But gradually he became aware of his surroundings, and his first thought after that was: *I'm in Verona's house!* He sat bolt upright and instantly pain struck through his brain like the blow of a sledge. Faint, he fell over sideways on the bed.

He had made some small noise, and it brought Rose Healy on a run. She caught him by his shoulders and laid him back in bed.

Several minutes later he again opened his eyes. This time he saw the girl. She had eyes of a dark, soft brown. Her smooth skin was tanned and her hair, yellow as quaking-aspen leaves in early fall, was tied behind her head with a ribbon. Street looked at her for a moment, then made a weak grin and said: "This is the point where I'm supposed to say . . . where am I?"

Her smile was friendly, natural as a cloud drifting across the sky. She said: "You're at Chain, and I'm Rose Healy."

Street liked her voice. It was calm and gentle. It had a throaty, vibrant quality he found most attractive. He liked her instantly. "Mind telling me what time it is?"

"Almost noon."

"I've been out all night?"

Her smile faded. "Three nights and two days. We thought you were going to die."

Street took a few moments to digest this,

finding it hard to believe. Yet neither could he believe this girl would lie. His eyes took on a sudden look of panic. "Did I talk?"

She nodded, sober and unsmiling. "What did I say?"

"You talked of your wife. You talked of Verona Ormsby." There was both disapproval and disappointment in her. Street rose to his elbow, savagely ignoring the pain in his head. "Then you know who I am?"

She nodded. She stooped and pushed him firmly back onto the pillow. She said: "Sleep some more. When you wake, I'll give you something to eat." Street's eyes weighed her, and she said woodenly: "You needn't worry. You are safe here." And, turning, she left the room.

Street stared at the door through which she had passed. Then his head moved, and he looked around him. He was in a small room, furnished only with a dresser, chair, and the bed upon which he lay. A washstand stood beside the window holding a basin, pitcher, and an assortment of bandage and antiseptic. A bright, hand-made rag rug was upon the floor. The wallpaper had some striped pattern to it that was cheerful and attractive. Street's eyes saw these things, but his brain was busy elsewhere. His brain was bleakly contemplating the ruin that had come to his plans ever since the stage had left Montezuma. It was as though fate were stubbornly determined to defeat him. The muscles along his lean jaw played briefly. His eyes narrowed and turned hard. Fate be hanged! Nothing was going to defeat him. He had spent two years of his life working and staying out of trouble so that he could return to Verona. Now he was here. He had done nothing to spoil his two-year record. Whatever had happened had been forced upon him. Surely Verona would see that. Yet somehow, all he could remember was the hate in Verona's eyes. Frowning, he closed his eyes and slept again.

VIII

Street awoke the second time to the smell of chicken broth and toast. He sat up, and this time the pain in his head was less. The girl, Rose Healy, propped pillows behind him, then brought basin and water and firmly and wordlessly washed his face and hands.

Her face was somber, her lips unsoftened by any smile. Street spoke with some embarrassment: "I think I owe you a great deal for taking care of me. I hope I'll have a chance to repay it."

Rose frowned. She said stiffly: "It was not done with the thought of repayment." She sat down beside the bed, picked up a bowl, and put a spoonful of scalding broth in his mouth.

Street said: "You don't like me, do you?"

Her eyes met his briefly. "How could I know whether I like you or not? You have been unconscious." She was withdrawn, cool. Street, having known but one woman, could not know that her coolness was a defense. Not knowing this, aware that all she knew of him was what he might have babbled in his delirium, he said: "Then it is possible that you don't like what I am . . . what I stand for."

"What do you stand for?" Her gaze, so steady and still, was disconcerting. He had a suddenly overwhelming desire to make this girl understand.

He said: "When I was sixteen, I caught a man stealing a horse from my father's pasture. I was hunting at the time. I was carrying a rifle. I yelled at him to stop, and when he didn't, I fired."

"Was that the first man you killed?" Her voice completely lacked expression.

"Yes. And I didn't mean to kill him. I think it must have been almost automatic, my shooting at him."

The girl said: "You needn't have made a career of it."

"No, I guess not." He was angered by her calm hostility. He shrugged. "I won't bore you with the rest."

"No. I'd like to hear it. I'd like to know how a gunfighter is made."

Street scowled at her. On the point of refusing, he changed his mind. Perhaps his need for understanding was greater than he had realized. In brief, uncolored narrative, he told her the rest of it. He told her of the past two years, of his putting aside the gun. He told her of Rawlins's attack on the stage out of Montezuma. As he talked, he stared beyond her, out the window at the rolling grassland of Chain. When he had finished, he looked at her face.

Her eyes were wide. Her lower lip was full and trembling. She blinked and looked away. She murmured: "I think you must love Verona very much. Are you quite sure she deserves it?"

Street failed to answer that.

Rose said: "Yes. You're very sure, aren't you?"

Street nodded.

There was a silence in the room for a long while. At last Rose said, looking down at the floor: "And if you discover you have been wrong, what will you do then? Will you slip back into your old ways? Will you take out your anger and disillusion on the world in general?"

But she did not wait for his reply. Hastily gathering up the tray of half-eaten food, she hurried out of the room, closing the door firmly behind her.

Street was puzzled by her behavior. He was puzzled and upset. Had he known that she was crying bitterly as she carried the tray to the kitchen, he would have been even more disturbed. For he might have understood then what she had been trying to tell him all along. That Verona today was not the Verona he had known two years ago. That Verona had changed. Not knowing, he simply thought: *I've got to get out of here. I've got to leave and I've got to see her. The longer I stay in this country the harder it's going to be.*

Experimentally he swung his legs over the side of the bed. But he did not stand up. For dizziness claimed him and he knew that if he did, he would fall down. He lay back on the bed. Reflectively he rubbed his jaw, was surprised to find it clean-shaven, at least where there were no scabbed wounds. He thought: *Why, good Lord, she's even been shaving me.* And suddenly the full weight of his obligation struck him. Except for this girl, for Chain, he would be dead. If he'd almost died *with* her care, he'd undoubtedly have died without it. Yet this obligation was one he would have to ignore. Because he knew that to pay it would be to lose Verona forever. Chain was at war with Gunhammer. Perhaps no shots had been fired as yet, but it was war all the same. Street, nominally owner of the Rawlins spread, stood in the middle. If he sold to Gunhammer, they would move in on Chain, would steal the major part of this fabulous kingdom of grass. If he did not sell to

Gunhammer, he would have to fight. And if he fought, he would lose Verona, assuming of course that he had not already lost her.

Street closed his eyes. Impatience gnawed at him. But he was wise enough to know that he could not leave Chain yet. He also knew that the quickest way to regain strength, to heal, is to sleep and rest. He rested. But already he was planning, was yearning for the time when he could leave the haven of Chain and ride back to Escalante. *We'll go away together,* he thought. *We'll get the fresh start we've both waited so long for.*

It was fortunate, perhaps, that Street did not know Gunhammer had no intention of letting him leave. It was also fortunate that he did not know that Frank Jagger even now was heading toward Escalante, $1,000 in his poke and triumph in his heart.

The next morning, Rose permitted Street to get out of bed. She provided him with Levi's, faded from many washings, and a plaid flannel shirt, which Street judged belonged to her father. She brought him his boots that had been cleaned and polished. She left the room while he got dressed although Street realized with a sudden heat of embarrassment that he had no privacy left where Rose was concerned. She had cared for him three days and nights.

Afterward, feeling weak and dizzy and only partially recovered from his embarrassment, he made his way through the house and out to the verandah where Rose was waiting. More tired than he would have liked to admit, he sank gratefully into a wicker rocker. Perhaps the vast impatience he felt with his own weakness showed in his face, for Rose said: "Don't be so intolerant with yourself. Even a strong body takes time to mend."

Street gave her a meager smile. He said: "Two years of waiting make a man impatient. Hell, I've been here four days and I haven't even talked to Verona yet."

Rose stared at the horizon. Silence fell between them, silence that became increasingly awkward. Street wondered why Rose did not like Verona. The girl seemed above feminine jealousy, but what else could her dislike be? He fished automatically in his shirt pocket for tobacco, failing to find it. Rose got up wordlessly and went into the house, returning shortly with sack tobacco, papers, and matches. Street fashioned a cigarette and lit it.

He was painfully aware of this girl beside him, was also aware that she disapproved either of him, of Verona, or of both of them. It puzzled him until he thought: *It's the way I've lived that she disapproves.* Yet with Rose he felt, in spite of that, a deep sense of companionship such as he had never known with Verona. His life with Verona had been tempestuous and full of fire, always. There had been no moments of peace and understanding. Moodily he stared out at the land that was Chain. Peace and understanding lay ahead, down the years. Youth was the time for fire. Yet why could not the two go hand in hand?

Perhaps Rose thought he was noticing Chain, for she said: "We put up no hay on Chain, as you've probably noticed. There is shelter in the timber over there for the cattle during winter storms. And grass aplenty when the storms are over. Cattle winter fat on Chain. They always have." There was unconscious pride in her voice.

Street followed the direction of her gesture with his glance. Chain, the whole length of it, lay nestled like a lover against the plateau rim and was sheltered by it. There was a strip of hilly, timbered country between the foot of the rim and the open grassland. Street's eyes wandered across the bench to the other side where the grass ended abruptly at the cañon drop off.

Rose murmured: "Chain is a cowman's dream, Mister Street . . . fenced by Nature with the rim on one side, with the cañon on the other. Except at roundup time in the fall and branding in the spring, we don't even need a crew. All the cattle need is to be let alone, for there's grass and water everywhere."

Street said: "No wonder Gunhammer wants it. Will they leave you anything at all?"

Rose Healy made a small, bitter laugh. "Oh, yes. They're being very generous. They won't bother our home, because it stands on patented land. The Laceys own Sheriff Coe, but they're terrified of doing anything that would bring in a U.S. marshal. So they won't bother our patented land."

"How about graze?"

"They'll take all of that. They have offered to let us run three hundred head of cattle on a pool arrangement. I won't even have to hire riders. Gunhammer will do my branding, my roundup work, my shipping." Rose's lovely face was bitter.

"Just like a pension . . . or a hand-out. Take what they give you and be grateful." Street was angry. He asked: "What are you going to do about it?"

She made a pathetic shrug. "What can we do? My father is an invalid, confined to his bed or to a wheelchair. For a while Will Rawlins stood between Gunhammer and Chain, but he only did it in hope of profit. He was asking Gunhammer ten thousand dollars for that little hundred and sixty acres down there. So you see, he was only using our misfortune as a lever to pry money out of Gunhammer."

"What happened to him?"

Again Rose shrugged helplessly. "Some things you know but cannot prove. He was found dead in Escalante's shack town, a knife in his back. There was a bottle beside him and signs that a woman had been with him. And likely Max Bauer wielded the knife."

"So now nothing stands between Gunhammer and you. Nothing but a man who doesn't even own the name he carries." Street had a dark suspicion, which was that Rose had brought him here and cared for him in the hope of using him as a buffer. It must have been a great shock to her to discover he was Street and not Rawlins.

Rose looked at him steadily. "I know what you're thinking. It isn't true, though I can't ask you to believe it. It does look bad, doesn't it, bringing you here and caring for you, and you a total stranger?"

Street smiled wryly. "I've considered the possibility that you wanted my help."

Rose flushed. She said: "We're beyond the help of any one man. And you're not to let it worry you. We'll continue to live, even after Gunhammer takes over. It's not your problem at all. You've troubles enough of your own, which are worse because of us."

"Ever think of fighting for Chain?" Street asked dryly.

"Of course we've thought of it. But we have also realized that we cannot win. Gunhammer is too big, and they're ruthless, which we could never be. The only thing we might gain by fighting would be delay, and the cost would be too great. Men would be killed. Children would be orphaned, women widowed. Is a little delay worth that?"

Street's admiration for this girl grew. He suddenly wanted to pitch in and help her himself. Then he thought of Verona again and remained silent.

IX

He rocked, feeling strength returning and staring moodily out across the land of Chain. A feeble voice raised inside the house and Rose excused herself. Street heard her talking within the house, patient, tender. After a while she returned, pushing a wheelchair. Street got up and helped her through the door with it.

Sean Healy, he saw at once, had been a big man. The story was there in his massive bones, in the wide spread of his shoulders, now so wasted and thin. Sean's face was hollow, gaunt, shrunken, yet its color told a story of exposure to sun and weather; its seamed good humor told of a lifetime of work and lusty living. The body was wasted, but the eyes were bright and lively. Sean smiled up at Street and asked wryly: "Another victim of Gunhammer, Mister Street?"

It came as something of a shock to Street to hear his name used. He was getting accustomed already to being called Rawlins. He inclined his head with unconscious respect. He grinned with genuine liking. "No one likes to be considered a victim. The word implies complete helplessness."

"And aren't we helpless?" Vast bitterness was reflected in the old man's face.

Street's grin faded. He said: "If we admit it, we are. I haven't admitted it yet."

"And I have?"

Street's glance was an apology, a protest, but the old man waved it aside, smiling gently. "Do you blame me, Mister Street? Can a man fight from a wheelchair?"

"Others have. There are men who fight for money. Have you thought of them? Fighting men have been directed from a wheelchair before. They will be again."

"Not on Chain they won't. Because it is a battle that cannot be won without heavy casualties. Seguro has been on Chain as long as I, and he has nine children. He would fight with the others and he might be killed. I couldn't have that. Neither could I have Chain turned into a fortress, liable to attack and burning at any time. No, Mister Street, I will keep part of what is mine at least. I will keep it so that I can pass it on to Rose when I die. Perhaps someday a man will come along, a man with the strength to fight Gunhammer, who will marry Rose and recover what rightfully is hers."

Rose exclaimed: "Father!"

Sean glanced at her and grinned. "All right. I'll be still. But you see how I feel, Mister Street?"

Street nodded. "I do. And I had no business criticizing. After all, I'm not fighting, either."

Rose argued stoutly: "It's not your fight."

Street shrugged. "Tell Bauer that." The subject died, but Street had the feeling it was still alive in all their minds. Rose had said that it was not his fight, but Rose was wrong. Gunhammer had made it his fight when they beat him up. Rose had made it his fight when she'd taken him in and nursed him back to life. Only he couldn't pick up this fight. Because to do so would cost him what he had come here for. Instead, he would take Verona and leave the country to its own solution of the problem. This realization made him feel vaguely guilty.

Rose excused herself and Street sat on the verandah and talked with old Sean until dinner was ready. Sean, in his cracked voice, went back in time to the beginning, to his coming here with his wife, his small daughter, and Seguro Martinez, to found Chain.

Just before noon, Seguro, an aging, wizened Mexican, came riding in and dismounted before the porch. He bowed to Sean, then took Street's hand.

"You are better, *Señor* Street. *Seguro. Seguro.*"

Sean laughed gently. "You see why we call him Seguro? He keeps saying . . . 'Sure, sure.' . . . in Spanish."

Seguro reported briefly to Sean on the results of his morning's ride. His face was dark, wrinkled like a shriveling apple, but his eyes were young and full of humor. When he had finished, he crossed the yard to the log tenant house where he lived with his family.

Sean said: "Seguro's nine kids attend school down in the cañon. His wife helps Rose in the house."

"And he is your only 'puncher?"

"Yes. Except for spring and fall we need no more. Soon we will need none at all."

"And Seguro?"

"We will keep him, of course. As long as there is anything at all, this is Seguro's home, and his family's home."

As long as there is anything at all. The phrase lingered in Street's thoughts, repeating itself. Then, in his heart, Sean believed what Street believed. That there was no compromising with Gunhammer—that Gunhammer would eventually take it all. Right now, all Gunhammer wanted was the grass. But their greed could have no end. When they had Chain's grass, they would discover they needed the buildings as well, and the campaign would begin. Not a warring campaign, perhaps, only a campaign to make

90

existence at Chain intolerable for Sean, his daughter, and the family of Seguro Martinez. Then an offer. Give ground to greed once and there is never an end to it.

Rose came to the door announcing dinner, and Seguro came and wheeled old Sean Healy inside. Seguro and his wife sat down at the table with them, but Mrs. Martinez was up often, replenishing the food on the table. Street ate, not tasting the food, and feeling increasingly guilty. Conversation ran to generalities, the weather, the state of the grass, to the wolf-killed calf Seguro had found this morning. It was interrupted by the barking of dogs in the yard, by the drum of hoofs on hard-packed ground.

Rose hurried to the kitchen door and looked out, her face mirroring the uneasy terror that must live with her continually these days.

A harsh voice demanded from the yard: "I want to see Ben Rawlins."

"Why?" There was fear, undisguised, in Rose's voice.

Seguro had risen. He left the room and returned with a rifle. He jacked a shell into it and crossed silently to the window.

Street was touched. But he was also angered because Bauer had come. He knew a sudden, trapped feeling because he could neither let these people defend him nor take another beating at Bauer's hands. He knew he would kill before he would let Gunhammer touch him again. He got up, but Rose spoke sharply over her shoulder: "Sit still! You are not well enough. Don't come to the door!"

Street ignored her. He came up behind her and put his hands on her shoulders, gently moving her aside. Bauer had not bothered to dismount. He sat with his right side to the door, and his hand rested lightly on the pommel of his saddle, within instant reach of the cross-draw gun.

Street scowled, thinking—*There was a time when I'd have made you show your speed.*—but he said nothing.

Bauer was arrogant, riding the crest of what he believed to be Street's fear of him, He said: "Rawlins, we won't touch you while you're here. But you can't stay forever. When you leave . . ." He smiled cruelly, showing his white, even teeth. He was shaved today but his jaw still showed the bluish cast of his beard. His hair was as wildly unruly as ever. His eyes were oddly hot as they gazed at Street as he said: "I don't quite know why, but I feel something personal in this. I don't like you, mister."

Street's voice was dry. "That makes us even." He could feel something rising in him, something that had been unknown to him for more than two years, something that might have been the tense excitement that always preceded a gunfight. He made himself think of Verona.

"You didn't ride 'way up here to tell me that."

"No. We need Chain's summer graze. We've two thousand head of cattle on the trail, coming here from Texas. Brandt Lacey says to double the offer. A thousand dollars. Forty a head for your stock."

Street said: "Tell Brandt Lacey to go to hell."

"Nobody tells Brandt Lacey that." Bauer's expression showed little change, just a slight narrowing of the eyes, and Street knew he had been prepared for this answer. Bauer said to Street, tightening up the reins preparatory to leaving: "There was something more Brandt Lacey said to tell you. Seems Bruce noticed the way you and Verona couldn't keep your eyes off each other. Brandt says to tell you Verona's got Gunhammer's brand on her. She's been living with Bruce for a good long time now."

Street lunged out of the door, his face suddenly chalky. But Bauer, seeing he was unarmed, only laughed tauntingly, and reined away. Street stood in the yard, stunned, watching Bauer ride away. He turned, looked at Rose, and saw in her face the devastating admission that what Bauer had said was true. He began now to remember the way Rose looked whenever Verona's name came into the conversation. So this was what he had waited two long years for? This was why he had avoided trouble, demeaning himself, torturing himself. Blood rushed to his face. With it came a terrible rage, a fury such as he had never before known.

He asked: "Rose, why didn't you tell me? Didn't you know it would make me fight them?"

Her voice was scarcely audible. "Do you think I wanted you to fight on those terms? I'd rather have lost Chain than to have been the one to tell you."

Street stalked into the house. He found his hat and coat, and put them on. Outside again, he said: "Loan me a horse?"

Rose opened her mouth to protest, but she must have seen how useless it would have been. She nodded. "Take your pick out of the corral."

They were her last words to him. She watched him catch and saddle a horse, watched him mount, and did not miss the way he swayed for an instant in his saddle. Then he raised a hand to her, and rode away.

Tears dimmed her last view of him. He would be killed, of course. No man could buck Gunhammer and live—not even a man such as this. For an instant, Rose envied Verona. It must be a wonderful thing to have this man fighting over you, a glorious, wonderful thing.

Rose whirled and ran into the house. She fled to her room and flung herself face downward on the bed. For a while she lay still, trembling. And then, all at once, more tears came, and with them a cruel despair. She knew now what she would not have admitted before. She was in love with Street. She was in love with a man who would be dead before the day was out.

X

For the first ten minutes, Street's mind was a blank of tortured fury. But gradually, as his mind calmed, he began to see that he had no chance whatever of reaching Escalante in daylight. He had no gun. And he must pass directly through Gunhammer, the stronghold of his enemies. So, although it was perhaps the hardest thing he had ever done, he found himself a place down beside the creek where high willows would conceal both himself and his horse, and here he waited.

The daylight hours whiled away for what seemed an eternity. Stretched on the grassy bank of the creek, Street rested and marshaled his strength. The sun sank, and dusk dropped down over the land. In the first full dark, Street mounted and rode.

He passed warily through Gunhammer without incident, for it was just past suppertime, and no one was stirring in its broad fields. And, later, he entered the streets of Escalante carefully. He felt an ever-increasing nervousness now, aware of his helplessness without even a gun with which to defend himself.

A challenge came from the side of the street so suddenly as to be completely unnerving. "Who the hell's that?"

So Gunhammer had posted watchers on the roads leading into town.

Instead of answering, Street drove spurs into his horse's sides. The animal leaped ahead, surprised by the sudden nervousness of its rider. He thundered down Main, and the Gunhammer riders' shouts rang out behind excitedly: "Hey! It's Rawlins! It must be. I know that Chain horse!"

Cursing silently, Street reined savagely over and rode the horse through a weed-grown vacant lot to the alley. Here he dismounted, and, tying up the reins, slapped the horse on his muscled rump. The horse sprinted away, heading back the way they had come, heading back toward Chain.

Perhaps they would miss the horse in the dark. Perhaps he would get clear. Or perhaps they would see him and chase him without realizing that Street had dismounted. Breathing shallowly, harshly from exertion, Street ran through the lot and back toward the street, keeping to the building wall for more adequate concealment. He could hear the town stir and come to life. Voices began to shout all along Main. One, clear and separate from the rest, yelled: "There he goes!" And an instant later: "I got the horse! Rawlins ain't on him. He's hidin' somewheres."

Street felt a savage desperation. Here he was, hunted, in a hostile town, without a horse, without a gun. But it wouldn't stop him. Nothing would.

A group passed on the walk, their running boots making a rumbling thunder against the worn boards. Dogs were barking now all over town. Doors opened, and women's voices asked, querulously: "What is it? What's the matter?"

Somewhere the noise had awakened a child and it began to cry.

Street backtracked carefully to the alley. He guessed at the number of Gunhammer riders he had seen so far, deciding it had been five. But how many more were here? And where was Bauer? He moved along the alley until he came out on a narrow lane, then headed along this toward Main, knowing only one thing. He had to get his gun, and that was in the sheriff's office down on Cougar.

Fifty feet from the place where this narrow lane intersected with Main, he halted. Before Street, looming only as shapes in the dark, were three men who had just turned the corner. There was little chance of hiding, little chance that they would pass without seeing him. Street felt an empty kind of sickness. He could almost feel their fists thudding into his face, the solid blow of a gun barrel against his skull. Nausea surged through him. It angered him to realize that he was trembling. Better a bullet than another beating. He turned to run back in the direction from which he had come, then halted abruptly for a second time. For blocking his path in that direction were two more men and one of these carried a lantern. The search was well organized already. It was proceeding in systematic fashion, section by section of the town.

In an instant the men behind Street would glimpse his silhouette against the approaching lantern light. Probably they would do no shooting for fear of hitting each other. But they would close in on him in this narrow lane, two from the one direction, three from the other. And then he'd get the beating Bauer had promised this afternoon. Still weak from the last beating, he'd have little chance even to inflict his share of punishment on the Gunhammer men. He'd be strictly on the receiving end this time.

His anger was cold, but controlled and careful. He edged along the brick wall of the two-story building, waiting nervously for the shout that would reveal that he had been discovered. Luck was with him for once, and he was able to get to within fifteen feet of the lantern carrier before the man spotted him.

Street sprinted directly at the man, whose shouted surprise was instantly echoed by the three behind Street. Street's batting hand collided with the hot lantern and it made a loud crash as it struck the brick wall of the building. It broke, flamed briefly, and went out. In utter darkness, Street was past. Behind him, a gun flashed orange, and a bullet ricocheted off the wall and into the night, whining. Street reached the alley, and swung right, running hard, growing breathless and dizzy from exertion.

Behind him an instant later he heard a shout: "Which way did he go? Damn it, didn't anyone notice?"

And a resentful reply: "Did you see him, Buck? It's blacker'n Hades. How d'you expect . . . ?"

They wrangled peevishly for a few moments, then split up. Two came toward Street, one waited, and two went the other way.

Street stopped and took off his boots, folding them under his arm, and began to run soundlessly along the alley. He was not foolish enough to think he could tackle and whip two armed men. His only chance was to reach Coe's office and get his gun. If he could do that, by Judas, he'd show this Gunhammer outfit a scrap.

Headquarters for the search turned out to be Verona's house. Old Brandt Lacey sat on the porch with his sons around him, taking reports as they came in, directing the search. His anger was monumental as Bauer reported Street's escape from the five who had apparently had him cornered.

"Fools!" he raged. "A damn' jewelry salesman, unarmed at that, and you let him slip away!"

Behind him, Verona spoke triumphantly, gloatingly: "You're wrong, old man. You're not chasing a jewelry salesman named Rawlins. You're after a man named Walt Street, and if he gets a gun . . ." She left the sentence dangling.

"Then the dead one *was* Rawlins?" Bruce Lacey had a brutal grip on her arm, and she cried out involuntarily.

Old Brandt, his face purple in the light streaming from the open door, suddenly bellowed: "Douse that damned light! Quick! If that's who he is, we can expect him here before long."

Verona began to laugh hysterically. One of Brandt's sons ran inside and blew out the lights.

Brandt's voice was bitter. "So all this was for nothing! Hell, Rawlins has been dead all the time. And now we've got Street on our tails." He was silent a moment, and when he spoke again, his voice had chilled. "Max, send a man down to the hotel to tell Jagger nobody's earned that bounty yet. Tell him Street's still alive and here in town. Then you take the crew and find Street, if you can, before Jagger does. I'll add five hundred to Jagger's bounty on him. Now get going! I want Street dead!"

Behind him there was a faint rustle of silk, a quickly indrawn breath. Verona's heart was pounding. Why, oh, why hadn't she kept still? She'd thought to frighten Brandt into leaving Street alone. And she'd only succeeded in signing his death warrant. She slipped into the house, unnoticed. She went unerringly to the drawer where she'd put Bruce's Schofield .45. She took it out and, holding it against her dress, drew back nervously: "Max, wait! I think I can tell you where he's gone."

Brandt said: "You've told us enough, you damned Jezebel! Besides, Max is gone."

Verona put the muzzle of Bruce's gun deliberately against Brandt's old neck. "Call him back or I'll pull the trigger."

Brandt laughed. "You haven't got the guts," he said scornfully. "Besides, it's too late to call him back."

Verona could sense someone, maybe Bruce, moving toward her in the darkness. She said, her voice now trembling with hysteria: "Call him back!"

Brandt laughed again nastily. Someone lunged against Verona, throwing her aside. At the contact, she pulled the trigger. Brandt choked and fell forward out of his chair. The shot drew half a dozen men of the Gunhammer crew. They came running from the darkness and, with Brandt's sons, bent over the old man. Verona they ignored for the moment.

Standing in a shadowed doorway, Street heard the shot, heard the sound of running footsteps as the searchers now converged on the house at the upper end of Main. It was his chance, he knew. Without hesitating, he ran down toward Coe's office.

Alerted by the sound of the shot, Coe was just coming out of his office. Street halted in the shadows and let him pass. Then he went into Coe's office. He struck a match and by its light riffled through the sheriff's desk until he found his gun. He loaded it, strapped it on, and turned toward the door.

His eye caught the movement of a shadow in the doorway, and only instinct dictated his sudden lunge to one side. Flame laced from a waist-high gun in the doorway, and the sound of the report was deafening. Street heard Max Bauer's low, triumphant laugh. Perhaps he could have cut Bauer down with his gun, killed him outright then and there. But his anger, his fury at Bauer was too great for that. Bauer was the one whose fists had helped beat him to insensibility, almost to death. Bauer was the one who had given the order for the beating. A quick death would be too easy for Bauer.

Street said softly: "Get me fast, Bauer, if you can. Because I'm going to beat you until you'll wish you were dead."

His answer was a second shot from beside the doorway. And now he began to move, as silently as a stalking panther, testing each footfall before he would let his weight down. He could hear Bauer's hastened breathing, and grinned coldly when Bauer panicked and fired again. Bauer had no liking for this, now that he knew who Street was, that was plain. So Street watched the square of lighter gray that made the doorway, to see that Bauer did not escape.

Bauer fired a fourth time, but this bullet missed Street by a full three feet. But he had seen Bauer's crouched form in the flare from the gun—no more than ten feet away—the hated sneering face, whose sneer now had an odd, fixed quality. Sudden fury overpowered Street. He lunged, gun raised, and brought the muzzle of it savagely down upon Bauer's forearm. A low-pitched sound of pain broke from Bauer's lips. Street jabbed the gun muzzle into his belly, and heard the sound choked off. Bauer's gun clattered to the floor. Almost without thinking, Street jammed his own gun into its holster. His fists struck out, given added power by his vengeful fury. They struck rhythmically against Bauer's heavy face.

Bauer's hands came up, but Street's savage fists beat them aside. Again he could feel his knuckles smashing Bauer's face, his nose, his mouth, his eyes, and throat. Bauer choked, gasped, and would have retreated but for the wall at his back. Street's eyes were more accustomed to the darkness now. He could see his adversary dimly. Bauer choked: "Street, let up! Look, Street, the two of us could take over this whole damned range if we'd work together. . . ."

Street saw Bauer's gleaming white teeth as the

man smirked hopefully. With all the power of his shoulder behind it, his right went out. He felt those gleaming teeth crack beneath its force. He felt his knuckles split. And Bauer slid down the wall to the floor. Street said hoarsely: "Get out of the country, Bauer! If I see you again, I'll kill you!"

He stalked out the door. The job was begun, but not finished. Only now there was a difference. Street was no longer the hunted. Now he was the hunter. What he did not know was that behind him, Max was groping around for his gun. Bauer found it, loaded it, and hurried after Street, heading for the hotel verandah. There, Bauer knew, Jagger was waiting patiently. Between them, Bauer figured, they could get this crazy gunman.

Street stalked from the sheriff's office up toward Main. He turned toward Verona's house, which was now ablaze with light. Street's mind was sick with fury and outrage, only partially appeased by his victory over Bauer. Verona, his wife, living with Bruce Lacey, and Rose Healy, badgered, was about to be pushed ruthlessly off Chain. The restraint was off him. The two years were past. Tonight some things were going to be changed.

He walked toward the tall frame house at the end of Main, cautiously, slowly, taking advantage of all available cover. And his slowness made it possible for Bauer to reach the hotel verandah even as Street came abreast of it. Afterward, two figures left the verandah and fell in behind him, Jagger and the hurt, maniacal Bauer. Jagger carried a rifle at the ready. Bauer carried his revolver in his hand.

Coe was within the light circle before Verona's house. So was Verona, and Bruce Lacey, and Bruce's two brothers. But old Brandt was down on the porch floor, dead. Doc was rising from beside Brandt's body, shaking his head.

Street walked into the circle of light. His voice was like a whip. "So the king is dead?"

Bruce's hand flashed toward his gun. The compulsion was strong in Street to kill him. But in the split second of decision, he rose above it and put a bullet into Bruce's shoulder. Bruce was driven back across the porch. He collapsed against the house's front door.

Behind Street, Jagger raised the rifle. Bauer kept moving closer, face twisted and bleeding, wanting a sure thing this time. Verona's eyes, meeting Street's briefly, were stricken.

Street said: "I did what you asked. I put my gun away. What happened on the stage was no fault of mine. Why couldn't you have waited?"

Verona's eyes shifted and fell away. They went beyond him, saw Jagger drawing his bead. She screamed. Street whirled, his gun finding Jagger's body and centering. The bellow of the rifle and Street's revolver sounded in savage unison. Jagger's bullet buzzed like a bee past Street's head, struck a building behind him, and ricocheted angrily off into the night. But Jagger was beginning to fold, his eyes already glazing over.

A bullet twitched at Street's sleeve. He ducked into a crouch, and a second bullet, which would have pierced his heart, grazed across the hard, flat muscles of his shoulder.

Bauer panicked then. As fast as he could thumb back the hammer, he flung the shots in his gun wildly at Street. Calmly, almost abstractedly, Street centered his gun on Bauer's chest. There was no hatred in him now, only the strong instinct to survive. He squeezed the trigger and saw Bauer jerk under the impact.

Verona's screaming was continuous. But it stopped abruptly as Nick Lacey began to fire at Street. Only the awed fear engendered by Street's reputation had saved him so far. They'd all been too anxious, and too afraid. But it wouldn't save him forever. Before he could complete his turn toward Lacey, Verona fired for the second time tonight. The huge Schofield bucked in her slim hand.

Hurt, Nick turned on her. Between clenched teeth he whispered: "Why, damn you! Damn you anyway!" At pointblank range, he fired.

Verona was flung back like a limp rag doll. She

struck the wall and slumped down it as though she were only very tired.

Street's head was ringing. His arms and legs felt like lead. There was shock to all this killing, but he knew he wasn't hit. This was only his weakness coming back. The Gunhammer crew seemed dazed, but that would pass, and when it did, they would be dangerous. Street said quickly, harshly: "Gunhammer's through. With Brandt and Bauer dead, Gunhammer's finished."

He heard Doc's voice: "Verona's gone, too."

The old fury came roaring back to Street. For a moment he stood like an executioner, staring at Nick. Nick shuddered, and licked his lips. "Street, don't! I'll leave Escalante forever. Don't kill me. For Christ's sake, don't!"

Street fought hard for control. At last he said bleakly: "You'll all leave. Before morning. Send in someone to settle up your damned ranch for you, but don't ever come back."

He heard swift-running feet coming toward him along the street. He heard a voice, Rose's voice. "Walt! Oh, Walt, are you hurt?"

He shook his head. And now, Coe spoke up at last. "I'll make what Street said official. Get out, the three of you. And stay out!" Coe's rifle was steady and his voice was strong.

Street looked at him. Coe was late, but perhaps he had finally found his strength, with old Brandt and Bauer dead. Perhaps now, with the memory of his weakness and humiliation strong in him, he would cling to his newfound strength. Street had found his own strength too—in the warm arms that now encircled him, in the tear-wet cheek against his own. He had found a woman who wanted him exactly as he was, who wanted both his strength and his weakness. He had found a woman who would help him live down the past, to build the future.

Rose murmured brokenly: "We can go home now, Walt. It's over, darling."

Street made a grin that had no bitterness in it. "No. It's not over. It's just beginning."

Rose smiled with a woman's tender triumph. And led him out of the lantern light into the darkness.

LAWLESS TOWN

I

At first they were only two small specks, materializing out of the vast and empty land lying to the north, rising whorls of dust behind them the only evidence that they were moving. But as they drew closer they became elongated and, approaching through the shimmering, distant waves of heat rising from the sun-baked land, became wagons, big wagons drawn by four mules each and loaded high with hides. Sloan Hewitt drove the lead wagon, hunched forward with his elbows on his knees, the reins held competently in big, callused, sun-blackened hands. His body leaned and swayed, compensating automatically for the jolting movement of the wagon, but he seemed as comfortable as though the seat were cushioned or his buttocks made of iron.

He was a big man, with everything except muscle and sinew and bone sweated and worked from his six-foot frame. A beard, reddish and ragged, and a floppy wide-brimmed hat all but hid his face. But his eyes peered out, blue as the sky above his head, watchful and narrowed against the glare. Also visible was his nose, a bit sharp but prominent and shaped like the nose of a Cheyenne chief. Shaggy, stinking hides behind —shaggy, stinking men ahead. He grinned wryly as his mind drew the comparison. Then he began to think of what lay ahead. The town. A market for the hides and wagons, too. A bath, a shave, and a change of clothes. He was a man who could grin—whose grin touched every part of his face and not his mouth alone. But a man, too, with something brooding behind his eyes, of bitterness, or disillusionment, that never went away.

Sid Wessell drove the second wagon, his feet spread and braced. They drove in silence because everything they had to talk about had long since been talked about, and because the noise of wagons and mules made conversation difficult. Withal, they were a companionable pair, with no hidden resentments or angers between them.

Ahead, the town materialized as a few moments before these two had materialized out of the empty distances to the north. Prairie Town was not very large or prepossessing, but it was larger than when they had seen it last. A town composed of crooked streets lined with one-story frame buildings, their false fronts a shoddy attempt to make them appear more imposing than they were, and eternal dust rising from the streets until it made a thin haze over the entire place. The herds, trailing in from the south, were bunched on the grass within a ten-mile radius to north and west and east, with riders going between the waiting herds and the waiting town. A twin ribbon of steel linked the town with the East. Along this tenuous link of steel puffed a locomotive, drawing a seemingly endless string of cattle cars.

Skirting the waiting herds, Sloan drove his wagon in and stopped at the crest of a little knoll to stare down at the bustling place. Wagons and riders churned the dust in the streets, the noise of their voices and their rigs making a kind of buzz clearly audible in the summer air. Closer were the residences of the townspeople, simple frame dwellings for the most part, some with lawns, some without. Sloan's gaze lingered on a woman hanging clothes in the backyard of one, and now, all at once, the brooding loneliness in his eyes became more obvious. She was dressed in a blue gingham gown, her dark hair pinned loosely out of the way atop her head. Her sleeves were rolled above her elbows, and her arms were brown. A little girl was playing with a doll on the lawn nearby. She was too far away for Sloan to see her features. But there was a picture in his mind of what they would be like.

His face twisted briefly into an expression something like a frown, and then he put his wagon into motion again with the briefest of glances over his shoulder at Sid. Down the slope to the waiting town he went, and along the quiet residential street, all too recently cut from the prairie sod, down the main business street and across the tracks, and thence westward, away from the cattle pens, to the hide warehouse, easily recognizable by its size, its smell, and the towering pile of bleaching bones behind it.

He pulled the mules to a halt and tied the reins. He jumped down, waited for Sid, then crossed the yard with him. This was Sloan's first venture as a buffalo hunter, and it would be his last—in spite of the fact that it would pay handsomely for the time he'd spent.

A man in leather apron, black sleeve protectors, and black skullcap came out of the warehouse to stand in the shade beneath a sign that read: IKE SOLOMON—HIDES AND BONES.

Sloan leaped easily to the dock, Sid following. Sloan said: "I'm Sloan Hewitt, and this is Sid Wessell. We've got five hundred and sixty-eight hides, more'n ninety percent bulls. We got two wagons and eight mules. What'll you give for the lot?"

"Quittin'?"

Sloan nodded.

Solomon was a dour, smallish man with shrewd eyes behind gold-rimmed glasses pinched to his nose. "Too hard or too dirty?"

Sloan's eyes narrowed at the unpleasantness in Solomon's tone. "You a hide buyer or do you make your living asking questions?"

Solomon frowned. "Market's three dollars and seventy-eight cents for bulls. I'll pay three-fifty. Half that for cowhides." He got out a stub of pencil and figured a moment on his celluloid cuff. Looking up, he said in a take-it-or-leave-it tone: "Three thousand."

Sloan said: "Thirty-two hundred."

"Thirty-one. And I'll dock you for every spoiled hide you've got."

Sloan nodded. "A deal."

"Come back this evening. I'll have your money then."

Sloan nodded again. He turned to grin at Sid. "Somebody say something about a bath?"

He hadn't known it would be so bad—that slaughtering animals for their hides could so remind a man of the war and the slaughter of men. But it had, and that was why he was quitting now.

As they got their guns and personal gear out of the wagons, Sid said exultantly: "Take off six hundred we got in the mules and a hundred in the harness and four hundred for the wagons and we still come up with a profit of a thousand apiece. Not bad for two months' work."

No, Sloan thought. *It wasn't bad. If a man stayed with it he could make himself a stake, a start that would put him well along the road to being rich. That is, if a man didn't think. If a man thought about it at all, he realized that every rotting carcass out there on the plain meant that some Indian lodge would feel the pinch of hunger during the months to come.*

He flung his saddle to a shoulder, hefted his rifle and war sack in his left hand, and trudged away toward town, Sid keeping pace. And now he began to see the changes that had come in the last two months, that had come with the herds and their crews. For one thing, the cattle pens were full. Men, sitting on a fence, tallied cattle into a car. When it was full, another moved into place. And this went on all day.

The pair left the tracks behind and started up Texas Street. There was a bustle about the town and, even at this hour, a wildness, an untamed quality you didn't notice until you mingled with the people on the streets and became a part of it. The signs over the saloons were riddled with bullet holes, and one hung from a single chain, the other having been parted by a lucky or remarkably accurate shot.

Sloan and Sid trudged uptown until they reached a hotel, wide verandah stretching across its face, balconies above the verandah. A bullet-marked sign hung above the steps: DROVERS REST.

The pair went in, a bit self-conscious about their appearance and, after registering at the desk, disappeared up the stairs, both grinning a little, both anticipating the feel of being clean, the feel of beds beneath their bodies once again. And, as they did, a volley of shots sounded at the lower end of Texas Street, and down there in the dry dust a man died and stained the dust with his blood. Watching him die, the expressions of concern deepened in the faces of some of those in the street. This town had a man for breakfast every day. This town had a savage and insatiable taste for blood.

At sundown, Sloan Hewitt came down the stairs to the lobby, leaving his partner behind in the room, mouth open, snoring noisily. He was dressed now in soft-tanned Texas boots, wool pants tucked into their tops, and a faded Army shirt. He wore no hat. He paused on the verandah, squinting slightly against the orange glare in the western sky, and lit one of the cigars he had purchased at the desk. Then he turned briskly toward the mercantile store across the street and several doors north.

A dozen riders came thundering down Texas Street, raising a blinding cloud of dust. As they passed the hotel, several of them emptied their guns at the sign in front of the hotel. Sloan had to jump to get out of their way, but he did so cheerfully enough and with no resentment. He watched them disappear into their own cloud of dust as they thundered on down the street.

He went into the store and bought a hat, fitted it on his head, and stepped out into the soft dusk of the street with it cocked, uncreased, over his right eye. Now something was noticeable about him that had not been noticeable before—his gun and belt stood out because the rest of him was so clean and new. The belt was cracked and caked with buffalo grease and dust. The revolver holster, hardened by countless wettings, was formed exactly to the shape of the gun it held. The gun itself, the part of it that showed, was different. The grip was scarred, the blue worn off cylinder, hammer, and frame, but a light coating of oil shone on the gleaming metal, and there was not a speck of rust.

He walked downstreet, his cigar firmly clamped in his big, strong teeth. He heard the barkers before the larger saloons. He heard the tinkle of pianos, the hum of voices, and occasionally a woman's laugh. He let himself be jostled by drunks and others too intent on what they were doing to watch where they were going, good-naturedly, because out where he had been, there was nothing but silence, loneliness, and the smell of blood and death.

He walked past the saloons and beyond—right along the tracks, toward the gloomily towering bulk of the hide warehouse. A single lamp glowed dimly through the dirty office window. Sloan knocked and went inside.

Solomon sat at a scarred roll-top desk, wearing a green eye-shade, still wearing black sleeve protectors and his black skullcap. He glanced up, then fumbled for a sheet of paper among the others on his cluttered desk. He said: "It tallies three thousand seventy-one dollars."

Sloan nodded. Solomon got up and went to the tall wall safe at the rear of his office. Shielding the knob with his body, he twirled it and a few moments later swung open the ponderous door. He said without turning: "Gold or specie?"

"Gold's too heavy. Give me paper."

Solomon came back to the desk, carrying a black enamel box. He opened it, counted out the money, closed it, and returned it to the safe. Coming back, he counted the money again, then shoved a receipt at Sloan. "Sign for it."

Sloan signed. He picked up the bills and stuffed them into his pants pocket. He'd go back to the hotel and put the money in the hotel safe. In the morning he could put it in the bank.

It was wholly dark outside. He stood for a moment beside the door, letting his eyes become accustomed to the dark. Then he jumped down off the dock and headed along the tracks toward the foot of Texas Street.

The soft, velvety breeze of a summer night blew off the prairie, blew away the smells of the town and the hide warehouse at his back. It was laden with the smell of crushed sage, with the vague, faint smell of horses and cattle, with the elusive smell of a thousand endless miles of grass. For some reason the soft night breeze reminded him of things—of another place and another time, of a woman faintly scented with lilac and soft and warm, of a promise made that was never kept, and, remembering her, Sloan thought of another woman, the one he had seen hanging clothes on a line today while a small child played nearby.

Something, some odd uneasiness, made him glance behind, and he saw Solomon standing at the end of his warehouse dock, a dim figure in the faint light shining out of the open office door. He felt the beginning of a chill along his spine, a chill that was premonition, a warning sense bred out of men when they came out of their caves ten thousand years ago but present still in some. His hand dropped toward his gun but too late, for they were suddenly all around him. A hard-swung two-by-four torn from a fence row nearby slammed him on the side of the head and neck, stunning him like a hard-sledged steer.

Down he went, still conscious but paralyzed and wholly unable to move, thinking: *You fool! You poor, damned, stupid fool! You walked into this like a greenhorn straight off the farm!* His thoughts stopped, and he could feel the pain of their boots in his ribs, his thighs, his shoulders, and his face. The one with the two-by-four belabored him with it whenever he could swing without hitting one of his savage companions.

Sloan's consciousness faded. The last thing he felt was his pockets being searched, the last thing he heard a growling voice: "Got it, Lane?"

"Yeah. Let's go."

"Is he dead?"

"If he ain't, he damn' soon will be."

"Come on, then."

Three of them, one called Lane. Faceless men coming out of the shadows and returning now to the shadows from which they had come. But not voiceless men. He'd know their voices if he ever heard them again. Consciousness left him, and he lay unmoving, as though dead. The rise and fall of his chest was slow and labored, the sound of his breathing rasping but very faint.

It was cooler when he regained consciousness, and he knew he had been lying there a long, long time. With returning consciousness came the pain, splitting his head, running like knives down his neck to his collar bone and into his chest. One leg felt broken, and his face burned savagely. His mouth was so puffy he could scarcely lick his lips. But, when he did, he tasted blood.

He heard someone coming along the tracks and putting forth a supreme effort, managed a voiceless croak. And then, the unbelievable, a girl, running toward him, kneeling beside him. Her voice was crisp. "Are you drunk or hurt?"

He didn't question fate. He groaned: "Hurt. Help me to my feet."

He found out at once that his leg wasn't broken, for it bore his weight. Gritting his teeth against the pain, leaning heavily upon the strong and slender girl, he went with her along the tracks to Texas Street. And, as he did, anger came to him. It began as a tiny stirring in the back of his mind, but it grew as a fire in dry grass grows until it blazed white-hot all through his brain. Anger. Not because he had lost the money nor because now the months of bloody work were for nothing. Not even because of the pain. No. This fury was partly at himself for making it so easy for them, partly at the town, at the times, at the thing in men that makes them live like beasts of prey.

This was pure, consuming rage because he was sick of violence and death and because he could see, more clearly than he ever had before, that there could be no end to it for him. It followed him, clung to him, lived with him. He'd tried to avoid it but would never run from it. He walked painfully along toward the lights of the noisy town, the girl half supporting him. Two voices and a name were sharply remembered things in his mind.

II

The girl, whose face he still had not seen, turned at the first intersection off Texas Street and after that led him along quieter business and residential streets until she reached a small white cottage sitting at the very edge of the prairie.

While he stood silently on the porch, she went in the unlocked door and lit a lamp. She held the screen open for him, and he stumbled inside to collapse into the first chair he reached.

He realized at once how bloody and dirty he was and tried to get up, but she pushed him back. "Never mind the chair. Good heavens, what did they hit you with?"

"A two-by-four, I think." He stared up at her, trying to make his eyes show him a clearly focused picture of her.

She was a tall girl, he remembered that much. The top of her head had come well above the point of his shoulder. Her hair was dark, braided, and the braids were coiled around her head. Her eyes, resting on him, were steady and appraising, her mouth firm. He wondered what she had been doing, walking along the railroad tracks in the middle of the night. She wasn't a saloon girl, that was plain enough.

"Did they rob you?"

Her voice, though crisp, had a disturbing timbre, a throaty quality he found pleasant. He nodded and said wryly: "Three thousand."

She said: "I'll get some water and things. Do you think you have any broken bones?"

"I doubt it. Ribs maybe, but nothing else."

She disappeared. He heard the back door, the squeak of the pump in the yard. He heard the back door again, the clatter of a pan, a sound like that of a tea kettle being replaced on the stove. Then she came into the room, carrying a basin of water and an armload of towels.

"Take off your shirt."

He got up. Wincing, he removed the torn and dirty shirt. She probed gently at his ribs with her fingers, finished, and glanced up at him. "Two broken. You haven't asked me what I was doing down there at this hour."

Sloan said: "Not my business."

She didn't answer that. She was busy washing him with a wet, soapy cloth. The skin had been scraped off in a good many places, and, while his face remained expressionless, his skin twitched and pulled away from the cloth. But she finished at last, dried where she had washed, and then began to wind strips of sheet tightly around his mid-section.

Finishing this, she asked: "What will you do? There is no law in this town."

He said: "I'll make some. I'm sure not going to let it go."

"You saw them?"

"No. I didn't see them . . . their faces, that is. But I heard one of their names and I heard their voices." He reached for his shirt and shrugged into it. The pain was considerably less than it had been before, due to the bandages tightly wound around his middle. He said: "Ma'am, I'm obliged."

There was an odd expression in her face.

"Forget what you're planning. Ride on out. If you don't, they'll be burying you in the morning." She studied his face for several moments, then turned away with a little helpless shrug. "Good bye."

The coolness of her voice disturbed him, and he felt ungrateful. He turned to the door and stepped outside. He started down the walk, then halted as he heard her voice. "You lost your hat. See if this one fits."

He returned, took the hat from her, and put it on. She said: "It was my father's."

"Thank you, ma'am."

She came out onto the porch with him. She said, in a small furious voice: "Damn you!" Then, unexpectedly, she took his face between her hands and kissed him on the mouth.

Sloan caught her and held her for a moment. There was no response in her, and she held her body stiff. He released her, puzzled, feeling a strange sense of frustration. He didn't understand this one at all.

She stepped away into the darkness. "They say this town has a man for breakfast every day. My father made one meal for it. You'll make another. I guess . . . oh, hell, go on and do what you think you have to do." Sloan didn't move, and her voice turned sharp. "Go on! Why should I worry about you?"

"You shouldn't, ma'am." Sloan turned and

tramped along the graveled walk to the street. Reaching it, he turned. He could see her standing in the doorway. As he watched, she closed the door.

He walked away toward the noise and the lights of the town. Walking, his hand dropped to his gun, touched it, and came away. He passed the hotel where he had left Sid without looking at it. He needed a new shirt, but he didn't want to let Sid know what had happened. He didn't want Sid horning in on this, maybe getting himself killed.

He started with the first saloon he reached, the Bullshead, knowing his search would take a long time unless he happened to be unusually lucky. It was a big town. There were at least twenty-five saloons. He had a drink in the Bullshead, listened, circulated, and afterward moved on.

He watched the gambling tables. He watched for heavy spenders. He listened—for those voices, for that name. And the hours passed.

He was halfway down Texas Street when the sky began to turn deep gray in the east. The barkers had gone inside. Sullen drunks, boisterous drunks, quarrelsome drunks filled the street. Occasionally a burst of gunfire echoed from one of the flimsy buildings. Sloan turned in at one of the more pretentious of the saloons, called the Longhorn. He heard no familiar voices. He heard no names. But he knew as he stepped through the swinging doors that the three were here. He knew which three they were. Because, of all the men in the saloon, only these three saw him or paid him any mind.

Their scrutiny was brief and soon over. But their faces held, in that short instant, fleeting wonder—a touch of uneasiness—a flash of recognition and surprise. Surprise that he was still alive. Surprise that he was here. They were together at the bar. They were all a little drunk. Sloan paced purposefully toward them.

He felt right now as he had felt on a number of occasions during the war—before he led his cavalry down into the woods where he knew the gray-clad infantrymen were—before he led a charge over a stone wall and up a hill into the withering fire from the top. Emptiness came to his belly, coldness to his spine. They were familiar symptoms. But his face was like a rock, and his hands were steady and sure.

He stopped ten feet away. He said: "Lane!"

One of them jerked. But he didn't look up, and he didn't turn. Instead he muttered something to his companions, who immediately pushed away from the bar and sidled to right and left. And then he turned. "Who the hell are you?"

He was a couple of inches shorter than Sloan, but he was broad. A red-faced man, he wore several days' growth of reddish whiskers. His sweat-stained hat, pushed back, revealed reddish hair thinning over his temples.

Sloan said: "You've got something of mine. I want it back."

"What the hell are you talking about?"

The voice was familiar, the same voice Sloan had heard earlier as he lay on the ground down by the hide warehouse, helplessly waiting to be killed. He knew what they were doing. He understood their strategy in separating. He couldn't keep his eyes on all three at once. And he couldn't fire his gun in more than one direction at a time.

He took several evenly paced backward steps. A drunk jostled him, and he sent the man sprawling to the floor with a savage sweep of his arm without taking his eyes from Lane. There was no real fear in him—only that emptiness in his belly, the old coldness in his spine. He supposed those were the symptoms of fear, and yet he had faced death too many times to shrink from it now. A certain fatalism was in him—a belief that when his time came he would die, regardless of all other considerations, that until that time came he would live.

Lane's eyes, close-set and strangely piggish, flicked from one side to the other. They were bolder when they again met Sloan's. The man had looked to his companions for reassurance, and found it.

Sloan said: "Don't pick the hard way, Lane.

Give me the money and I'll overlook the bumps."

There was a nervous laugh from one of Lane's companions, but Sloan didn't look at him. The man said: "Listen at that, fer God's sake! We got him boxed."

Sloan put his eyes on the man. Whatever he had intended more to say died in his throat. Beyond Lane the bartender scrambled out of the way. And behind Sloan a path of emptiness opened. The drunk Sloan had flung aside got up and advanced on him gloweringly.

He saw the flicker of decision touch Lane's piggish, close-set eyes, but he was moving before Lane began to move. He moved toward the drunk, swept his gun from its holster, brought it up, and slammed the barrel into the side of the drunk's head. He lunged beyond the drunk at the one on Lane's right, striking him with his shoulders and bowling him back. Whirling, just as Lane's gun flamed, he released the thumbed-back hammer of his gun and felt it buck against his palm.

Lane slammed back against the bar and hung there, motionless, for the barest instant. But Sloan's eyes weren't on him now. The muzzle of his gun swung, belching smoke and flame. The one beyond Lane got off two shots, the second of which raked a furrow along the muscles of Sloan's forearm. Sloan fired again, knew where this bullet struck, and whirled, falling, to face the one he'd bowled aside before. That one was on

129

the floor, fanning the hammer of his gun from there. Sloan struck the floor, let himself roll, then brought his feet under him like a cat. Freezing all motion for the briefest part of a second, he put a bullet into the third man's throat.

Breathing hard, he got to his feet. Lane was crumpled over the bar rail. The second man was spread-eagled on his back. The third was gurgling as the last of his blood and his breath mingled in his shattered throat.

Sloan saw the bartender stoop and, when the man raised up, a double-barreled shotgun in his hands, he was ready for him. Leaning over the bar, he slashed competently with his fisted gun. The barrel and the front sight raked the bartender's forehead, bringing an instant rush of blood. The shotgun rattled on the bar.

Sloan seized it, holstered his revolver, and swung around. If there had been thought of interference from any of the trio's friends in the crowd, it died suddenly. Sloan spoke over his shoulder: "Bartender, come on out here."

The man shuffled from behind the bar, mopping his bleeding forehead with a wet bar towel. Sloan said: "These three beat me and robbed me of three thousand and seventy-one dollars. If anyone wants to check the amount, he can see Ike Solomon." The man stared at him fearfully. Sloan said gently: "Go through their pockets and lay their money on the bar. Count out three thousand

and seventy-one dollars, and I'll be on my way."

He waited while the bartender kneeled to rifle the pockets of the dead. He watched the stack of money grow as the bartender went from one to the other. He waited impassively while the man counted money with hands that shook almost uncontrollably.

He finished. Sloan said: "Pick it up and hand it to me."

The bartender complied. Sloan stuffed the roll into his pocket. He broke the shotgun, tossed the shells into the spittoon, and put the shotgun on the bar. He walked down the lane that had opened up and went out the door.

He was hurting now—from the broken ribs, from the places on his face and scalp where the two-by-four had struck, from the bullet burn along the muscles of his arm. His anger was gone, and in its place was only the sickness, the bitterness that violence always brought.

III

Sloan Hewitt did not awake until noon. When he did, he stared up into the face of his partner, into Sid's bloodshot eyes, his gray, sick face. He stirred and sat up on the side of the bed, remembering now all that had happened the night before. He'd returned to the hotel room to find Sid passed out cold, an empty quart of whiskey beside his bed.

Sid said: "There's some men outside looking for you. God, what a night! You look like you've been in a fight."

Sloan said: "I was." He grinned at Sid. "You look like you tried to drink the damned town dry."

He got up, and Sid fell across the bed, both hands to his head. Sloan felt stiff this morning, and there was pain, but he pulled on his pants and boots, belted his gun around his middle, and, shirtless, went to the door.

Three men stood in the hall, their hats in their hands. Sloan said—"You want to see me?"—relaxing immediately as he saw them. All three were unarmed, dressed in respectable business suits. One had mutton-chop whiskers along his jaws, brown and silky, but the other two were clean-shaven.

The one with the mutton-chop whiskers nodded and extended a hand. "I saw you in the Longhorn last night. I . . . that is, we have a proposition to make you."

Sloan shrugged. "Come on in."

He stood aside, and the three filed into the room. Sloan closed the door, went over to the wash-stand, and poured a pan full of cold water. He washed thoroughly, ignoring the pain soap and water brought to the lacerations on his face. His mouth felt puffy. He dried his face and turned. "What is it?"

The mutton-chopped man said: "I'm Will

Dryden. I own the bank. This"—he indicated the man next to him—"is Lucian Lake, and"—indicating the third man—"this is Frank Graham. Frankly, Mister Hewitt, we're concerned about our town. We're concerned about our safety and that of our families. It's time we had some law."

Sloan said: "Get some, then."

"That's why we're here, Mister Hewitt. We want you to take the job as town marshal. We saw you work last night, and, if anyone can do it, you can."

Sloan shook his head without hesitation. "You've got the wrong man. I'm no lawman. Besides that, whoever takes the job will be dead in twenty-four hours."

"An ordinary man would."

Sloan rummaged in his war sack and found a clean shirt. He shrugged into it gingerly, saying: "You're crazy. Why should anyone take on a job like that? There's not enough money in the world. . . ."

"No. There isn't. We realize that. A man would have to want something besides money to take the job."

"Like what?"

Dryden shrugged. "Satisfaction, maybe. You risked your life last night to recover your three thousand dollars, Mister Hewitt. Was it just for the money, or was there something else?"

"The money," Sloan growled, but he knew it

wasn't true. A man didn't put a price on his life, even though sometimes he risked it for a price—and for an intangible something else.

Dryden said: "The pay for marshal would be three hundred a month. Three hundred more for expenses and deputies."

Sloan shook his head. "No." And now a vague anger touched him.

"Why, man, why? You can do it. And the pay is right."

Sloan's anger grew. He said sourly: "Money's your answer, isn't it? You've stood by and watched this happening to your town and you let it happen because the money was rolling in. When you could have stopped it, you didn't, because you didn't want to stop that flood of money. Now you're scared because you've suddenly realized there's a lion loose in the streets, but you still think in terms of money. You think you can buy safety from the thing you allowed and even encouraged." He shook his head again. "Go find someone else."

"Mister Hewitt . . ."

Sloan said coldly: "The answer is no. Get out of here."

Dryden opened his mouth to protest further, then closed it abruptly. Hat in hand, he backed to the door, then turned and followed the others out. Sloan went over and kicked the door shut. He looked at Sid. "Hungry?"

Sid groaned. "Hell no." He rolled and sat up on the bed. His eyes pinched shut as the pain of his throbbing head struck him. "What were they talking about?"

Sloan grinned. "I got robbed last night. When I came to, I went looking for the three that robbed me."

"Find 'em?" There was quick anxiety in Sid's tone.

Sloan nodded. "And I got the money back. I'll go over and put it in the bank right now."

Sid sighed with relief and lay back on the bed. He closed his eyes and groaned. "I think I'm going to die."

Sloan picked up his hat. Seeing it reminded him of the girl who had given it to him last night. He didn't even know her name, he realized. He went out quietly and closed the door, thinking of the girl. She had puzzled him. She had seemed so crisp and efficient, yet she had kissed him and cursed him within the space of a few seconds, and neither had been an act of crispness or self-assurance. He smiled faintly to himself. He'd have to see her again, today, and thank her for helping him.

He walked through the lobby and out into the glaring sun. He crossed the street to the bank, deposited the money, and tucked the receipt carefully into his pocket. He lit a cigar, then went downstreet to the mercantile store, and bought another hat. With the one she had given him wrapped in brown paper, he hunted along the eastern edge of town until he found her house.

In daylight, it was a pleasant place despite the lack of trees. Its lawn was green, and there were beds of flowers on either side of the porch. He knocked and heard her steps coming, and a moment later she faced him through the screen door, dressed in a flowered dress and looking fresh and clean.

He grinned. "I'm returning the hat you gave me. And I want to thank you, too."

The expression on her face was a puzzling combination of conflicting emotions. But she seemed genuinely glad to see him. She opened the screen door. "Come in. I was getting dinner for myself, but I hate to eat alone."

He said: "I don't even know your name. I'm Sloan Hewitt."

"I'm Merline Morris. Come on. It's warmed-over chicken and cold dumplings, but if you're not too fussy . . ."

"I'm not fussy, ma'am. I've eaten nothing but buffalo for several months."

There was a fresh tablecloth on the kitchen table. He sat down, and she poured him a cup of steaming black coffee. "I hear you recovered your money last night."

Her voice held a note of disapproval, of censure. He said: "You don't approve?"

"I'd rather not answer that."

"Why not?"

She turned, and her eyes touched the gun hanging at his side. "Isn't there ever any way but that way? Three men are dead."

He said: "They didn't want to give the money back. What other way was there?" His eyes mocked her good-naturedly.

"There's such a thing as law."

"Not here there isn't."

"There could be." Her back was to him, but he sensed that she knew, not only about the fight last night in which Lane and his two companions had been killed, but also about the offer made to him this morning by the banker and his friends.

He said: "You get around, don't you?"

She turned. "I get around. I'm a cattle buyer."

"You think I ought to have taken the job?"

"Someone's got to. Sometime. Or this town is going to destroy itself."

"Why should I care? The town could have stopped what was happening any time it wanted to. Now it's too late."

"Not if the right man took the job as marshal."

He peered closely at her. "You're not very consistent. You don't like the fact that I killed three thieves last night, but you want me to take on a job that will mean killing more. What kind of reasoning is that?"

She grinned at him unexpectedly. "Woman's

reasoning, I guess." She put a plate of chicken and dumplings in front of him. "Go ahead and eat."

She sat down across the table, and, as she began to eat, he looked at her closely. Her skin was tanned, but clear and flawless, the healthy skin of a girl who is out-of-doors most of the time. Her eyelashes were long and delightfully curved, and her mouth was full and red. Her cheeks were slightly hollow beneath high, prominent cheek bones. A lovely girl, without the artfulness and artificiality Sloan had found to varying degrees in other women he had known. When this girl met a man's eyes, her gaze was disconcertingly direct and forthright.

He ate ravenously and polished off a second helping the same way. He leaned back, fished a cigar from his pocket, and bit off the end. "All right if I smoke?"

She nodded, rose, and began to gather up the dishes. He stared at her thoughtfully, and, while she avoided his glance, her face flushed faintly with awareness of it. Her body was straight and strong, but it was an exciting woman's body that he knew would be eager and satisfying to the man she chose. He felt the stirring of hunger in him and lowered his glance so that she wouldn't see it in his eyes.

With her back to him, she asked: "What will you do now?"

He shrugged, savoring the taste of the cigar. "I haven't decided. I think I'd like a ranch. Where . . ."—and this slipped out—"where there's no killing and no dying."

She turned her head, and he felt the impact of her eyes. "That's a strange statement from a man who . . ." She stopped suddenly.

He finished it for her, a touch of bitterness in his voice. "From a man who has just killed three of his fellow men? From a man who has slaughtered buffalo by the hundreds for their hides? From a man who has been through four long years of war? Maybe that's why I want the ranch."

"I'm sorry. I didn't mean . . ."

He changed the subject abruptly. "How did you get to be a cattle buyer? It's a strange occupation for a woman."

"My father was a cattle buyer. When he was killed, I just took over where he left off. There aren't too many ways for a woman to earn a living out here. This seemed preferable to the others."

He rose. "I'm obliged for the dinner, ma'am."

"For heaven's sake, stop calling me ma'am. My name is Merline."

"All right, Merline. I'm obliged. You're a good cook."

He went through the house to the door and stepped out onto the porch. He turned to find her watching him, and now he suddenly remembered the way her lips had felt touching his own last night. Her forthright glance did not conceal her thoughts, and he knew she was remembering that, too.

She said: "Good bye."

"That sounds pretty final. Do you want me to leave?"

She frowned. "I think I do. I think if you stay, you'll take that job, and if you take it, you'll be killed."

"Then I'd better leave."

Walking back toward Texas Street, he frowned faintly, not liking his own conflicting thoughts. He wanted to stay, and admitted to himself that Merline Morris was the reason. Yet he also admitted that what she had predicted was at least a probability. He was at loose ends, and he was not the kind of man to be satisfied with remaining idle long.

He wandered aimlessly along Texas Street, letting the early afternoon sun beat hotly against his back. Even this early there was a crowd of Texas trail drivers in the street, some squatting in the shade talking, some going from saloon to saloon, some already drunk. The barkers had begun their monotonous chant from in front of their respective saloons, shamelessly exaggerating the attractions to be found inside.

Farther up the street, the people of the town went about their business. There seemed to be an invisible dividing line between the lower end of the street and the upper end. A lion was loose in the streets. The lion was drowsy now. But before the day was over he would become hungry again. Sloan shook his head angrily. It was not his problem. He had not helped create it, and this was not his town.

Ahead of him, the batwing doors of a saloon banged open and a man staggered out, to be followed by another. They came together and pounded each other briefly with fists, until one fell back. Then, so quickly that it startled Sloan, the downed man's gun came out and barked rapidly several times. The other man collapsed and lay quite still. Sloan stopped to avoid the gathering crowd. The noise in the street mounted.

Sloan became aware that a woman was screaming farther up the street. Puzzled, he glanced around. Then, without thinking, he whirled and began to run toward that lost and awful sound.

IV

Behind him a circle of men gathered around the dead cowpuncher. Ahead of him a crowd began to gather around the screaming woman. By the time Sloan reached the scene, they obscured his sight of the woman herself. But he had caught a glimpse of her as he swung around—and had been struck by recognition. Running, he realized who she was—the woman he had watched hanging clothes on a line while a small girl played on the lawn nearby.

He reached the scene as the crowd parted to let a man come through. He was an elderly, bearded man, and he was carrying a limp, pitiful burden —the little girl Sloan had seen playing on the lawn. He stalked away, his face white and furious, toward the bank. The distraught, hysterical mother followed. And now, with a shock, Sloan knew why this woman had drawn his attention so. Out of the past, out of his memory of another time and place her identity came to him. Stunned, he watched her follow the doctor up an outside stairway to his office over the bank.

Sylvia Flint. She had promised to marry him before he went away to war. But, when he returned, she'd been gone—leaving no word for him, leaving no clue as to where she might be found. He'd searched for a while, but he'd found no trace. And now—to find her here . . . She was married. She must be married to have a little girl.

He scarcely heard the talk in the street. But he couldn't miss the tone of it—outraged, angry, indignant. Frowning, he crossed to the hotel and went inside.

The town had had its breakfast—a hearty one

today. A man and a little girl. Sloan's mind was stunned. He stared at the stairway leading upward from the lobby. He turned and stared at the outside door. His mind was crowded with memories. Abruptly he turned and strode outside again.

The crowd had not dispersed. He saw the banker, Dryden, in the crowd. Dryden was watching him closely. Sloan scowled and turned away.

He walked to the edge of town and beyond, out onto the wide, golden prairie. Dust rose from his rapidly striding feet. His fists were clenched at his sides, his face cold and hard as he sought to bring order out of chaos in his mind. The shock of seeing Sylvia after all these years. The shock of seeing a child shot down in the middle of the street. The stupidity of it all—a stray bullet fired from a drunken, quarrelsome cowpuncher's gun. The expression on Dryden's face was suddenly very plain in Sloan Hewitt's mind. His anger stirred like a sleepy giant.

Accidental death—that was the verdict a coroner's jury would bring in, if there had been one here. But it wasn't accidental. Sylvia's little girl had been murdered by the public greed and apathy that had allowed a situation such as existed here to flourish and grow. Like spectators who had idly watched water wash through a hole in a dam, they were looking around now for something to throw into the breach. They wanted to throw Sloan in first, and when he was gone, they would throw others in, at a frightening rate, until by their very numbers the men sacrificed would slow and stop the flood. A flood that needn't have started at all. Sloan suddenly barked a savage curse, turned, and strode quickly back toward the town.

Sun heat beat mercilessly now into the dusty streets. A few people moved about, but they did it silently, almost furtively. The barkers at the lower end of Texas Street were quiet. As though in defiance of this self-imposed respect, a piano tinkled from one of the saloons, and Sloan faintly heard a woman's laugh.

He stopped in the shade across from the bank and stared up at the doctor's office. He knew they were still up there, for others were waiting, too. The doctor came out at last, and helped a still-faced, numbed Sylvia Flint down the wooden stairs. He walked with her up the street toward the edge of town. The full shock of what had happened was plain in the faces of those who watched. The little girl had still been alive when Sloan had left, but she had died, else the doctor would have stayed with her. Sylvia's hysteria had obviously given way to shock.

Sloan walked slowly in their wake. He knew that now was not the time to renew their relationship, but he also knew that Sylvia was alone. She needed her friends. Suddenly he frowned. Where were her friends? Where was her husband? Why was she alone, save for the old doctor taking her home?

He increased his pace. He saw them go into her house, saw the door close behind them. He went up the walk and knocked on the door.

The doctor answered it, scowling. "I don't know you, and it's a damned poor time to call. Come back some other time."

Sloan said: "Tell her it's Sloan Hewitt. I think she needs all the friends she has, and I'm a friend."

She must have heard his voice, heard his name, for she came running to the door. Seeing him, her face turned even whiter than it had been before. She swayed and would have fallen but for the doctor's steadying hands. "Sloan." The word was the barest whisper, but the intensity of her voice was frightening.

The doctor said irritably: "Come in. Come in!"

Sloan went in, removing his hat as he did. He closed the door behind him. He stared at Sylvia uncertainly, wondering what to expect. And then she was in his arms, her body cold and trembling uncontrollably. Her tears came like a flood.

The doctor looked at Sloan over the top of her head. His eyes mirrored satisfaction, and he said: "Good. Crying is what she needs."

For a long, long time she wept, and at last Sloan picked her up bodily and carried her to the sofa under the window. He laid her down, kneeled beside her and wiped tears from her cheeks with a gentle, callused hand. Her face relaxed, and her lips smiled faintly. She murmured: "I'm glad you're here, Sloan. I'm so glad you're here." And then she slept.

Sloan got up and walked softly across the room. He opened the door and stepped outside. The doctor followed.

He studied Sloan briefly. "You're the one Dryden was talking about. The one he wanted to take the marshal's job?"

Sloan nodded.

"Are you going to take the job?"

Sloan said: "I don't know." But he did know, even though he had not yet admitted to himself that he did.

"You know Sylvia?"

Sloan nodded. "From before the war. She was going to marry me. When I came home, she had disappeared." That had been a long, long time ago, he realized now. Three years. With a shock it struck him that Sylvia's daughter had been older than three. Or had seemed so. He asked harshly: "How old was the little girl?"

"Five. Why?"

Sloan turned his face away. With a hand that trembled violently, he reached in his pocket for a cigar. But his voice was calm enough. "Know when her birthday was?"

"A month ago. June seventeenth, I think."

Sloan's mind was racing. He'd had a leave. He said suddenly—"Take good care of her, Doc. I'll be back."—and he strode away toward town.

The town had touched him now, had taken something from him he didn't even know he had. The man-eating town had made its first mistake.

A part of the crowd had dispersed, but a few remained, gathered into little groups. Their talk was low, their faces sober—worried. Sloan saw Dryden and walked toward him.

Dryden's eyes lit as he glanced up. Sloan said: "I want to talk to you."

"I was hoping you would."

Sloan moved away, and Dryden followed. Sloan said: "I'll take the job, but there will be conditions. Conditions that you may not like."

"I'll get the others together. Would you mind waiting in my office at the bank?"

Sloan shook his head. He crossed to the bank and went inside. The lobby was cool. His boot heels pounded noisily on the white-tiled floor.

He was directed to an office at the rear of the bank, an oak-paneled office with furniture upholstered in red velour. He removed his hat and sat down to wait. He found another cigar in his pocket, bit off the end, and lit it. He tried to study himself, his own emotions, dispassionately. But he found that underlying everything he felt was anger, deep-rooted, smoldering anger that made such an analysis impossible. He knew it was enough—enough to make him take the job—enough to enforce the town's acceptance of him on his own terms. And he knew his anger would neither fade nor die in the days to come. It would be with him while he lived; it would be with him when he died. Die he surely would, but maybe not before he had brought some kind of order to the town, had tamed it to a point where someone else could take over and finish what he had started.

He had waited less than five minutes when Dryden arrived, accompanied by the pair who had come with him to Sloan's room earlier today, and three others.

Dryden introduced them. And then he waited.

Sloan said: "I told Mister Dryden I'd take the job. I also told him there would be conditions he probably wouldn't like."

No one spoke. Their faces were grave, the faces of men who would accept anything that promised to eliminate the condition now existing in their town. Sloan realized with a flash of insight that because they now accepted the conditions willingly did not mean they wouldn't repudiate them later.

He said: "I'm to have a free hand. There's to be no interference with anything I do. A week from now you may begin to wonder if a man for breakfast every day wasn't mild. But this town's completely out of hand."

They glanced at each other, then nodded agreement.

Sloan said: "I want a contract for a year. If I'm still alive at the end of the year, which isn't likely, your town will be clean."

They glanced around at each other, then nodded again.

Sloan said harshly: "I'll be hated . . . by every man in town. I'll hurt you in your pocketbooks. Trail hands like a town that's wide open, the way this one is. Saloonkeepers like it, and gamblers do, and so do the prostitutes. I have an idea you gentlemen like the way the money's rolling in. It won't roll in as fast in the next few months, but you'll be alive to spend it. If that's what you want, then we can go ahead." There was some hesitancy this time, so Sloan got up. "Talk it over. Be sure you want what I'm offering you. If you decide you do, prepare a contract and bring it to me at the hotel."

He put on his hat and went out, leaving utter silence behind. The sun was low on the western horizon now. The heat of the day was fading slightly. Down at the lower end of Texas Street the noise was increasing, and the barkers were back at their posts in front of their respective saloons. His face somber, Sloan stepped to the corner of the building and climbed the outside stairs to the doctor's office.

V

He stopped in the hall and stood there, hat in hand, for a long, long time. His eyes seemed to have sunk into their sockets. His mouth was a thin, straight line. His hands shook slightly, and there was an ache in his chest, an unaccustomed tightness in his throat. Slowly, softly he turned the knob and stepped inside. He closed the door quietly behind him.

Now he stood with his back to the door, smelling the smells peculiar to a physician's office, seeing the small body lying there on the table covered with a sheet. Like a sleepwalker he crossed the room. Carefully, gently he took the edges of the sheet and folded it back. He stared down into the white, pale face of the little girl. She was a pretty thing with dark, silky hair framing her waxen face. Her eyes were closed, her long, dark lashes lying on her cheeks. If only he had known. If he had only known that Sylvia and her daughter were here. They might not have been in the street today. Perhaps he would have been with them some place else. But he hadn't known, and now it was too late. The little girl was dead, and nothing could bring her back.

He heard the door behind him and swung his

head in time to see the doctor enter. The man was gaunt and untidy and ugly, but his eyes held an incredible amount of sadness as he glanced at Sloan, then glanced away. Sloan said—"You weren't here."—wondering at the need he felt to explain himself.

The doctor said: "It's all right. I wish every man in town would come and look at her."

"How's Sylvia?"

"Sleeping. You know I gave her a sedative. A neighbor woman is with her now."

"Where the hell is her husband?"

The doctor frowned. He walked to the window and stared down into the street. With his back to Sloan, he said: "She has no husband." He turned, his face a study of indecision. "Are you going to stay here? Are you going to take that job as marshal?"

Sloan nodded briefly.

The doctor shrugged. "Then I suppose I had better tell you. Sylvia is . . . oh, for Christ's sake, I'm getting as mealy-mouthed as some of the women hereabouts. Sylvia is living with Jeff Burle. She has been for a couple of years. It's why she's alone now, except for that neighbor of hers that I had to practically drag over there just now."

Somehow or other the news did not surprise Sloan as much as he thought it should. He supposed he had expected something of the sort when he saw no one come forward to comfort Sylvia in her grief. He asked harshly: "Then where the hell is Burle?"

The doctor tossed his head in the direction of the lower end of Texas Street. "Down there, I suppose. He never liked the little girl much. Thought she was in the way."

"How long before Sylvia will wake up?"

"Two or three hours, I suppose."

Sloan nodded. He took a last, long look at the still face of the little girl, realizing that he didn't even know her name. He felt his throat constrict and his eyes begin to burn. He went angrily out into the hall, closing the door firmly behind him. He strode down the outside stairs into the noisy street, across the street, and into the hushed hotel lobby, then up the stairs to his room.

Sid Wessell was washing noisily at the washstand. He turned his head as Sloan came in. He was a bit white and shaky, but otherwise appeared all right. It was hard for Sloan to believe that so much had happened to him in the past twenty-four hours, while Sid stayed here in the room getting drunk and sleeping off the subsequent hangover. He said: "You look better. Maybe you're going to live."

"I feel like I might, now. For a while there I didn't even care."

Sloan asked abruptly: "Want a job?"

"What kind of job?"

"Marshal's deputy."

"Who's the marshal?"

"I am. Or at least I think I will be."

"Are you crazy? In this town a star will just make a damn' good target."

Sid was tall, stringy as a bean. There was surprising strength in him, however, and Sloan had never seen him tired. Sid's face was heavily freckled, his eyes blue, his whiskers spotty and thin. His nose was always sunburned and peeling, and when he was out in the sun too much, it sometimes got raw and scabbed.

Sloan said: "Maybe so." And waited.

Sid peered at him while he dried his face. "How many men are you going to hire?"

"Just you."

Sid stared. "Why the hell are you taking the job, anyway? You don't need the money. This town doesn't mean anything to you."

Sloan didn't reply because he hadn't yet answered that question to his own satisfaction.

"You won't last three days."

"Maybe not."

He heard the heavy tread of many feet on the stairs, heard them approach along the hall. At the first knock, he opened the door.

Dryden, Lake, Graham, and the others were standing in the hall. Sloan jerked his head in a curt gesture of admittance and stood aside while they filed in.

Dryden said: "We've accepted your proposition. We have a contract here."

Sloan said: "Leave it. I'll look it over and bring it to the bank."

Dryden said: "One thing . . ."

Sloan stared at him, puzzled at the way his anger flared. He said: "Let's get something straight right now. There are no conditions. I clean up this town just as I see fit. I'll be honest with you. I don't think that drunk killed that little girl at all. I think you did. You watched this town turn wild and did nothing to stop it because you were afraid you might lose business if you did. I don't want this job, and I'm taking it purely for reasons of my own. But I'll do it my way or not at all."

He could see hostility growing in their faces, and he didn't care. Better that they be hostile from the start. Better that they understand exactly where he stood because, after the first day on the job, the whole town was going to hate him anyhow. Nor could he expect support from anyone—save perhaps from Sylvia, from Merline Morris, from Doc, and from Sid. Before he was through, the things he would have to do might turn even them against him.

Dryden nodded curtly and led the way into the hall. The delegation marched angrily down through the lobby and into the street.

Sid stared at Sloan for a moment, his forehead touched with a puzzled frown. Sloan glanced up.

He was beginning to understand his own anger, his own unpleasantness in the face of it. In the first place, he didn't want the marshal's job. The war had sickened him of killing and the stink of death. The months of hunting buffalo had compounded that sickness. In the second place, he understood how he would be feared and hated if he tackled the taming of the town in the only way it could be accomplished successfully. He said: "This town's been wild too long to accept law and order now without a fight. There's only one way to make it stick . . . knock the damned town flat on its ass, then kick it every time it starts to get up again. By the time I'm through, I'll be lucky if there's still one person in the whole place that has any use for me."

"Then why are you doing it?"

Sloan's face was sober. "Go over to Doc's office and look at that little girl they killed. That might have been my daughter if it hadn't been for the war. I was going to marry her mother."

He sat down and read the contract Dryden had left. He went over to the desk, dipped a pen in ink, and signed it. He got up and crammed his hat onto his head.

Sid said abruptly: "I'll take the deputy's job."

"Good. Go get yourself some supper. We'll start tonight." He went out, down the stairs, through the lobby and into the street. He crossed to the bank and went inside. Dryden and the others were grouped in Dryden's office. The place was blue with smoke.

Sloan laid the contract on the desk. Dryden opened the drawer of his desk and took out a gleaming, silver star upon which the word MARSHAL was engraved. "I had this made today. I'm glad you're taking the job, Mister Hewitt. You can count on us to back you all the way."

Sloan nodded.

Dryden said: "I don't know whether I've got the authority to administer an oath or not, but as long as there's no one else to do it, I will. Raise your right hand."

Sloan did.

Dryden said: "Do you solemnly swear to uphold the laws of this town and the State of Kansas to the best of your ability?"

Sloan said: "I do."

"Good. We've got men working right now converting that empty building next to the hotel into an office and jail for you. I'll serve as judge until we can get a real judge to take over." He stepped around the desk and pinned the star to Sloan's shirt front. "We're indebted to you, Mister Hewitt."

Sloan grinned wryly. "Tell me that a week from now."

He went out and strode downstreet to the livery barn. He bought a horse and saddle, the tallest, blackest horse in the place, and rode out on the horse's back. He had learned in the cavalry that there is a certain advantage inherent in looking down upon others from the back of a horse. He also knew he would need every advantage he could get.

Dusk lay softly in the street. The voices of the barkers had raised in pitch, as each vied with the other for customers wandering along the street. At the upper end of town, storekeepers were locking up for the night and heading home. The day had ended for them, but down here it was just getting started. In the cattle pens a bull bellowed, and behind Sloan, in the corral behind the stable, a horse nickered shrilly.

Sloan drew rein and stared at the town. He could feel tension mounting within himself, the same tension that had come to him during the war, just before an attack. He thought about Sylvia, sleeping in the house at the upper end of town. He wanted to see her, and yet he felt reluctance, too. The thing between them was over. He wondered at the reasons that had made her leave and disappear before he returned from the war. He thought of the little girl lying dead in Doc's office over the bank and wondered if the child was his. It was a possibility chronologically, he knew.

Sitting there, he saw a man come from one of the larger saloons and stand before it while he carefully bit the end off a cigar and lit it. The

157

man watched him steadily for several moments, then crossed the street to him. He was not an exceptionally tall man, but there was something in the assurance of his walk that seemed to convey upon him a height he did not possess. He was broad through the shoulders, and his chest was so deep that his shirt stretched tight across it. There was a diamond stickpin in his tie that caught the light and gleamed yellow each time it did. He wore a sweeping mustache, and as he came up before Sloan, Sloan saw that his eyes caught the same yellow light as the stickpin did. The man said affably: "I'm Jeff Burle. You must be Hewitt, the marshal."

"I'm Hewitt."

"You've taken on a man-size job."

Sloan didn't reply. He knew he shouldn't start off disliking Burle, but he couldn't help himself.

Burle studied him carefully in the growing darkness. "How far are you going to go?"

"I'll let you know."

Burle's voice grew a bit tight. "Nothing's accomplished in a day. These things take time. I'd advise you to go a little slow."

Sloan said sourly: "Thanks for your advice."

Burle puffed thoughtfully on his cigar, studying Sloan. "The people in this town don't want a clean town. They just want a non-violent town. They'll make you walk a narrow line."

"I'll walk it then." He stared down at Burle,

trying to fathom him. What kind of man was it who could know that death had come to the daughter of the woman he was living with and not even go to her? An arrogant man, certainly, and an unfeeling one. He fished his watch from his pocket and looked at it. Three hours had passed since Doc had given Sylvia the sedative. She ought to be waking soon. He said: "Doc gave Sylvia a sedative to make her sleep, but she ought to be awake by now. Are you going to see her?"

"You know Sylvia?"

"I knew her before the war. I was going to marry her."

"Was Debbie your daughter?"

"I don't know. Are you going to see her?"

"Not tonight. I'm afraid I just can't abide a hysterical woman."

"Then I'll go." Watching Burle, he thought he sensed a change in the man.

Burle turned his head and his eyes gleamed yellow. Burle said evenly: "I don't think I'll like you, Marshal."

"I wouldn't want you to."

Burle stared up at him for a moment more, his face hidden in shadow. Then he turned on his heel and stalked away. There was a peculiar, cat-like grace about the way he walked. There was animal power in him not concealed at all by the clothes he wore. Sloan sensed that Burle, while undoubtedly attractive to women, was completely ruthless, without gentleness, without concern for anyone but himself.

Then, forgetting the man, he turned his horse, lifted him to a trot, and headed up the street toward Sylvia Flint's small house.

VI

He dismounted before her house and tied his horse to the fence. There was a single lamp burning inside. He went up the graveled walk, onto the porch, and knocked lightly on the door.

A woman answered it, a middle-aged, sour-faced, gaunt-bodied woman, who scowled at him. Sloan said: "I want to see Sylvia Flint. Is she awake?"

"Who're you?"

"Sloan Hewitt."

She opened the door a bit wider. The light apparently glinted from his badge, for her manner changed. "You're the new marshal, ain't you? Come on in."

News certainly traveled fast, thought Sloan. He went in, removing his hat as he did. The woman said: "Wondered what you'd look like. Wondered what kind of man would take on a job like that."

Sloan said: "Now you know. Is Sylvia awake?"

"She's awake." She turned her head and called shrilly: "Marshal's here to see you."

A door opened, and Sylvia came into the room. Her eyes were red, her face very pale. Her hair was disordered, and she put her hands up to smooth it. She had obviously wakened only a few moments before, because her face still showed signs of heavy sleeping. She said: "Marshal? Sloan, are you crazy?"

"Maybe."

"It would take a troop of cavalry to tame this town. I hope you didn't . . . because of Debbie . . ."

Sloan asked softly: "How are you now?"

Her eyes glistened with fresh tears. "I'm all right, Sloan."

The woman said harshly: "Then I'll be getting on. I got work to do."

Sylvia turned to her. "Thank you, Missus Pugh. Thank you for staying with me."

The woman grunted, but did not reply. She got her hat, put it on, and stood before the mirror while she pinned it to her piled-up hair with an eight-inch hatpin. She went out the door without further comment.

Sylvia waited until the door had closed. Then she said: "Sit down, Sloan. Sit down a minute and let me look at you."

He went over and sat down on the sofa. She met his glance for a moment, then looked away. "You're wondering why I left before you came home."

"Yes. I'm wondering. But you don't have to tell me unless you want to."

"You have a right to know. But . . . Sloan . . . I just can't talk about it now." She turned her head and met his glance again. "You've changed. You're bigger . . . older . . . you're more handsome than ever."

"It's been a long time."

"Yes. Yes, it has." Sloan thought she had twisted her face and brightened her eyes again. He asked: "Is there anything I can do to help?"

"Not right now. But will you come . . . to the funeral, Sloan?"

"Of course."

Dimly, he heard a faint burst of gunshots from the direction of the lower end of Texas Street. He got up quickly. "Will you be all right?"

"I'll be all right. Be careful, Sloan. Please be careful."

He nodded and hurried to the door. He flashed a quick smile at her, then mounted his horse, and pounded away in the direction from which the shots had come. He was realizing, as he rode, that this would be a test in the eyes of the town. This would be the most important action he would take, however long he remained as marshal of the town.

He passed the hotel at a hard gallop and thundered down Texas Street. He watched the entrance to each saloon closely, and swung down before the one belonging to Jeff Burle, the Cowman's Pride, when he noticed that the barker was not in his accustomed place out front. He looped the reins of his horse over the rail and stepped through the swinging doors.

Immediately every eye in the saloon was on him, almost as though they had been waiting for him to appear. In a small, cleared circle halfway to the bar, a man lay on the floor face down, a pool of blood leaking out from beneath his chest. Another man stood in the cleared area, a defiant look in his angry eyes. Jeff Burle was behind the bar, a shotgun in his hands. This was more or less what Sloan had expected, and yet there was something wrong. He sensed it, though he knew there was no basis for such a suspicion. He pushed his way through the crowd, reached the cleared circle, and stopped. "What happened?"

The man stared at him truculently but did not reply. Burle spoke from behind the bar. "Only thing I know, Marshal, is that the dead man wasn't armed."

Sloan stared hard at the truculent one, then let his eyes drift swiftly, appraisingly, over the faces of the waiting crowd. He said: "I'll take your gun."

"By God, you're goin' to have to take it! Because I ain't goin' to give it to you!"

Burle's voice broke in. "Take it, Marshal. If he moves, I'll blow him apart."

This was the jarring note that Sloan, without realizing it, had been waiting for. Now he saw others. The truculent man's scowl was a bit too deep. The others seemed a shade too expectant. There was a nervous grin on one cowboy's face, and his eyes fell away guiltily when Sloan's touched them. Sloan understood. This play had been engineered by Burle. When he had disarmed the killer and placed him under arrest, the man on the floor would get up, and everyone in the place would roar with laughter at the marshal's discomfiture. He would become an object of ridicule. Any chance he'd had of establishing authority would be gone. Clever. Easier than killing him. Everyone would have a good laugh, and the town could go on as lawlessly as before. Only it wasn't going to work. Blood began to pound hard and fast through his veins. His stomach felt flat and empty, his hands as though every nerve in them was jumping.

He approached the "killer," circling as though wary, circling so that he had to pass the "corpse" on the floor. Passing, he swung a savage boot. The toe sank into the ribs of the man on the floor.

He reacted as Sloan had expected. He yelled, rolled, and came to his feet. He charged furiously. Sloan side-stepped at the last instant and, drawing his gun, brought the barrel around with numbing force against the side of the man's head. The man pitched forward into the crowd and fell as they scrambled to get away.

Sloan's action had startled the "killer," and for

an instant he was motionless. Then his hand streaked for his gun. Sloan shot without hesitation. The man drove back into the crowd, upon whose faces there was no humor now. Sloan swung toward the bar, very aware of that shotgun in Jeff Burle's hands. In the act of raising it, Burle stopped. He froze, with the shotgun halfway to his shoulder. His face lost color, and his eyes took on the startled look of fear. Sloan said evenly: "Lay it on the bar. Easy."

Burle complied. The fear in his eyes faded, to be replaced by uncontrollable fury and hatred more vitriolic than Sloan had ever seen in the eyes of a man before. Sloan said: "Your saloon's closed. You're under arrest." He waited, a wicked light growing in his eyes. He could see Burle's thoughts through the changing expressions on his face. Incredulous disbelief. Then the raw fury again. Then recklessness that made his glance drop toward the shotgun on the bar.

Sloan said softly: "Grab it, Burle. Go ahead. Then I can close your damned saloon for good."

Those in the crowd had been prepared to laugh. Taken by surprise, they had not yet recovered sufficiently to become dangerous. Burle, glancing at their faces, apparently understood their mood.

Sloan stepped to the bar and picked up the shotgun. He turned his head and shouted: "This place is closed. You got ten minutes to finish your drinks and leave." He glanced back at Burle. "Come on. Let's go." Burle was trembling with rage. His face was white. Sloan said harshly, with savage emphasis: "You son-of-a-bitch, I don't care whether you walk out or whether I have you carried out on a door. Now move, before my patience all runs out."

Burle came from behind the bar. Without looking at Sloan, he pushed his way angrily through the crowd to the doors. Sloan followed.

There would be no more jokes. The lines were drawn, and the fight was in deadly earnest now. But that was the way he wanted it. That was the only way he could even hope to win.

In front of the Cowman's Pride, he paused to untie his horse, mounted, then followed Burle up the street. The man walked angrily, swiftly. Behind them, the saloon began to empty its occupants out onto the walk and into the street.

Sloan had made an implacable and powerful enemy, but this episode tonight could not have worked out better from his own standpoint. While he regretted the necessity of killing the make-believe killer, he'd had no choice. The man had been trying for his gun and would have killed him without hesitation if he'd been able to get it out.

He reached the bank and rode beyond to the new marshal's office and jail. He swung down and tied his horse. There were lamps burning inside, and there was the sound of a hammer. Apparently the carpenters were still at work.

He said coldly: "Go on in."

Burle turned his head. "What's the charge?"

Sloan gave him a savage push. "Don't crowd me, Burle. I don't need to charge you to hold you overnight."

"You'll regret this, Hewitt."

"Sure. Sure I will. Why don't you take a look at things the way they really are, Burle? You're not the big man you think you are. You're just a two-bit saloonkeeper."

Burle opened the door and stepped inside. Sloan followed, the shotgun still cradled on his arm. There were two carpenters working, one a middle-aged man in overalls, the other a boy, obviously an apprentice. Sloan asked: "Got any cells ready yet?"

The man nodded. "All finished back there. It's a wooden building, though, so I wouldn't say it was very strong."

Sloan nodded. He gestured with his head to Burle. "Go on."

Burle glared at him, then stalked back to the rear of the building. There were four small cells, two on each side. The bars were made of iron pipe set in holes drilled in four-by-fours, which were spiked to ceiling and floor. A two-by-four, also drilled, made the bars rigid between ceiling and floor. It would take a powerful man to break out without tools, but anyone with a crowbar, an axe, or a sledge could break out in a matter of minutes.

Sloan closed one of the cell doors behind Burle. He snapped the padlock shut and pocketed the key that had been in it. He returned to the office.

The carpenters had begun to clean up. The older one said: "Dryden promised to get some furniture in here first thing in the morning."

Sloan nodded. He stepped out on the walk, fished for a cigar, bit off the end, and lit it. Downstreet he could see the last of the crowd pouring from the Cowman's Pride. He could see the place begin to grow dark as someone went around blowing out the lamps. For the first time he began to realize what a monstrous job he had undertaken. He began to comprehend the extent to which opposition would develop. Burle might be a two-bit saloonkeeper, but he could muster considerable support among the other saloon-keepers. Next time their play wouldn't be a joke.

Down in the cattle pens a cow bawled for her calf, and out on the plain a pack of coyotes yammered and yipped. A warm breeze blew in from the south, bringing its wild, free smell, bringing, too, the smells of the town, of manure in the loading pens, of horses in the corrals behind the livery barn, of hides and bones at the hide warehouse. It brought the smell of loco-motive smoke and, a few moments later, the lost, eerie sound of the locomotive's whistle as it pulled out going east.

Sound on the walk made Sloan whirl nervously, his hand streaking toward his gun. A bit sheepishly, he let it fall away as he recognized Merline Morris coming toward him.

If she noticed his nervous reflexive action, she didn't comment on it. She said simply: "Good evening, Marshal."

He nodded.

She came up close to him and stood looking up into his face. There was a fresh, faint fragrance about her he found vaguely stirring. She said: "I see you took the job. I wish you luck."

"Thanks."

"What made you change your mind? Debbie?"

"Partly, I suppose."

"You knew her mother before, didn't you?"

He stifled the irritation that touched him and stared down into her steady eyes. He weighed the tone her voice had possessed, and his mouth twisted in a small, wry grin. He said: "I knew her. We were going to be married after the war, but when I got mustered out, she had gone away."

Merline's eyes were large now, troubled. Sloan knew she was wondering—about Debbie—wondering if Sloan had been her father. Her glance lowered and a faint flush stained her cheeks. She said: "I'm sorry."

He did not pretend to misunderstand. "Don't

apologize. Your curiosity is natural enough."

She changed the subject. "I saw you bring Jeff Burle to jail." He didn't reply, and after a moment she looked up and met his eyes again. "Be careful, Sloan. And watch Jeff Burle. He's a dangerous man. He'll kill you if he can."

Sloan said: "I'll watch him."

Merline murmured something and turned away. He watched her until she disappeared into the darkness of the street.

VII

He stood there in the shadows idly, staring down Texas Street at the trail hands clogging the lower end of it. Faintly he heard the cries of the barkers, and sometimes the tinkle of a piano, or a woman's singing voice. The air blew softly in off the prairie, and, after a few moments, Sloan saw Sid Wessell come from the hotel and turn toward him.

Behind him, the carpenters finished cleaning up and came out, carrying their tools. "Good night, Marshal."

"Good night."

Sid stepped up beside him, and Sloan said: "I've got Jeff Burle, one of the saloonkeepers, in a cell. Stick around here and keep an eye on things."

"Sure." Sid hesitated, packing a stubby pipe. He lit it, puffed a few moments, and then said: "That was a joke down there in the Cowman's Pride, Sloan." He stopped, and the silence grew awkward between them.

Sloan glanced at Sid wryly. "And you don't think I should have used my gun?"

"Well . . ."

Sloan felt a touch of bitterness. It had begun already. He felt a compulsion to justify what he had done down in the Cowman's Pride, opened his mouth to speak, then snapped it shut angrily. He said: "I've got to go. Look after things."

He stepped to the rail, untied the black, and swung astride. He reined the horse down toward the lower end of Texas Street, riding in the exact center of the street, riding straight in the saddle, and holding the nervous horse to a steady walk. He wanted the town to see him now—see him plainly, conspicuously, and often. He intended to set up a route through town, rounds that he would make several times every night. Doing so would make him a target, and he fully realized this. It would also announce that he was not afraid of them, that he intended to keep the peace, that he was on the job.

Coming out of the darkness here at the upper end of the street and into the light of the lower end, he saw the way they turned to stare at him, saw, too, the hostility in their faces. He knew these Texas men, these Southerners. He'd met them often enough during the war. He understood their pride and knew how recklessly they would defend it if they thought it had been challenged. This time he passed along the street unchallenged, and he rode beyond to the cattle pens, to the railroad depot, which he circled, still at a steady walk. Then he went west past the hide warehouse, in which a faint light burned, threaded his way between the piled-up bones and bales of hides to the street west of Texas Street, which was lined with cribs. Most of these were dark and relatively quiet, for the hour was early. In the shadows before each one the crib girls stood talking, some clad in low-cut dresses, some in wrappers. Their perfume was strong and tangible even out in the middle of the street. A few of them spoke to him, and he touched the brim of his hat by way of reply, but most of them were silent, watching, wondering what he intended to do about them, wondering whether he would tolerate them or run them out of town.

He reached the intersection of Fourth, the street on which both the hotel and the bank fronted, and turned east here, continuing until he reached Texas Street and Fourth. He rode over to the jail and stared down at Sid standing in the shadows. His anger having mellowed, he said: "That was not a joke down at the Cowman's Pride. It was a deliberate attempt to make a laughingstock of the law. If I'd allowed it . . ." He let the sentence dangle, having gone as far as he ever would to explain himself. And now, looking inward, he was mildly amazed at the position in which he found himself. He had not wanted the marshal's job. He had wanted it least of all the things that had passed through his mind in the last few days. The money meant nothing, and he had never been a man to whom authority was important. Nor did the welfare of a town that had allowed lawlessness to get out of hand concern him.

Sid said: "I . . . hell, Sloan, I didn't think, I guess. I'm sorry."

"Forget it." For some reason he felt better as he turned away to begin another round of the noisy town. The opinions of others were important to him. He had never thought they were before, but he had been wrong. And this realization brought a rueful twist to his mouth. Hell of a job for a man who cared what others thought. Because everything he did in the next few days would be bitterly denounced, at both ends of Texas Street, out on the plain, and even in the respectable residences at the upper end of town.

In front of the Cowman's Pride, he stopped, as half a dozen riders whirled from the rail to halt, fighting their plunging horses, in the street before him. He let his gaze rest steadily on them, but the nerves in his body grew tight. One of the riders was a tall, middle-aged man with a sweeping, cavalry-style mustache and a Confederate officer's hat, from which the insignia had been removed. The man said intemperately: "Hold on there, Marshal. That was one of my men you killed a while ago."

"Too bad."

"Too bad? Why, God damn you, suh, you'll have to do better than that. They was funnin' you an' . . ."

Sloan's lips firmed out. He stared at the cowman with icy eyes. "When a man draws a gun on me, mister, it isn't fun. What's your name?"

The cowman sputtered a moment, then said: "Towner. Jeb Towner."

"The one they call Maverick?"

"The same. And I'm goin' to kill you, suh."

Anger stirred in Sloan. He said evenly: "Are you, Mister Towner? All by yourself? Or is it going to be you and your five helpers?"

"You Yankee pup!"

Sloan eased his horse closer. "You brought the war into this, Mister Towner, not me. But, now that you have, I'll tell you something. You're a type. You're arrogant as hell, but you're a god-damn' bag of wind. I've seen . . ." He was close to the man now, close enough. As Towner's hand streaked toward his holstered gun, Sloan snatched his hat from his head and batted Towner's horse squarely between the eyes. As he did, he dug heels into his own nervous mount and uttered a howling yell.

The Texan's horse shied, reared, and swapped ends before Towner could get off a shot. Sloan's black thundered past him, then whirled as Sloan hauled back savagely on the reins and dug a heel into one of the horse's sides. As Towner's horse came down, Sloan was there, and ready. His gun slammed against Towner's forearm with sufficient force to snap the bone. Before the cowman's gun struck the ground, he had holstered his own.

Now he seized Towner furiously with both hands, yanked him from the saddle, and dumped him on the ground. His right side was toward Towner's companions, so he swung off to the left. A shot blasted, then another, from the milling group in the center of the street. Both missed cleanly. Sloan reached Towner and yanked him to his feet. He was raging now, as furious as he had ever been in his life. His voice was a whip. "Damn you, call 'em off!"

Towner bawled: "Hold it!"

The shooting stopped.

Sloan yelled: "Dismount! All of you!"

They got off sullenly. Sloan could sense, rather than see, the crowd gathering behind him. He said sharply, authoritatively: "Shuck your belts!" They hesitated. He repeated: "Shuck 'em! Now!" One by one the holstered guns and belts thudded to the ground. Sloan gave Towner a push toward them. He ordered harshly: "Take him over to Doc and have his arm set."

Towner staggered toward the five, recovered, and whirled, his face twisted with pain and rage: "You bastard! You dirty bastard, I'll kill you for this!"

Sloan heard someone coming at a run and turned his head to see Sid approaching down the middle of the street, gun in hand. Sid hauled up, out of breath, and positioned himself on Sloan's left side. Sloan said: "Pick up their guns and take 'em back to the office." He stared coldly at the five. "Be out of town in an hour or go to jail. And don't ever let me see any one of you carrying a gun in town again."

He swung to his saddle deliberately, turned his back, and rode away, holding the black to a walk. He could hear the indistinguishable muttering in the crowd and grinned humorlessly to himself. He was doing fine, but he hoped his luck held out. All the challenges had been made openly so far—Burle's and Towner's both. But when open challenges repeatedly failed, either to discredit him or result in his death, other means would be brought into play. Bullets would come without warning from dark places. There would be other, more devious attempts to discredit him.

He threaded his way between the stock pens, past the railroad depot, through the stinking, cluttered yard of the hide warehouse, noting that the light in the office had gone out, wondering now as he had wondered before if Ike Solomon had had anything to do with his being beaten and robbed. Oddly, he discovered that he was enjoying one part of this job, enjoying the feel of danger, of walking along the edge of a yawning precipice.

He rode up the crib street, staying in the center of it, but halted as one of the girls called: "Marshal!"

He waited, and after several moments one of the girls detached herself from the others and came toward him. His horse fidgeted nervously at her approach, but Sloan held him still with an implacable hand. The girl stood looking up at him for a moment, her face a blur of white, and when she spoke there was something of defiance in her throaty voice. "What are you going to do about us?"

"Nothing. As long as you're orderly."

In this dim light she made a strangely appealing figure standing alone there in the middle of the dusty street. Sloan wondered briefly what pressures forced girls into this way of life. He touched the brim of his hat, said—"Good night, ma'am."—and rode on up the street, leaving her there, staring after him.

He rode up to Fourth, then right to Texas Street, across it to the jail, where he dismounted, and went inside. It was a bare place, without furniture, with the smell of fresh-sawed pine heavy in the air. Sid was sitting uncomfortably on a box.

Sloan asked: "Burle all right?"

"Sure. Quiet, anyhow."

Sloan took a cigar from his pocket and bit off the end. There was a peculiar excitement in him as he thought of his next round through the town, because he knew that the next time there would be a serious, organized attempt to get him. He'd taunted the town, and slapped it down ruthlessly both times it had risen to the taunts. He'd drawn the line between himself and Texas Street. Unless they killed him, the quarrel would not be decided tonight, perhaps not for many nights to come. But the quarrel would continue to one of two inevitable conclusions—with Sloan dead or with the town subdued.

VIII

With the cigar clamped in his teeth, Sloan crossed to the door and stepped outside into the cool night air. His horse fidgeted at the tie rail, occasionally lifting his head, nostrils flared, to smell the breeze blowing in off the prairie. Sloan grinned, his mind drawing a comparison between himself and the horse. The difference was that Sloan was listening only to sounds in the town, alert for those that meant danger to himself.

Down there at the lower end of Texas Street, the racket of revelry went on as the evening progressed. Innocuous enough. Yet it seemed to Sloan that there was an undercurrent of menace flowing in the air tonight. The lion was at bay, teeth bared wickedly in a snarl, muscles gathered for a slashing leap. He puffed luxuriously on the cigar and watched the bluish smoke lift in the faint breeze and drift lazily up the street. Out on the plain there had been no cigars, no small comforts, and he was enjoying those to be found in town to the fullest. He finished it and threw it regretfully into the street, watching the shower of sparks as it struck. Then he walked to the rail, untied the black, and swung to the saddle.

Tension grew in him as he turned toward the lower end of the street. They would have his route marked now and would know all the dark, safe places for laying an ambush. He supposed the most likely of them would be between the foot of Texas Street and the hide warehouse, but perhaps for this very reason it would not be used. Down Texas Street he rode, in the exact center of the street, his alertness as sharp as the honed edge of a skinning knife. Tall in the saddle, riding straight, as a cavalryman learns to ride, right hand hanging loose and easy with the thumb touching the saddle skirt.

It was not only the saloonkeepers, the lawless element that was out to nail his hide to the wall.

He had affronted the Texas cattlemen and trail drivers when he killed one of their number, again when he braced Jeb Towner and broke his arm. He had pricked their pride, and they would now be able to persuade themselves that killing him was not an act of murder but an act of vengeance for a wrong. The star gleamed dully in the lamplight shining from the windows of the saloons. Barkers stopped in mid-cry to watch him pass. Silence followed him along the street like a current pushing a leaf down a tumbling mountain stream.

In front of the Bullshead, he saw Dryden step from the boardwalk and moved to intercept him. He tugged the black to a halt.

Dryden looked up. His voice was soft, but it was touched with shocked amazement. "Man, do you *want* to be killed? You're a target for every drunk with an itchy trigger finger and a yen for fame."

Sloan grinned sourly. "Do you want your marshal skulking along in alleys? Or do you want him hiding in his office?"

"We want him alive."

"And I want to stay alive, believe me." Sloan paused, and then he said: "An ambusher is a coward, Mister Dryden, or he wouldn't be an ambusher. It's easier for a coward to kill a man who's afraid than one who is not. I don't intend to make it easy, that's all."

Dryden studied his face in the faint light. Then, shaking his head, he retraced his steps to the walk. Sloan moved on, down the length of Texas Street, with a spot in the middle of his back aching in expectation of a bullet striking it. His ears were tuned to the sounds of the street, waiting for one that would mean someone was about to strike.

He rode around the depot and through the dark alleys between the cattle pens, thence back to cross Texas Street and start along the tracks. As he rode, a peculiar certainty grew in him. There would be an attempt made to kill him before he reached the jail again. Yet he was equally sure that if this attempt failed, there would be no more tonight. They had tried to discredit him by making him a laughingstock. They had tried to get him openly through Maverick Towner and his men, who, Sloan had no doubt, had been stirred up by inflammatory talk on the part of the saloonkeepers. Now they would try the third way, by ambush, by cold-blooded murder. That spot in his back began to ache again. He passed the place he had been attacked and robbed, and his nervousness increased. He was like an animal now. Danger seemed to have sharpened his senses. A man who knew horses, who knew how much sharper than man's were their senses of smell and hearing, he watched his horse's head, the animal's sensitive ears. He realized, as he had not consciously realized before, that there had been another reason why he chose to make his rounds on horseback.

He turned into the stinking yard of the hide warehouse and this smell brought back sharply his memory of the previous months out on the plain hunting buffalo. It brought back memory of Ike Solomon. He glanced at the warehouse windows, but they were dark. He passed the bleaching pile of bones, swung over, and entered the crib street, which, so far as he knew, was unnamed.

For the hour, the street was quiet. A drunk staggered from one of the darkened doors and stumbled up the street, a dimly seen shadow from a hundred yards away. Otherwise, Sloan saw no one. It was almost as though the street had gone to sleep. Here, then, was where it would happen. Here, bullets would come cutting out of some dark doorway. Here the town would see its marshal die, or see him win and live. The sleeping anger awoke in him as he rode along the street. His faith in human nature waned. Every person along this street knew that an ambush had been laid. Its silence told him that. It was disillusioning to realize that not a single person of all those who knew would speak. Every nerve and muscle tense, he kept his eyes straight ahead, as though in contempt of what he knew. But he was not as foolhardy as he seemed. His eyes were on his horse's head, his full trust in the animal's alert senses.

Ahead, a little light filtered between two buildings from a garishly lit gambling room in the rear of one of the saloons on Texas Street. And, since it was the strongest light along the length of the street, Sloan guessed the attempt would be made as he passed through it. Nearing it, the tight, empty feeling in his stomach increased. His chest was cold. The war had been easy compared to this. There is security in companionship, strength in the knowledge that you do not face death alone. Yet his left hand holding the reins was steady, his right not visibly tensed to seize his gun. A dozen paces—half a dozen. The horse's ears pricked the instant he entered the light. His head swung nervously to the left.

Sloan leaned forward; his heels touched the nervous animal's sides. The horse lunged ahead at the precise instant the first gun flared from the shadows on the left, at the precise instant a woman screamed: "Marshal, look out!"

As though this first shot had been a signal, now others lanced from the darkness, from right and left, from straight ahead. The horse reared as one of the bullets ticked his chest, reared in the middle of that deadly shaft of light. Sloan whirled him as he came down. His gun was in his hand, hammer back, and he fired twice at a flash on the edge of the street. Outnumbered, he knew he had no chance as long as they could *see* him and he could not see them. He slammed his revolver down against his horse's rump and the animal leaped as though he had been shot. Straight out of the light, straight toward those flashes to Sloan's left. They broke as he thundered down upon them, one scurrying to the right, one to the left, still a third down a narrow passageway between two buildings. Sloan rode one of them down, heard the man's high scream as the black struck him, knocked him down, then plunged on over his prone body.

Again now, Sloan whirled the horse, fired at a running shadow and saw it melt into the shadows lying close to the ground. Bullets were still coming from the other side of the street. Thoroughly furious, with both caution and fear gone before his raging anger, Sloan turned and thundered across the street. A bullet slashed across his thigh, bringing instant numbness, an instant rush of blood. Involuntarily he swung the black, veered aside, and left the saddle. He hit the ground running, but the wounded leg gave way and he fell, rolling in the deep, dry dust. He heard their pounding feet, heard their high, exultant yells: "Got him! Got the son-of-a-bitch!"

Hidden by darkness and the cloud of dust he had raised himself, Sloan scrambled to one side, felt the boardwalk under his hands, and pulled himself up. Let them come. Let them come as close as they would. Surprise at seeing him up, at seeing his gun flare from an unexpected place should make them break and run as the others had.

They were coming, sweeping across the street like a wave of wind rippling a high stand of prairie grass. Sloan's leg was wet all the way to the ankle, wet with blood, and suddenly he felt the weakness come. It swept up from the pit of his stomach, closed his throat, and made his head swim dizzily. His eyes blurred until he could not have shot accurately at a man two dozen feet away. He clung to the post beside which he stood and knew he was doomed.

The past days had been too much—the beating, the strain, the sleeplessness—and now this wound, which, while it hadn't crippled him, had made him lose enough blood to weaken him disastrously. A sibilant sound on the walk behind him made him turn his head, made him tense and raise his gun, but had the sound been made by one of his enemies he would have been too late. He felt a small, soft hand touch his arm, heard a throaty voice he had heard in this street before: "Don't stand there, fool. Come on."

Those in the street had slowed; caution had slowed them, and they were coming more carefully now. To each, death and danger had become personal things that lurked in the shadows toward which they walked. Only this circumstance made it possible for Sloan to edge back from the post, to enter the door a dozen yards downstreet toward which the woman had drawn him.

The air inside smelled of cheap perfume that was strong enough to be a tangible and almost solid thing. He heard the bolt eased into place on the door and stood blindly in the darkness, swaying nearer to the void of unconsciousness than he had been in a long, long time.

There was a rustling of skirts, and the woman came up beside him, caught his arm, and pulled him gently across the tiny room. "Come on. Lie down. The windows are shuttered so I can light a lamp. Maybe I can tie up that leg or something."

"How did you know . . . ?"

Bitterness faintly touched her voice. "You forget, Marshal. We live in the dark . . . particularly those of us who aren't as young as we used to be. I saw you limping and saw your leg give way."

Sloan sank down onto the perfumed bed. A match struck and touched the wick of the lamp. A moment later she came toward him, carrying it. She was dressed in a red wrapper. Her hair was long, and also red. Brick red originally, he guessed, for there was a bridge of pale freckles across her nose. Now her hair, dyed with henna, was a deep, auburn red. A woman who looked forty—who was probably less than thirty. Yet there was something in the depths of her eyes right now that was very young.

Sloan closed his eyes as she lifted his leg to the bed and cut the cloth of his pants leg awkwardly with a small pair of scissors. He said: "Your bed . . . the blood . . ."—and tried to move, but she pushed him firmly back.

She found the wound, and he smelled the strong, raw stench of whiskey, felt its acrid coldness against his skin and against the raw flesh of the bullet's gash. He entered a world neither altogether unconsciousness nor consciousness and hung there for what seemed an eternity. With gentle hands she washed the wound, not with water but with whiskey, then bound it up and soaked the bandage liberally out of the bottle. She pried open his mouth and poured a little of this same antiseptic into it. He choked, gagged, swallowed, and opened his eyes.

There was a racket in the street now to which she seemed oblivious. He said: "Blow out that lamp."

She did. He eased the leg over the side of the bed and sat up. His head swam, and he shook it angrily. He said: "Help me up."

"No. You're not strong enough. . . ."

"Damn it, I've got to be." His voice was harsh. "I was bleeding like a stuck hog out there. If they've got lanterns, they'll trail me straight to your door."

He crossed the room, staggering, sometimes blundering into a piece of furniture as he went.

He came up against the wall and edged along it to the window. He shoved the curtains aside, groped for the latch on the inside shutters, found it, and eased the shutter back the slightest crack.

He saw the light in the street instantly. It was very close. He latched the shutter and turned. "Back door? Window?"

"There's a door. Over here."

He crossed the room, feeling stronger and less dizzy than he had before. The back door opened, and the freshness of air straight off the prairie blew inside, only contaminated slightly by the smells of the town. He said: "How about you?"

"I'll yell bloody murder the minute you leave." Her voice was a little breathless—excited—and not as it had been before. He started to move past her, but she blocked his path. She stood in tiptoe and kissed him on the mouth. "Good luck."

He put a big, callused hand on either side of her face, then bent his head and kissed her back, missing her mouth and kissing her nose instead. He said: "Thanks. Any time I can . . ."

Someone pounded on the front door. She said: "Hurry. Go on."

He stepped out into the alley and heard the door close quickly behind him. He cut across, through vacant lots and tin-can dumps, to the rear of Texas Street, thence between two buildings and out into the busy street again.

He heard her screaming behind him, her

screams muffled by the walls at first, unmuffled later as his pursuers opened the back door and streamed into the alley in search of him. But he was safe. He was moving unnoticed along the darkened upper end of Texas Street toward the jail.

IX

He was almost exhausted when he reached the jail, and was wryly considering contrasts in his mind. He had ridden out with the pleasant aftertaste of a good cigar in his mouth, his nerves alive and alert to the threat he knew he faced. He had ridden down Texas Street like a tall, immovable rock, had ridden into the planned ambush as though unaware that it was there or as though he didn't care. Now he was returning, dizzy, sick, weak from this wound, and still smelling of the perfumed bed on which he'd lain. His trouser leg flapped around his bloody shank, and he reeked of the whiskey that had been used to disinfect the wound. But the very contrast gave him an idea, one that he knew would set his ambushers back on their heels for the rest of tonight, at least.

He pushed open the door and stepped inside. The sight of him brought Sid rushing toward him. "God! What happened? I heard the shots and I almost . . ."

"Good thing you didn't. It's ten to one they had someone waiting to grab Burle out the minute you left."

He sat down. Sid looked at the leg and saw that it had been bandaged. His nose wrinkled as he smelled the perfume and whiskey, and suddenly a grin was born behind his pale blue eyes, a grin that reached out and lightly touched the corners of his wide, thin mouth. He said: "By God, there's nothing I admire more than a man that can fall in the outhouse and come up smelling like a rose. Or is it rose? More lilac, seems like."

"Shut up."

"And whiskey, too." Sid's eyes were exaggeratedly solemn. "Mebbe being a marshal's deputy ain't going to be so bad after all. Man could learn something in this job."

"Shut up and go over to the hotel. Get me my extra pants and a clean shirt."

Sid grinned at him impudently and went outside. Sloan got up and found a wash pan and a bucket of water. He poured the wash pan full and splashed water into his face and over his head. He lathered with strong soap, rinsed, then toweled himself dry. He found a cigar that wasn't broken too badly and lit it. He sat down and waited, drawing the smoke into his lungs.

Back in the cell-block, Burle was quiet. After a few moments Sid returned with the clothes Sloan had sent him for. Sloan put them on with considerable difficulty while Sid looked on, grinning unsympathetically. At last Sloan said with good-natured irritability: "Damn you, I could've got myself killed."

Sid sighed with mock delight. "What a way to die."

"Ahhhhh!" Sloan buckled on his gun belt and sat down to pull on his boots. He stood up and set his hat at a jaunty angle. "Go down to the livery barn and get my horse. He's probably standing outside the corral fence."

"You're not going to ride this town again?"

"I sure as hell am. Just like nothing had happened."

Sid studied his face a moment, sobering. Then he nodded, turned, and went outside. Sloan called out: "Bring the horse up the alley!"

He waited again, and as he waited, he began to grin in spite of the gnawing pain in his leg. Seeing him ride down the street, unruffled, apparently unhurt, ought to set them back on their heels. They were sure they had hit him; they'd seen him go down. They had followed a trail of blood to the red-haired woman's door. But by the time they were through speculating, they'd be thinking either that Sloan was the devil come to life or that they'd ambushed an unsuspecting cowhand who happened to look enough like Sloan in the darkness to be mistaken for him.

He heard the sound of hoofs out back, and a

few moments later Sid came in the front. Sloan nodded to him, said—"Thanks."—and went on outside. He reached the horse by tramping around to the back through the weeds, mounted, and rode back the way he had come. He was hurting for sleep, and was groggy enough to have difficulty sitting straight in the saddle without swaying from side to side. But for all the town could see, there was a ramrod in his back and calm, implacable strength in his steady eyes.

He rode down Texas Street in the exact center of the street, looking neither to right nor left, past the noisy line of saloons that faced him from both sides of the street, and he heard the silence that followed him along like an ominous calm in a storm. He circled the depot and rode through the dark alleyways between the cattle pens, thence back through the depot to cross Texas Street at its foot. Then to the hide warehouse and beyond, to the street of the prostitutes, which he traversed in an almost complete silence broken only by the measured sound of his horse's walking hoofs.

On Fourth, he turned right and returned to Texas Street, and now, as he rode into it, a stillness hung over the entire brawling town, a stillness that reached into the saloons, into the bagnios, and lay in the streets like a cold, wet fog. With a grim, tight grin on his nearly colorless lips, he dismounted before the jail and stepped inside. He said: "Blow out the lamp. Then go over to the hotel and borrow a cot. If I never do another thing, I've got to sleep right now."

Sloan Hewitt awoke at sunup, to the sounds of Burle bawling to be released. He sat up, startled, not immediately remembering where he was and what had happened. But the sharp, immediate pain in his leg reminded him quickly enough. He winced, and his face twisted with pain.

Sid, who had been sitting on a box outside in the street, now came in, carrying it. He put the box down. "Feel better?"

Sloan nodded, rubbing his eyes and running his hands through his hair.

"You'd better see the doc about that leg."

Sloan nodded again. He gestured with his head toward the cell-block in the rear. "Turn him loose."

Sid went back and unlocked Burle's cell. He came out again, following a sullen, angry Burle. Burle said: "Damn you. I'll see you in hell for this."

Sloan stared at him steadily. "You sure won't be seeing me any place else." He didn't stand up, and he didn't move. He doubted if Burle knew he had been hurt, and he didn't want the man to know. Burle could hardly have been directly responsible for the ambush last night, but Sloan didn't doubt it had been laid by Burle's friends and probably by his employees, too.

Burle glowered at him and headed for the door. He met Doc coming in. Doc glanced at the marshal and then at Burle. He said: "Jeff, you lost a couple of men last night."

"What the hell you talking about?"

"About Hughie Revel . . . and Dan Purdue. They were working for you, weren't they?"

"I'm not their keeper."

"No, I guess you're not." Doc stepped aside, but he kept his sour, steady glance on Burle's face until the man was past and out the door. Then he turned to Sloan. "You look like you might've lost some blood."

Sloan said: "Leg. Come on back here in one of the cells and take a look at it. Don't talk about it, though. I'd as soon they didn't know."

He got up, turning pale and breaking into a sweat. He limped toward the rear. Doc said grumpily: "I don't know how the hell you're going to keep it secret. You're limping like a man with a wooden leg. Your face is as gray as the belly of a toad."

Sid carried the cot back, and Sloan sank down upon it. He gritted his teeth as Doc unwound the makeshift, blood-soaked bandage. He felt his consciousness slipping as Doc pulled the last of it free.

In a haze of half-consciousness, he began to think bleakly that he'd bitten off more than he could ever chew. One man couldn't face down a whole town that was determined to have his hide. Not a whole man, nor half a man like he was now. This wound would sap his strength for several weeks to come, and he needed all his strength if he was going to stay alive.

He gripped the sides of the cot as Doc re-dressed and cleaned the wound. Doc growled at him: "Don't fight so hard. You've got all day."

"Can you make me well by night?"

"No. You damn' well know I can't. But if you'll listen to me, I can make you well enough to do your job."

"How?"

"Get a good breakfast and then hole up here and sleep until the sun goes down. Nobody'll think anything about it . . . you've been up all night. Get up at sundown, drink some whiskey, and eat a steak. Remember to move real easy and slow and you'll be all right."

"How bad is the leg?"

"Clean, round hole. Bullet went in and came on out. Tore up some flesh and muscle and cut some veins. But, unless it infects, it will heal. Whoever tied you up did a good job. Who was she, by the way?"

"Red-haired woman down on the crib street. If she hadn't let me in, I'd be dead right now."

Something made him open his eyes, and he saw Merline Morris standing in the door of the cell.

Doc said: "That would be Rose."

Behind Merline, Sid chuckled, and Sloan scowled briefly at him. He let his glance rest closely on Merline's face and knew she had overheard. She was, he knew suddenly, the reason he had stayed here, the chief reason he had taken on this job. She was the one he wanted most in all the world, but every time he thought he was making progress with her something like this came up, or something like his past relationship with Sylvia Flint. He looked at Merline with a bit of defiance in his eyes and said: "She helped me when I needed help. Is there anything wrong with that?"

"No. There's nothing wrong with that. Get the chip off your shoulder."

"Then, damn it, don't look at me like that."

"Like what?"

"Like you're doing."

Doc said: "Quit bickering, you two. Merline, be a good girl and go get him some breakfast."

"Shouldn't he stay . . . ?"

"In bed? Hell yes, he should. But I won't waste my breath asking him to. He wouldn't do it anyhow."

She let her eyes rest briefly on Sloan's face. They softened, and clung, and then brightened. She turned and hurried almost angrily from the door. Sloan said: "Now what the hell was that all about?"

"If you don't know, you're a sight stupider than you look." Doc glowered at him, then followed Merline out, untidy, whiskered, looking as though he had slept in his clothes. He probably had. Sloan stood up and followed, trying furiously not to limp but failing miserably. Sid brought the cot. He put it down, and Sloan sat on the side of it gratefully, stretching his hurt leg out before him.

He saw Doc standing across the street talking to a man, then saw the two hurry away and turn the corner on Fourth. One doctor wasn't enough for a town this size, he thought. And then he forgot both the doctor and the town, for he saw Merline crossing the street carrying a covered tray.

Sid put a box in front of him, and Merline came in and put the tray on it. Sloan was ravenous, yet the smell of food emanating from the tray made his stomach knot with nausea.

Merline's expression was one of mixed pity and anger. She stared down at him, hands on hips, and said truculently: "You can't do it. No one man can."

He grinned weakly. "Why don't you make up your mind? I thought you said the right man could."

"Maybe you're not the right man." She hesitated. "Oh hell, I don't mean that at all."

Sloan's grin mocked her. "Mind if I eat before all this gets cold?"

"I don't care if you never eat. You smell . . . you smell more like a carousing cowboy than a marshal!" She sniffed. "Lilac."

Sid said solemnly, "You know, I thought it was lilac, too. But Sloan says it's rose."

Sloan grunted sourly, shifted his leg, and bent forward to eat. His face twisted involuntarily. Watching him, concern touched Merline's face. Sloan glanced up and saw an expression in her eyes that made him want to get up and seize her in his arms. But he didn't move. He drank half a cup of scalding coffee, then determinedly forced down the food. His nausea mounted, but he didn't stop until the plate was empty. He finished the coffee and leaned back.

There were two cigars beside the plate. He lit one and put the other in his pocket. He sat there broodingly, puffing on the cigar, while the others watched him furtively. He was thinking that a lame marshal wasn't much better than no marshal at all. He was thinking if in the next few days his life depended on moving fast, he'd be dead. Then he thought of Sylvia Flint's small girl, limp in the doctor's arms. His chances of survival were less today than they had been yesterday, but he wasn't going to quit.

He saw Doc round the corner of Fourth and cross the street diagonally toward the jail. He knew from the set of Doc's face that something had made him furious.

Doc stamped in and slammed the door. He glowered at Sloan. Sloan said: "What's the matter with you?"

"Rose. She's dead!"

Sloan didn't speak. He got painfully to his feet.

Doc said irritably: "Sit down. Sit down, damn it! She's dead, I said, and there's not one damned thing you can do about it now."

"What killed her?"

Doc's voice was savage. "Fists. A lot of fists. She was beaten." He shuddered, almost as though he were cold.

Sloan asked evenly: "Who were the dead ones you told Burle about?"

"Hughie Revel and Dan Purdue."

"You treat any wounds this morning? Gunshot wounds?"

Doc shook his head no.

"Who are Revel's and Purdue's friends?"

Doc shrugged. "Burle. The rest of the bums that work for him. But you'll never prove a thing. There'll be a dozen men to swear that bunch was in the saloon all night."

Sloan said grimly: "I don't have to prove. All I've got to do is know."

He limped to the door, gritted his teeth, and stepped outside. His face turned pale with the effort, but he walked without a limp.

Merline watched him helplessly, her expression plainly saying she knew she couldn't stop him now. Sid hurried out and crossed the street at Sloan's side. Together they marched down Texas Street toward the Cowman's Pride.

X

There were, perhaps, half a dozen men in the Cowman's Pride besides the bartender and Jeff Burle, still rumpled and untidy from his night in jail. Sloan pushed open the door, and Sid followed him closely, stepping immediately to his left as they cleared the door.

Burle, at the end of the bar, was just leaving to go upstairs. He swung angrily as they entered. "What do you want?"

"The men that were with Purdue and Revel last night."

He thought he saw a glint of triumph in Burle's eyes, but it was gone so quickly that he could not be sure. Burle said sarcastically: "Want to get rid of the witnesses against you? That it?"

"That'll have to be a sight plainer than it is."

Burle walked behind the bar. He kneeled before the safe, and when he straightened, he held some papers in his hand. "Know what these are?"

"How the hell would I know that?"

The glint of triumph was back now, and plain. "They're affidavits."

"By the men who ambushed me? Let me see those."

"Oh no!" Burle hastily stuffed them back in

the safe and slammed the door. "I'm not going to give you their names. Not until the trial comes up."

Sloan felt a rising, impatient anger. He said: "What do these so-called affidavits have to say?"

"That Rose Lauck was dead when they arrived. Beaten to death with *your* fists. All of 'em say the same damn' thing."

"Get those men down here."

Burle smiled. "Uhn-uh, Marshal. They're out of your reach. They left for Maverick Towner's cow camp fifteen minutes ago. They're halfway out there by now. 'Course, if you want to ride out to Towner's camp and take 'em . . ." He let the sentence dangle suggestively.

Sloan felt balked. He wanted the men who had killed Rose, and he wanted them badly. When he thought of her paying with her life for a simple act of decency and mercy . . . but it would have to wait. Burle was right when he said the men were out of Sloan's reach. Sloan doubted if he could ride to Towner's camp, let alone take on the three, and Towner's men to boot, when he arrived.

Burle said: "Now the people of this town are going to find out what kind of a bastard they hired. I'm going to see to it that they read these affidavits."

Sloan said—"Do that."—and strode from the saloon. He forgot his wounded leg as he went out

201

the door and put his weight on it as he stepped down the single step. It gave way, and he fell heavily.

Sid helped him up. Sid's face was white with anger, and the expression in his eyes matched that in Sloan's. He grunted under his breath: "The son-of-a-bitch."

Sloan didn't reply. He was bathed with sweat from the pain, and, try as he would, he could no longer walk without a pronounced limp. He felt as though the blood had all flowed out of his head, and the street swam dizzily before his eyes. Wait. It was something he had never really learned to do. He'd had to wait often during the war, and he'd had to wait out there on the plains when he and Sid were hunting buffalo. Yet then there had not been this merciless urgency to prod him. He remembered the way Rose had looked at him last night. He remembered the gentleness of her hands. She had been a prostitute, one on the long, downhill grade. But last night she had been a compassionate woman, too. She had saved Sloan's life when no one else would even try. She would be avenged. He promised himself that she would. But it would simply have to wait—until he was stronger—until he was ready for a showdown with the cowmen's group. By going out there now he would only get himself killed, and that would help no one. Rest. Sleep. How in the hell was he going to sleep while the men who had beaten Rose to death with their fists laughed at him from Towner's camp on the plain?

He gritted his teeth. As they entered the office, Sid said: "Dryden and a bunch of the others are going into the Cowman's Pride."

Sloan turned his head. He recognized several of the men who were with Dryden. They were the same ones who had pleaded with him to take on the marshal's job. Now they would listen to Burle's trumped-up evidence against him and would probably ask him to resign. And maybe, by God, he would resign. If they were so ready to believe the worst about him, they didn't deserve a lawful town. He'd quit, and he'd go out to Towner's camp and, if it was the last thing he ever did, he'd kill those three. He realized that his thoughts were getting wild. He felt hot, and knew he was feverish from the wound.

Doc was gone, but Merline Morris was still in the office. She asked no questions. She just took a look at his face and said: "You come here and lie down. You're going to get some rest, and I'm going to stay here and see that you do."

He collapsed to the cot, lay back, and closed his eyes. He felt as though he were floating, whirling through thin air. His body was weightless, and his head didn't even seem to be a part of it. But he felt her hand on his forehead, cool and soft and fragrant, and after a few moments felt his consciousness begin to fade. He would be stronger when he awoke, he thought dreamily. He would be stronger—perhaps strong enough to finish this dirty job he had agreed to do. After that he would sleep a week.

Sloan Hewitt had slept, but it was not an easy sleep. The things his mind knew as he slept seemed to be parts of disjointed dreams, and yet were not. Dryden and the others had come marching across to the marshal's office shortly after he fell asleep. Sid had met them just outside, but their voices carried in the door.

Dryden had said: "We want to see Mister Hewitt."

"He's asleep. He was up all night."

"He was limping."

"A little old bullet wound is all. What do you want to see him about?"

"Some affidavits that Burle has got."

Sid had said softly, contemptuously: "Get out of here. I said he was asleep."

"You can't talk to us that way. You're only . . ."

"Can't I? I both can and will. You hired Sloan to clean up your town. You gave him a free hand." His voice had held a note of unbelief. "You know good and well what those three tried to do last night. They tried to kill Sloan, and they almost did. If it hadn't been for Rose, they'd have made the grade. Now you want to believe the word of three murdering pigs instead of his. You're actually going to ask him to explain."

"We're responsible . . ."

Sid had uttered a single, contemptuous, obscene word. Then he had said viciously: "You're responsible, all right. For the mess the town is in. For every man, woman, or kid that gets killed in the streets."

"But . . ."

"You stupid fool, why would Sloan kill Rose? She helped him. She saved his neck. She doused his wound with whiskey and tied it up and then let him out the back door."

There had been some unsatisfied grumbling, but the group had broken up and gone away. And there was a time of deep, uninterrupted sleep for Sloan.

In midmorning, Burle had marched across the street and demanded to see Sloan. Sid had met him outside the door, as he had met the group of townsmen. He had refused to let Burle in, so Burle had stood and talked to him for almost ten minutes—about nothing—about the weather and the herds waiting their turn on the plain outside the town. Then he had gone away, leaving Sid with a puzzled expression on his homely face.

Sloan awoke shortly before noon to find Merline still sitting at his side. It was hot and sticky, and Sloan was damp with sweat. But the fever he'd had earlier was gone.

For a time he lay still, staring at the ceiling above his head. Then he turned his head and looked at Merline. It was good to see her here, good to know she'd stayed. He said: "I dreamed Dryden and some others were here."

"It was no dream." Her voice was angry.

"What did they want?"

"They wanted you to explain the affidavits Burle has in his safe. They wanted you to say you didn't beat Rose to death with your fists."

He looked at her closely. "Do you want me to say it?"

Her eyes snapped at him. "Of course I don't. That's an awful thing to accuse me of."

"I'm sorry."

"Well, I should think you would be."

He swung his feet to the floor and sat up. Pain shot from his thigh all the way up his back, and his face broke out in fresh beads of sweat.

Merline said firmly: "You can't do it. You're hurt and sick, and you've got to give it up."

He didn't look at her. He had been thinking the same thing himself, but hearing it put into words made him see how impossible it was. Quitting now would be like deserting under fire. He saw a young man, hatless, come from the direction of the bank next door. The man, who Sloan vaguely remembered as being an employee of the bank, entered and looked at him doubtfully. "Mister Hewitt?"

"Uhn-huh. What is it now?"

"Mister Dryden sent me. Someone's in the bank trying to make a large deposit to your account."

"Tell him I'll be right there."

The young man went out. Sloan got up, his teeth tightly clenched against the pain. He grinned ruefully at Merline.

She asked: "They're trying to smear you now, aren't they? They're trying to make Dryden think you've accepted a bribe."

He nodded, still grinning. "It's a good sign. First the affidavits, now this. It means they're backing up. They're scared."

She stood on tiptoe and kissed him on the mouth. "Don't you count on that." She looked straight into his eyes for the briefest instant. "And next time you smell of whiskey and perfume, see to it that it's mine. The perfume, I mean. Now I'll get you some dinner."

"That's the best offer I've had today."

"Which one?" Her glance dropped, but not before he had seen the expression her eyes held.

"The first."

Her voice was a mere whisper. "Don't wait too long to accept." Then she turned and ran out the door. A buggy, careening along, narrowly missed her as she crossed the street, and Sloan briefly held his breath. He could quit now, he thought. He could quit and Merline would go away some place with him. She'd never blame him for quitting. But he'd blame himself. He'd think about that little girl, Debbie, who might have been his own. He'd wonder how many other innocent ones had died before someone with more guts than he came along and tamed the town. He wondered, suddenly, how Sylvia was bearing up under her loss, and remembered her as she had been before the war, remembered how he himself had been. A long time ago, that, he mused. A long time. He had changed, and Sylvia had changed as well. What pressures had made her take up with a man like Burle, a cold animal who could give her nothing but a roof over her head? Pity for her touched him, and he began to understand her with speculation remarkably accurate for one who has been deeply in love and who has been hurt. The child had not been his. Affectionate, vulnerable with others as she had been with him, Sylvia had become pregnant by someone else while he was gone. But there had been too much honor in her to let Sloan think the child was his. And so she'd gone away. Burle had offered security, a roof over her and Debbie's heads. Safety and the necessities. Nothing more. Angrily he hobbled out the door, nodded briefly at Sid, then went to the bank next door.

The young man was behind the barred teller's window, but the depositor was gone. Dryden came immediately from the rear of the bank.

"He's gone, Mister Hewitt. We refused the deposit, and he left."

"Who was he?"

Dryden looked at him strangely.

Sloan said evenly: "Damn you, you're going to have to get off the fence. Two days ago, you were begging me to take this job. Now you're sorry, and you're trying to put the blame on me."

"But the killing, Mister Hewitt. There's been more. . . ."

"I said there would be."

"And those affidavits. And this."

Sloan put his hand on the marshal's badge. "You want this?"

"Now wait, Mister Hewitt. All we want is . . ."

"Do you want this now? It's the last damned chance you're going to get. You know those affidavits are phony. Those three and the two dead ones ambushed me. How much do you think those affidavits are worth? And this. If I wanted to take a bribe, do you think I'd let them deposit it in my account? What kind of fool do you think I am?"

"We don't think you're a fool, Mister Hewitt. It's just that . . . well . . . it's the other people in the town. We pretty much acted on our own when we hired you, and now we find that we haven't got much support from the others in town. There have been more bullets flying around and more men killed since you took over than there ever were before. People are beginning to think that when you've got the opposition licked, you'll be worse than they were. They're afraid of you."

Standing there, with his weight equally on the good leg and the wounded one, Sloan felt sick and angry and irritable. He needed support for the fight that was coming up. He couldn't face both the saloonkeepers and the cowmen without it. Yet now he knew that was exactly what he was going to have to do. Dryden's support was gone. So was that of Dryden's friends. The town had never given its support at all.

He turned and hobbled to the door. His hands were clenched. He knew if he stayed another minute, said another word, he'd yank the badge from his shirt and throw it on the floor.

XI

Walking from the bank to the marshal's office next door without limping required the greatest power of will Sloan had ever exerted, but he managed it, even though it soaked his body from forehead to shins with sweat. He was thoroughly infuriated, more so than he had ever been in his life before, but he was also sick inside. When the cowmen and the saloon crowd learned that he had no support from the town . . . ? Scowling, he stepped into the marshal's office. He looked at

Merline, and then at Sid, and snapped: "Burle sent someone over to try and make a big deposit to my account. A fool could see through it, but Dryden couldn't."

Sid said: "You can quit. All you got to do is take off the badge and walk outside. Nobody'll blame you. Hell, anybody'd be scared of a set-up like this one."

For some reason, Sid's tone and words only added more fury to that already seething in Sloan's brain. "Like hell I will. They've beat me and shot me and made me sore outside and in, and that's an end to it. Now I'm going to give them back some of what they've given me."

"You already have. The three that beat you are pushing up daisies, and so are two of the five that put the hole in your leg. Don't be a fool, Sloan. Quit while you're ahead. This town doesn't mean a tinker's damn to you."

Sloan sat down and began to eat from the tray Merline had brought. He glanced up at her. Sid was wrong. This town meant a lot to him. It meant a place to stop and stay. It meant a home, if the things he had read in Merline's eyes were true. It meant an end to the aching loneliness that had been a part of him ever since he returned from the war and found that Sylvia had run away. Something of his thoughts, his need, must have shown in his face and eyes, for Merline took an involuntary step toward him. Then she stopped and said almost angrily: "You look like hell, Marshal. Lie down and get some sleep. Do what Doc said to do or you'll never make it through the day."

He nodded. For now the fight was gone from him. His thoughts were sluggish, and his body felt like lead. He stumbled to the cot and flopped down on it. He had only to close his heavy-lidded eyes and he was asleep.

The afternoon passed while the marshal slept. On the streets, little groups formed and talked worriedly, broke up and formed again. Down at the lower end of Texas Street the saloons were open, but they had had only a few customers throughout the day. Not a single rider arrived from the held herds out on the vast, wide plain.

At 4:00 a group arrived and rode up Texas Street at a steady, purposeful trot. They drew rein before the bank and waited, while one of their number got down and went inside.

Sid watched from the marshal's office, and knew without being told why they were here. They carried a demand, he guessed, that the town get rid of its marshal or else. Or else what, he couldn't know. There could be a number of alternatives, all of them equally distasteful. They could refuse to patronize the town. They could attack *en masse*, kill the marshal, and tree the town. Whatever they threatened they could do. There were a dozen herds out there on the plain, and each had from ten to twenty-five men with it. Which added up to well over a hundred men.

Sid left the window and walked over to the cot. Sloan laid on his back, snoring heavily, his face drawn and covered with reddish whiskers. He touched Sloan's shoulder and shook him gently. Sloan opened his eyes instantly, and before he moved a muscle. They were red and fogged with sleep, yet they had a clarity about them that instantly comprehended his surroundings and his deputy standing over him. He said—"What is it?"—and his voice was harsh.

"Mebbe nothing. But I figured you'd want to be awake."

Sloan sat up stiffly, favoring the wounded leg as he swung it over the side of the cot. "What're you talking about?"

"The town's been quiet ever since you went to sleep. Too quiet. Until five minutes ago not a single man from the herds had ridden into town."

"And they're all here now?" Alarm showed in Sloan's eyes. He rubbed them and ran his fingers through his hair.

"Not all of them. About a dozen is all. They're sitting their horses in front of the bank next door, and one of 'em is inside."

Sloan got up and limped heavily to the door. Then he turned and walked to the makeshift washstand. He poured the basin full and slopped water into his face and over his rumpled hair. He dried hastily and thoroughly, then ran a broken piece of comb through his hair. "Glad you woke me. I'm ready for them now."

"You think they're coming here?"

Sloan's mouth twisted wryly. "Not the cowmen. Dryden and his friends."

"What do you figure the cowmen want?"

"Hell, you know what they want . . . my hide, nailed to the barn door. They've given Dryden some kind of ultimatum. Get rid of me or else."

Pressure was building up—steadily, relentlessly. Whole, unhurt, he'd have met it head-on, beat it back, and defeated it. But he was hurt. However much he hated admitting it, that clean, round hole in his thigh had sapped his strength. It would be weeks before he was as strong as he had been before. The worst of it was, he didn't have that much time. This fight would be decided— would be won or lost—in the next few days.

Moodily he limped to the window and stared outside. He saw one of the cowmen come from the bank and walk to his horse. The man, elderly, grizzled, stocky, and tough, mounted and sat his saddle like a rock while he stared at the marshal's office next door to the bank. His ice-blue eyes met Sloan's, flared with triumph, then looked away. He raised an arm, and the group whirled their horses and thundered away down Texas Street, staying exactly in its center until they were out of view. Still watching, Sloan saw Dryden come out. The man glanced at the marshal's office worriedly, without seeing Sloan. Then he hurried down the street.

Sloan turned away from the window. He looked wryly at Sid. "I don't know what I'm beefing about. I called it the way it would happen before I ever took the job. I knew they'd be more anxious to get rid of me before it was over than they were to hire me in the first place. I knew I'd end up being the biggest bastard in town."

"Then why'd you take it on?"

Sloan frowned. "I'm beginning to wonder. The funny thing is, I'd do the exact same thing again."

"Then tell 'em to go to hell. Ram yourself down their throats until they choke on you."

Sloan grinned. "That's exactly what I've got in mind."

He sat down, favoring the leg and letting it lie, stiff and straight, before him. Sid asked: "Hungry?"

"No, but I suppose I'd better eat. Go order me a steak, will you? A thick one, rare in the middle."

"Sure you don't want it raw? Raw meat might be what you need."

Sloan grinned at him. "Get it."

Sid went out and crossed the street, gangly and awkward-looking. It occurred to Sloan that Sid hadn't had much more sleep in the past few days than he had himself, but Sid showed no evidence of being tired.

Dryden arrived shortly after Sid had gone into the hotel, accompanied by Lake and Graham and, this time, by Ike Solomon, still wearing his leather apron, black with blood and grease.

Dryden cleared his throat and spoke before Sloan could. "We're going to take you up on your offer to quit, Mister Hewitt. We're willing to give you a month's salary and expenses. I'll deposit it to your account at the bank."

Sloan said dryly: "Don't bother." Dryden appeared relieved. His face slacked as Sloan added: "Wait until I've earned it. Wait until the month is up."

"You mean you refuse to quit?"

"I mean exactly that. I've got a contract, Mister Dryden. Or have you forgotten?" Sloan added implacably: "You promised to put some furniture in here today. It's late afternoon, and it isn't here. I want it. Now."

Solomon said hastily: "Now wait a minute . . ."

Sloan stared at him. "You wait. What're you doing here anyhow, Mister Solomon? You weren't one of the group that hired me. Getting scared?" Solomon's face lost color. He started to bluster, but stopped as Sloan turned his gaze to Dryden again. "How many buffalo hunters have been beaten and robbed in the past few months?"

"I don't know what that's got to do with this."

"How many?"

Dryden glanced at Solomon. So did Graham and Lake. Sloan knew the answer to his question by watching them. They didn't have to speak.

Sloan said: "I'll get you, Mister Solomon. It may take some time, but I'll get you before I'm through."

The whole group was shaken now. Dryden fought himself a moment, and then he said almost frantically: "You've *got* to quit, Mister Hewitt. You've got to! The cowmen have served notice that they're boycotting the town until you leave. There won't be a one of 'em in all day and not tomorrow, either, unless you quit and leave."

Sloan stared at them imperviously. "That's the price of the law you said you wanted."

"But we're geared to having the trail drivers' trade. The whole town is geared to having them come in. If they don't . . . Lord Almighty, Mister Hewitt, in the course of a year, those men spend upwards of a hundred thousand dollars here. Without them . . . well, the town would die, that's all."

"And you think they'll really stay away? They won't, Mister Dryden. They can't. A thousand Maverick Towners couldn't keep those men away from your liquor and women for very long. They've got three months of hell behind them and a pocket full of money. Towner can keep them out today and maybe tomorrow, but the day after that they'll all be back."

Dryden looked at him doubtfully. "I hope you're right. I just hope to God you're right."

Solomon broke in: "He's not right, and you know it. Next year the rails will be going west. There'll be a new town at the end of the track. If they haven't liked it here, they'll drive to the new town."

Sloan said: "Sure. They'll do that no matter what happens here. Because it's closer. A town fifty miles west of here will mean a shorter drive. Nothing we do or don't do is going to have any effect on it."

"Then why not give this up for now? Why . . . ?" Dryden didn't finish because Sloan broke in. "Why? Because the town will stay lawless whether the drovers come or not. Your crib street will stay and so will your saloons. Only, instead of preying on the drovers, they'll prey on you." He watched them and saw the indecision in them, the helpless confusion. He pitied them briefly, but he was weary of all the discussion and argument. He said harshly: "Get that furniture over here."

They filed out, waiting until they were out of hearing before they began to argue among themselves.

Sloan sank down stiffly on the cot. His nerves were edgy and tight. It went against his grain to hoard his strength when there were so many things he wanted to do. But he had no choice. He would need it all in the days to come. Towner's pride had been outraged, and his cause had become the cause of every drover on the plain. They would not be satisfied with a boycott long. When it failed, they would be coming to town in force. And Sloan must meet them and turn them back.

XII

Sloan had to force himself to eat the steak that Sid brought back, but he worked at it doggedly and was pleasantly surprised at how much better it made him feel. After he had finished, he took two stiff drinks from the bottle Sid had brought with the meal, then lit up a cigar.

A wagonload of furniture arrived as he was finishing the cigar, and he went outside while Sid supervised the placing of it. There were two roll-top desks with swivel chairs, an old couch, several benches, and a cot for each of the cells.

The sun sank rapidly in the western sky, and a breeze came up, blowing hot and dry off the wide, dusty prairie and bringing in the strong, rank smell of the bedded herds. Passers-by in the street stared hard and resentfully at Sloan, looked away when he met their eyes. No one spoke to him. It was an unpleasant experience for him. Already they hated him, already they feared him—and this was the way they showed it.

The two men who had brought the furniture finished carrying it in, got up on their wagon, and drove away. Sid brought a bench outside and placed it against the wall, and he and Sloan sat down. Sloan lit another cigar.

No need for patrols tonight. Texas Street was as quiet as a tomb. But Sloan knew, if the town did not, that the quiet was only temporary. The drovers wouldn't stay away. They'd try this—their boycott ultimatum—but if it didn't work, they would have to try something else. As though his thoughts had been running in the same channel as Sloan's, Sid asked: "What do you think the trail hands will do when they find out their boycott didn't work?"

Sloan shrugged fatalistically. "There's only one thing they can do. Come in and tree the town. Kill me and you when we try to stop them."

"Figured out what you're going to do?"

Sloan grinned. "Stop them without getting killed."

"And how the hell do you think you're going to manage that?"

"Haven't figured that far."

Sid stared at him helplessly.

Sloan said: "It can't be done without backing from the town. But maybe they'll come through."

"Like hell they will."

"Maybe we can make them help."

He hadn't the slightest idea how he would accomplish that, and yet he had staunch faith, both in himself and in others. When the chips were all on the table, most men displayed characteristics not evident in them when things were going well. He figured the townsmen would come through—enough of them, perhaps, to turn the tide. And he could count on Sid.

The sun went down, and a soft, hot dusk hung over the dusty prairie town. Smoke lifted from the tin chimneys of houses, and Sloan smelled cooking food in the breeze that stirred past him from the upper end of town. Saloonkeepers came from the doors of their saloons at the lower end of Texas Street and stared resentfully at Sloan and Sid, sitting comfortably in front of the marshal's office.

Something made Sloan turn his head. He saw Sylvia Flint coming toward him from the upper end of town. Sid saw her, too, and got up. "Maybe I can straighten up inside."

He went in, and a few moments later Sylvia reached Sloan, who stood up as she did. He tried to do so without giving away the fact that he was hurt, but apparently failed because Sylvia said: "For heaven's sake, sit down. Your leg is hurt."

He sat down, and she sat on the bench beside him. For several moments there was awkward silence between them. His eyes searched her face, and he tried to recapture some of the old fire that had characterized his feelings for her. He failed, because the fire was dead.

With startling perception, she said: "It's gone, isn't it, Sloan?"

He started to protest, but the protest died on his lips. He said slowly: "There was a time when I grieved for you and a time when I cursed you for going away. I loved you, but I never admired you more than I do right now."

She smiled, and the smile was only partly forced. "Thank you, Sloan."

He said: "I'm going to get Burle, Sylvia. I'm going to either kill him or run him out of town."

"I know."

"What will you do?"

She sat in silence for a long, long time. Then she said softly: "I think I will go back home. I do not think I am very well suited to living out here."

Her face was soft, softer than he had seen it. He said hesitantly: "It's an awkward subject, but if you need any money, you're welcome to whatever I have."

"No, Sloan. No."

He said: "Between friends money is only paper."

She changed the subject. "What will you do, Sloan?"

He stared at her closely in the failing light. "I don't want to hurt you."

"It's Merline, isn't it?"

"Yes."

"She won't hurt you as I did. I wish you luck in all you do."

"Thank you."

For a long time there was silence between them, still touched with awkwardness but more comfortable than it had been before. One thing remained between them, one thing—and when that was gone, there would be no more awkwardness ever again. But Sloan wouldn't bring it up.

Sylvia looked at him at last and smiled. "You'd never ask, would you?"

He didn't pretend to misunderstand. "No. I'd never ask."

"Then I'll tell you. Debbie wasn't yours. She could have been, but she wasn't. If she had been yours, I'd have stayed and married you when you came home."

Sloan murmured: "I have wondered."

Now her voice was touched with bitterness and self-blame. "And I let you wonder. I hated this town, Sloan. I wanted it tamed so that what happened to Debbie could never happen to another child."

"No one could blame you for that."

"I blame myself. Because it may cost you your life. Don't underestimate Jeff Burle, Sloan. He's as ruthless as a man can be. He'll get what he wants no matter what it costs. He'll do anything to win."

"I figured him that way."

Sylvia stood up. "And now I'll go. I've been noble enough for one day. What I really want to do is scratch that damned girl's eyes out."

"I'm not worth that."

"Don't be too sure, Sloan. Don't be too sure."

He started to get up, but she put a hand on his shoulder and held him down. She bent and kissed him softly on the mouth. She would be hurt again, he thought. Life would hurt her until she died. Because there was a rarely found softness in her, and a generosity that was just as rare. Now she was alone, or would be soon. But Sylvia would not be alone for long. Sloan realized that to think such a thing about any other woman would be a condemnation, but with Sylvia it was not. Sylvia's relations with the men in her life would never be cheap or sordid. Her motives were too unselfish for that. He watched her hurry up the street. She did not look back, and he had the uneasy feeling that the reason she didn't was because she was crying and didn't want him to see. She turned the corner and disappeared.

Sloan stared thoughtfully at nothing for a long, long time. He was remembering the war years, his brief leaves. He was remembering Sylvia and wondering if he were not a fool. Then he thought of Merline Morris and remembered the clear, straightforward eyes that could be so soft. There was fire in Merline as well as in Sylvia, but it would never spill over to include more than a single man.

He became aware that the activity in the street was not normal, and pulled his thoughts reluctantly from Sylvia and Merline to concentrate on the undercurrents flowing along the street. The saloonkeepers no longer stood before their saloons. The storekeepers, closing, did not walk past him toward their homes at the upper end of town, but rather turned downstreet to disappear into the Cowman's Pride.

Sloan's face was touched with a wry smile. A meeting was shaping up. The respectable and the disreputable were joining forces down there with a common purpose—that of ousting the marshal from their town. Each group had tried, in its own way, to rid itself of him. Burle and the saloonkeepers had tried ridicule, ambush, a smear. Dryden and his group had asked Sloan to resign and in their own conservative way had tried to buy him off. He wondered what they'd come up with next. A deal with the cowmen, perhaps, and this approach was certainly going to strain the consciences of the so-called respectable group. Because a deal with the cowmen's group could only be consent to murder, the price on that consent being the cowmen's agreement not to harm the town. Sloan was very close, in this instant, to getting up and walking down there to burst in on their meeting. He was close to giving them his resignation before they shucked their consciences and bought his death. A strain of growing stubbornness prevented it. The reasons he had taken this job were still valid ones. If anything, they were stronger than before. Sylvia had strengthened his resolve, whether she had realized it or not. And there had always been something about pressure that made Sloan stand like a rock in the face of it.

Dusk deepened into night, and stars winked out in the limitless black void overhead. The breeze died, leaving the town even more still than it had been before. Sid came out and sat down on the bench again. In the utter quiet lying along the street, Sloan could hear raised voices drifting from the batwing doors of the Cowman's Pride. Grinning, he said: "Argument. That's healthy." Then he thought: *It makes me nervous. It's not flattering when the whole town wants you dead.*

Down at the Cowman's Pride, the meeting broke up. First the town's businessmen filed out, to separate almost furtively before the door and go their separate ways, avoiding looking directly toward Sloan, detouring so that they would not have to pass close to him in the street. This, more than anything else, told him the things he wanted to know, and with the knowledge that the town's respectable citizens had made a deal with the lawless element came an intangible feeling of dread, a menace that flowed along the street like water. He couldn't fight them all, saloon-keepers and hangers-on, the respectable element, the cowmen, too. And if they didn't want him, then why cram himself down their unwilling throats?

He got up and walked slowly and carefully past the bank, then down Fourth toward the Morris house. And, walking, he saw still another segment of the town that he had not considered a few moments before. The women, who might not approve of his methods but who would certainly approve of the result. The children, whose lives would be safe if he succeeded in taming the lawless town. They yelled in the early darkness, and played along the dusty streets and through the grassy yards. They played the games that Sloan himself had played as a boy back home, and he smiled faintly to himself as he heard the old, familiar arguments between them. A wild prairie town, but one that would be here long after cattle, drovers, saloon men, and gamblers had gone. If he was lucky and lived through the next few days, he would be here, too, watching his own kids play in the soft summer night.

He reached Merline's house, limping more noticeably from his walk and sweating faintly from pain. She was sitting on the porch steps, her feet on the step below, her arms around her knees. She called softly: "Watch that broken board in the walk."

He avoided the broken board and stopped just short of the steps.

Her voice was a trifle nervous, as though she sensed what he had come to say. "The town's awfully quiet tonight."

"No drovers in town." He cleared his throat. "I've not got much to offer a woman. But I want to marry you. I think I've wanted that since I first set eyes on you."

Merline stood up, and doing so put herself only inches away from him. She said simply: "And I've wanted you to ask me almost that long."

"Is that yes or no?"

He could see her smile, even though the light was poor. "It's yes, you fool. What else could it be?"

He had been nervous and scared all the way here. Now he relaxed. He wanted to laugh with pure relief. He put out his arms and caught her to him with a hunger that flared like a fire but that was also strong and solid and good. It had been so long since he'd held a woman in his arms. He had never held a woman quite like this one before. She was less composed than he had ever seen her. She was like a girl, confused, eager, uncertain. He bent his head and kissed her on the mouth.

Now he had something to fight them for that he hadn't had before. He could feel strength flowing through his body, resoluteness through his mind. He had almost quit this afternoon, but there would be no thought of quitting again. This town was his, and before he was through it would be a decent place in which to live.

XIII

After Sloan had left, Sid Wessell went out and sat on the bench before the marshal's office, frowning thoughtfully into the warm summer night. There was a lamp burning in the office behind him, which softly bathed the boardwalk and street before him with light. A young couple in a buggy turned off Fourth, rounded the corner past the bank, and drove toward the upper end of town and the prairie beyond. From the darkness inside the buggy, Sid heard a delighted giggle and grinned to himself. The reins, he noticed, were slack.

Sloan had said nothing about his destination when he left, but Sid had a pretty good idea where he'd gone. There was a difference between them, he thought. Sloan liked a town and liked people around him even though he wasn't exactly the social type. Sloan had reached a point in his development where he wanted roots—a woman, a family of his own. Sid hadn't reached that point and maybe never would. He liked the open prairie, liked being alone with the vast and awesome stillness around him at night. He had a normal man's appetite for women, but an occasional visit to town took care of this need without cluttering his life with permanence and strings to tie him down. Sloan, if he lived long enough, would marry that Morris girl. He'd settle here and raise half a dozen kids and grow stocky and slow and get that quiet, thoughtful look in his eyes that married men developed. And it would be good for Sloan. Sloan, unlike himself, was deviled continuously with loneliness. Sloan needed to belong, and he would belong. Right here.

Sid would stay until the town was tamed, and then he'd go. Maybe he'd find another partner and hunt buffalo until the beasts were gone. Maybe by then he'd have enough to start some cattle of his own on a homestead grant of prairie sod. Or maybe he'd just drift. There was a lot of country to the west of here—where savages still roamed, where the land was new. Man ought to see all he could before it was too late. Someday there would be fences and roads and towns and schools out here just the same as there were in the East. Yes, sir. A man ought to see it all before it was too late.

He settled back, fished a plug of tobacco from his pocket, and worried off a chew. He stowed it comfortably in his cheek and let the warm stillness of the night flow through and over him. The showdown here was due in a day or two. At the prospect, the nerves in his body tingled expectantly. It never occurred to him that he might die and Sloan die with him. Whatever the odds, however uneven they were, he had unswerving confidence in Sloan and in himself.

The street was quiet. Those who had attended the meeting at the Cowman's Pride had disappeared from the street. The saloons were quiet, too, although they were still lit up as though expecting a flood of customers from the plain at any time. Sid remembered suddenly the way he'd met Sloan. Pure coincidence. He hadn't wanted to go home after the war because there was nothing particular to return for. He had no folks or family—only the granger for whom he'd worked when the war broke out. He'd been camped in the woods, roasting a weaner pig that he'd stolen from a farm. Sloan had walked into the circle of firelight, and Sid had invited him to stay and eat.

The brooding loneliness had been plain in Sloan's eyes then, he remembered, but not until much later had he learned its cause. Nor had he cared. They just seemed to get along well and so had stayed together. Sloan had a little money, and so had Sid. They both were pretty good shots. The buffalo-hunting venture had seemed natural and right. This was something else, and Sid still had moments of doubt about it. Seemed like a man was crowding his luck, taking on a job like this. It was like the war, only it was worse. You fought alone, and you fought craftiness and guile and murder from ambush. It was like fighting an enemy in his own camp because you fought hatred, too. That hurt Sloan much more than it did Sid because of Sloan's thirst for roots and a place to belong.

Impatient with his own thoughts, which he knew could scare him if he gave them a decent chance, he got up and went inside again. He wandered aimlessly through the office and the cells behind it, sometimes changing a piece of furniture and vaguely depressed for no particular reason he could name. The door stood open upon the street, and the man materialized there without sound. One moment the doorway was empty, and the next he was standing there.

Sid started, and his hand touched the grips of his gun. But the man didn't move. He was slightly drunk, whiskered, ordinary. The town-drunk type, Sid decided. He said unsteadily: "The marshal says for you to get a horse and make a couple of patrols."

"Where is he?"

"He 'n' Miss Morris took a buggy ride. I was down to the stable, so he sent me. He said you'd give me fifty cents."

Sid fished in his pocket and came up with a half dollar. He tossed it to the man, who caught it expertly as though used to having money tossed to him instead of handed to him.

Sid said—"All right."—and watched the man turn and slouch away downstreet. He blew out the office lamp, went out, and closed the door. He didn't see why patrols were necessary tonight, but if Sloan wanted them, it was all right with him. He walked downstreet to the stable, went in, and got a horse. He swung to the saddle and rode down Texas Street, staying in the center the way Sloan did. There was a reason for that, he thought. You were out in the open, and could plainly see both sides of the street. You had freedom of movement in case you were attacked. It also had a good effect on the town. Out there in the open you were the man on horseback, flinging a challenge into the faces of those who would like to cut you down. Whether you were or not, you seemed to be unafraid, contemptuous of danger and death.

Grinning, Sid held his horse in the exact center of the street. The doorways of the saloons were empty now; the town was like a tomb. No pianos tinkled from inside their batwing doors. No quarrelsome shouts were raised. Down past the depot he rode, on beyond to the cattle pens. The alleys between the pens were inky black, and cattle inside the pens spooked nervously away as he approached, to crowd together on the far side against the fence.

Vague uneasiness touched Sid, but he couldn't place its source. He quieted it by telling himself that no one wanted him. It was Sloan they wanted dead. He saw the shadowy movement at the end of the alleyway—saw it but didn't slack his pace. He thought it was a steer, loose from one of the pens. Too late, he saw that it was not. Flame, narrow, bluish orange, spat at him from beside the fence. He felt the bullet's impact and knew suddenly why they wanted him. Without him, Sloan would be wholly alone, without backing, without support, either moral or tangible.

He felt himself tumbling backward out of the saddle, felt his back and shoulders strike the ground. There were more bullets now, a veritable fusillade of them. From all sides they came at him, kicking dust and powdered manure over him, striking him, whining overhead. He never got out his gun. An angry curtain of red descended over his eyes. His last thought was: *That drunk! That god-damn' dirty drunk. . . .* And then he knew no more.

Sloan heard the shots from the porch of Merline's house, and was moving long before the last of them had died away. He forgot his wounded leg, and ran down the boardwalk toward the gate. Merline screamed at him: "Wait! I'll get my mare! She's . . ." She never finished. Sloan put his foot on the broken board, went through, and sprawled face down on the splintery walk.

She ran toward him, but he yelled: "No! I'm all right! Get the mare!"

He wasn't all right. He'd twisted the leg, and pain from it was a blinding white sheet of flame before his eyes. He rolled and sat up, keeping the leg stiff and straight before him. Carefully he eased himself to his feet. His head reeled, and he could feel the warmth of fresh blood soaking the bandage over the wound. Damn!

Now he tried to place the direction of the shots, and decided they had come from the direction of the depot. He felt immeasurably relieved and wondered why he had instantly thought of Sid as he heard those shots. Sid was in the marshal's office. He'd left him there less than half an hour ago.

Merline came running, dragging the mare behind her. Sloan took the reins from her, separated them, and swung to the mare's back. He thundered away down the street without glancing back.

God! They couldn't even let a man propose to his future wife without kicking up some damned fuss. Probably a pair of drunk cowhands shooting at . . . His thoughts stopped cold. There weren't any cowhands or trail hands in town. There was a boycott on. That realization started him thinking of Sid again. And suddenly he was scared. His spine was cold as ice, and the flesh on the back of his neck prickled. He wore no spurs, but his heels dug savagely into the mare's sides. Unused to this kind of treatment, she jumped as though she had been shot.

He took the corner at Fourth and Texas Street, heeled over, and swung wide to the opposite side of the street. He glanced behind him involuntarily and saw with increasing dread that the marshal's office was dark. Sid was down there . . . maybe hurt . . . maybe even dead. How he'd got there and why, Sloan didn't know, but now he under-stood why his thoughts had leaped to Sid the instant he heard the shots. Close as they were, there was something of their thoughts that leaped to each other across distances that voice or sight could never reach. Damn it! He'd thought the town was quiet for tonight. He'd let down his guard.

He passed the saloons at a hard run and rounded the turn into the depot, the mare's hoofs setting up a veritable thunder as they crossed the plank platform. The station agent, sitting at his tele-graph key, jumped and yanked his head around. Sloan yelled: "The shots! Where . . . ?"

"Cattle pens . . ."

Sloan didn't wait to hear the rest. Down across the tracks to the cattle pens he thundered, and down the main alleyway between them, con-temptuous of caution that would have slowed him down. His gun was in his hand, half raised and ready for anything that moved. But nothing did—not until he reached a cross-alley—and then he caught a glimpse of something large and dark that might have been a steer. He reined over hard, and the shadow spooked away from him. He recognized it now as a horse.

"One of theirs," was his thought, and he left his mount in a single easy movement as he spotted something dark and lumped upon the dusty ground.

He hit the ground running, cursing under his breath because once more he had forgotten his wounded leg. It gave, and made him lurch, but he caught himself and went on. Even before recognition touched him, he felt a stab of the same dread he had earlier felt, and something that was close to terror. Then he was close, and kneeling, and he knew that the man on the ground was Sid.

Gently he touched the man. He held his own breath while he listened for Sid's. Hearing nothing, he put his head down against Sid's chest and heard a faint, erratic heartbeat. Sid was still alive, at least. He started to slide his arms under Sid's body, but stopped as Sid stirred and tried to speak. Motionless Sloan said: "I'll get you uptown to Doc. . . ."

"Uhn-uh. Too damn' late for that."

"Who was it? How'd they get you down here?"

"Never saw 'em. They sent the town drunk to tell me you wanted me to get a horse and patrol the town."

Sid's voice was weak and growing weaker fast. Sloan knew he should let Sid remain quiet while he rode for Doc, but something held him here, immovable, and something made him ask urgently: "The town drunk, you say. What'd he look like?"

"Whiskers. Slouch. Red eyes. Made me give him fifty cents. I tossed it to him, and he caught it like he was used to catching coins."

"All right. That one shouldn't be very hard to find. And that one will talk until his guts run out." The terror was now like ice in Sloan's belly. He said: "Hold on, damn you! I'll get Doc."

"No. Stay. I don't want to die alone."

"You're not going to die."

Sid found his hand and gripped it hard. He murmured: "So this is what dying's like. I've wondered."

Sloan's throat felt tight. But he didn't argue now.

Sid's voice was very faint. "It's like standing on a cliff at night, looking out over the edge. You don't see anything. You feel it. How big it is. How empty. How cold." His hand tightened on Sloan's. Now Sloan had to strain his ears to hear. "You know you're going to step off in a minute but you don't want to . . . and float out there like a soaring bird . . ."

His voice trailed off. For the briefest instant his hand gripped Sloan's almost frantically. Then it relaxed and was limp. Sloan's throat closed tight. Scalding tears flooded his eyes and brimmed over onto his cheeks. God damn this town! God damn this stinking, dirty town!

He got up, walked to Merline's mare and picked up the reins. He led the animal back to where Sid lay. Cursing softly, savagely under his breath, he kneeled and slid his arms under Sid's gaunt, long body. He lifted him, angrily ignoring the pain in his leg the added weight brought. He almost fell as he stepped toward the mare. Like most mares, the smell of blood didn't bother her at all, and she stood like a rock while he laid Sid's body over the saddle, boosted it up, and hooked Sid's belt over the saddle horn. Then, limping heavily, he led the mare out of the cattle pens, across the lit depot platform, and out onto Texas Street.

Let them look. Let them look long and well at the marshal they had crippled, at the deputy they had killed. Because, damn them, they were going to pay. They were going to pay for Sid as they'd never paid for anything in their lives before. They'd better shoot now and shoot to kill. They'd never get a better chance.

XIV

He carried Sid into the marshal's office, laid him gently down on the couch, then crossed the room and lit the lamp. By the time he had that done, a small crowd had collected out in front. He went to the door and let his eyes drift over them coldly. "Get the undertaker."

A man detached himself from the group and hurried across the street.

Sloan said: "Somebody find Dryden."

He turned and went back into the office. He stared around cynically. This office was, he thought, symbolic of the brawling town's desire for respectability, and just as transient. The cells wouldn't hold an angry bear, and in a day's time it could be converted back to what it had been before—an empty store.

After fifteen minutes or so the undertaker arrived, driving his shiny hearse with four black horses hitched ahead. He and his helper put Sid on a stretcher, covered him, and carried him out. The black coach drove away.

Sloan's face was bleak. He'd accepted the fact that Sid was dead, but the mere removal of his body seemed to leave an aching void.

The crowd began to disperse outside. Dryden came walking in shortly after the hearse had left.

His face showed Sloan genuine regret. "I'm sorry about . . ."

Sloan cut him short. "Never mind that. Someone brought him a phony message to get him down there to the cattle pens where they could kill him without any risk. A man that slouches . . . whiskers . . . red eyes, a drunk that catches coins when they're flipped at him. Who is he?"

Dryden frowned. "Rafferty, maybe. Sounds like him. But I doubt if he even knew what was going on. You can't . . ."

Sloan stared at him coldly. "I can make him talk."

Dryden seemed relieved. There was fear in his eyes as he looked at Sloan's rigid face, at the icy set of his mouth.

Sloan said coldly: "Was Sid's murder part of the deal you made with Burle?"

Dryden turned red. His eyes flared angrily, and then the fire of anger died in them, to be replaced by a look of shame. He stared straight into Sloan's furious eyes and said: "No. There was actually no deal made, although I don't suppose you'll believe it. Burle called the meeting and most of us attended. He offered us a cleaner town if we'd get rid of you. He promised that the saloon-keepers would keep their own houses clean."

"Like hell they would."

Dryden said: "We told him you'd refused to quit, that you were going to wait out the boycott."

"But you didn't tell him I had your support, did you?"

Dryden colored again. His forehead was damp. "We told him we'd withdrawn our support. If that's . . ."

"An invitation to murder? What else do you think it is? God damn you, Dryden, get out of here!"

Dryden, taking a hasty look at his face, backed toward the door. He said—"Don't . . ."—but never finished. Sloan's eyes blazed at him, and he whirled and hurried away.

Sloan walked over and blew out the lamp. He stepped out on the walk and closed the door. He paused there a moment to let his fury cool, to let his hands grow steady again. Maybe they'd have killed Sid anyway. Maybe Dryden's public withdrawal of support hadn't brought it on at all. He didn't see how the support of a wishy-washy bunch like Dryden and his friends could have much effect one way or another. Yet he knew it had. Dryden spoke for the town, and while those behind him at first were few, eventually the way the town jumped would be the way Dryden jumped now. The saloon crowd knew they could buck Sloan and Sid. They knew they could buck a few of the town's respectable businessmen. But they also realized that they couldn't buck the town. Not for very long. Hell, the saloonkeepers knew that the trail drivers would be back. They were aware, as Sloan was, that a thousand Maverick Towners couldn't keep them away for long. Knowing this, they'd had to move fast— before the trail drivers returned, before Sloan regained the town's support. Ah, hell, a complicated business, but Sloan intended to simplify it just as rapidly as he could.

He walked down Texas Street and began the rounds of the saloons. His body was tense, his eyes hard, his disposition as edgy as that of a tormented snake. The attitudes of those he saw indicated they knew how dangerous he was. They glanced at him, then rapidly glanced away for fear he would read something into their glances and act on it. He'd never seen a guiltier-looking bunch of men in his life. Every one of them looked like a church-goer caught with his hands in the collection plate. He didn't ask after Rafferty, and he hoped Dryden would have sense enough to keep his mouth shut. He didn't want anyone to know that Sid had talked to him before he died. If those who had sent Rafferty knew Sloan was looking for him, Rafferty would simply turn up dead before he had a chance to talk.

He spotted a man shambling drunkenly down Texas Street near its lower end and knew immediately that this was the man Sid had described to him. He followed, aware that he was being watched by everyone on Texas Street. He caught his man where the street was dark, a few doors above the depot. He called—"Rafferty!"—and saw the man turn drunkenly to peer at him. He flipped a fifty-cent piece, said—"Catch."—and Rafferty caught the coin.

Sloan stepped up close, grabbed the drunk by the front of his greasy shirt, and shook him savagely. "I'm just going to ask you once," he said between clenched teeth. "Just once. Who sent you to the marshal's office with that message tonight?"

The drunk was mumbling, as though to himself: ". . . said it was a joke. Joke on the marshal, damn' son-a-bitch. Joke . . ."

Sloan shook him again. "Who said that?"

"Burle. Jeff Burle."

Sloan said harshly: "It wasn't a joke."

Rafferty's naming of Burle came as no surprise. Sloan had expected it, and would have been surprised if Rafferty had named anyone else. He released the drunk. Rafferty staggered over against the wall and slid down it to the walk. He went on mumbling to himself. Sloan turned away disgustedly, and behind him he heard Rafferty begin to sniffle as though he were going to cry.

Sloan had forgotten his wounded leg, had forgotten who he was and what job he held. He could only think of one thing—of Burle, sitting up there at the Cowman's Pride like a fat, hairy spider spreading his evil like a web over the town. He could only think that tonight he was going to kill Jeff Burle and that, when he did, he was going to enjoy it.

He limped, but as he walked up Texas Street no one noticed the limp. All they could see was the rigid, cold set of his face and the unholy light in his slitted eyes. Rose had died for helping him. Sid had died because he was close to Sloan. Sloan knew that if Burle wasn't stopped, Merline Morris was going to be next.

Jeff Burle stood behind the bar at the Cowman's Pride, his hand on a shotgun laid on a shelf below the bar. The place was nearly empty. What townsmen had been here earlier had left when Sloan brought the body of Sid Wessell up the street. Now, all that remained were Burle's employees—and the girls. Even so, he felt reasonably secure. Sloan might know who had engineered Sid's murder, but he could hardly prove it. There would be doubt enough in his mind to keep him from doing anything rash. And, if the doubt weren't enough, the shotgun would be. Jeff didn't intend to get more than a yard away from it until the showdown with Sloan was over with. Alone, hounded and threatened from every side, without even the support of those who had hired him, Sloan would probably quit tonight. He'd ride out, and things could go back to normal again.

Thinking it was Sloan, Burle started when Len Davenport came bursting through the doors. He realized that he had seized the shotgun and had raised it partway. A stunt like that would get him killed when Sloan came in. He was getting jumpy. He was giving Sloan credit for being something more than a mortal man.

Davenport hurried to the bar. He said in a low, urgent tone: "He found Rafferty. He talked to him. And now he's coming here."

"Rafferty? How the hell could he know Rafferty was . . . ?"

"Maybe the deputy wasn't dead. Maybe he lived long enough to talk to Hewitt."

Burle glanced around him. There wasn't time. He didn't have enough good men around him right now to be sure. Sloan Hewitt was hell with that gun of his. He'd killed the three who had robbed him less than a week ago and hadn't been scratched doing it. No. This wasn't the time for a showdown with Sloan. Because he'd be first to die when Sloan came in. The marshal would be out of his mind with rage. He'd be sure and not in doubt. It made Burle furious to think of running, but there was nothing else to do. He grabbed the shotgun and trotted heavily toward the back door. He went out through the kitchen and into the alley, and here glanced cautiously up and down.

Seeing no one, he crossed the vacant lot to the

crib street, then stopped in the shadows to think. He was panting softly and not in the least sure that he'd done the right thing. He'd let Sloan run him out of his own saloon, and that would play hell with his prestige. He'd admitted more or less publicly that he was afraid of Sloan, even when he had the odds in his favor. The truth of the matter was, he was afraid of Sloan. He'd tried to have Sloan killed, and it hadn't worked. Five men, good men, hadn't been able to kill him. Sloan must have the devil's luck with him. But he *was* only one man. The marshal could die like any other man. If he could just figure some way of keeping Sloan off his back until the cowmen came to town, they'd take care of him once and for all. Sloan wouldn't have a chance against them, no matter how tough or lucky he was.

Some way of keeping Hewitt off his back, some way of . . . ? Sylvia? Hell, no. Whatever had been between them was over, at least as far as Sloan was concerned. He hadn't been to see her except that one time. But Merline Morris—that was something else again. If Hewitt thought she was in danger, it would cool him off plenty fast. The way those two looked at each other . . . He still owned that little homestead shack along Squaw Creek that he'd won in a poker game. It would be an ideal place to take Merline, because Sloan wouldn't think of looking for either Burle or her outside of town. A couple of days, that was about all it would take the trail drivers to learn their boycott hadn't worked. Then they'd be coming to town in force.

Burle worked his way down toward the lower end of town and slouched across Texas Street near the depot, after carefully searching the shadows before he did. He reached the livery barn from the rear, climbed the corral fence, and plowed through the dusty, powdered manure to the rear doors. Apparently the stableman was asleep in the tack room, for Burle was able to hitch up a buggy without bringing him to the door. He got up and drove out, turned immediately off Texas Street, and then headed by a circuitous route for the Morris house.

He drove the buggy into the weeds beside the house when he reached it and hooked the weight to the bridle to hold the horse still. Then he went to the door.

Merline answered it. Burle opened the screen and forced his way inside. "Get what you need. You're going with me. Kick up any fuss and I'll have to knock you around. Come quietly and you'll be all right."

He thought for a moment that she'd fight, but she turned and ran instead. He reached her in a couple of leaps, swung an arm like a club, and knocked her sprawling. He was angry now, where he had only been nervous before. He said between his teeth: "God damn you, do as I say."

She got up numbly, her frightened eyes on his face. She said: "Sloan . . ."

He finished it for her. "Won't do a damned thing, when he knows I'll kill you if he does."

"How . . . ?"

He said: "I'll leave him a note, that's how. Now move."

He followed her into the bedroom and stood in the doorway while she packed a small valise. When she had finished, he demanded paper and pencil, which she got for him without protest. He didn't want to hurt her, but he wouldn't hesitate if she resisted him. Apparently she understood this thoroughly. He scrawled a note for Sloan.

He held Merline's arm tightly as he stuck the note between the screen door and the jamb. He held onto her all the way to the buggy. He was still holding her as he unhooked the weight from the bridle. Then he boosted her to the seat ahead of him. He picked up the reins and drove straight across the prairie toward the shack on Squaw Creek.

XV

When Sloan stalked into the Cowman's Pride, there was evidence that, in spite of the fact that it was only 10:00 p.m., it was closing for the night. The girls were trooping toward the stairway. A barman was straightening out bottles and glasses behind the bar. One swamper was sweeping, and another was emptying spittoons.

Sloan had a sense of being balked the instant he walked in. He briefly considered the possibility that this was window dressing for a trap, but discarded the idea immediately. It was too real. He said harshly: "Where's Burle?"

Nobody answered. Sloan walked to the sweeper and whirled him around. "I asked a question."

"He went out the back door a few minutes ago. When he heard you'd found . . ." The man stopped, shooting a fearful glance at the barman.

Sloan said softly: "Rafferty?"

The swamper averted his glance. "I got work to do, Marshal."

But Sloan had his answer. Burle knew he'd found Rafferty and knew Rafferty had talked. He whirled, nearly falling as he again forgot the wounded leg, and hurried out. He snatched the reins of a horse tied at the rail and swung astride. He reined around savagely and pounded up Texas Street toward Fourth. Burle was out in the open now. He had bought Sid's murder, and Rafferty was proof that he had. There were now but two courses open to him. One was to find and kill Rafferty, thus ensuring that Rafferty could not testify against him in court. Sloan didn't think he'd do it. In the first place, silencing Rafferty wouldn't help him except in court, and Burle must know this would never go to court. He knew Sloan would force a gunfight and kill him first. If Sloan's judgment was correct, if Burle wouldn't bother with Rafferty, then it left him but one other alternative—that of using Merline Morris as a hostage, to keep Sloan inactive until the cowmen took care of him.

He swung into Fourth at a hard gallop and pounded along it as fast as he could make the horse go. He stared ahead through the darkness, looking for lights in her windows. He saw nothing. The house was a dark shadow, blending with the blackness of the plain beyond. Worry stabbed him. Then he calmed himself with the thought that the hour was late—that the absence of lights in the house didn't necessarily mean anything. Perhaps she had gone to bed.

He swung off the horse at her gate, remembering the leg this time and favoring it. He couldn't afford a fall now. He couldn't afford any waste of time. But he knew even before he found the note. The thoughts he'd had that she might have gone to bed, that nothing could be wrong, had been empty reassurances to soothe his tortured mind. He saw the scrap of paper stuck in the screen door and snatched it out.

It was too dark to read. He opened the door with enforced caution, for it was still possible that Burle was waiting for him inside the house. He waited a few moments after he had stepped in, although the note was burning his hand. He waited, listened, and, at last when he heard nothing, fished a match from his pocket and thumbed it alight. He raised the lamp chimney and touched the match to its wick. He lowered the chimney, and then laid the note flat on the table and read:

Hewitt: Don't look for me or I'll kill her.

The note wasn't signed, but it didn't need to be. Sloan looked around the room. There was a straight-backed chair overturned near the kitchen door. He went to it and kneeled. There was a single, bright red spot on the floor and near it a bloody smudge where a hand had touched another drop. He'd hurt her, the son-of-a-bitch! That was why she hadn't fought—that and knowing that he was cornered and as dangerous as a man could be. Probably she'd tried to run for the kitchen door. Probably he'd caught her and knocked her down.

Fury soared in Sloan Hewitt's head. Scowling, he stared at the open door. His knees were trembling, so he sat down. Damn! What did a man do now? He couldn't go charging around town, looking for them, because Burle meant exactly what he said. He'd kill her or hurt her if Sloan got too close. Or he'd use her for a shield.

There had to be a way. He realized that his

thoughts were racing frantically from one impossible thing to another. He clenched his fists and jaws. Think! Take things logically and in order if you could. Burle wasn't a fool. Until Sloan got too close, until he became dangerous, Burle wouldn't do a thing. He wouldn't hurt Merline just for the sake of hurting her. Not now at least. He wanted Sloan off his back for a little while and had taken this means of ensuring it. He knew, as well as Sloan did, that the cowmen would eventually move against the town. That had to be what he was waiting for. Why should he risk his own neck beyond this point when he only had to wait for the cowmen to get rid of Sloan for him?

Sloan got up and nervously paced the floor, limping and favoring his wounded leg. Thinking of Merline, alone and afraid in Burle's hands, made him furious. The possibility, however remote, that Burle might not have to pay with his life for murdering Sid further infuriated him. No longer was he a lawman in the strictest sense. Perhaps he had never been. He was involved, personally, and had been from the very start. Impartiality was impossible under the circumstances. But perhaps impartiality could come later when the town had been tamed, if it ever was.

Quit, he told himself. Get a horse and ride out of town. Burle would know within an hour that he had gone. And he'd release Merline. Or would he? Burle was a prideful man, and Sloan had made him run publicly. He would never be sure that Merline was safe even if he rode away. And besides, there was Sid. He'd never square things for Sid if he let Burle go. There was a place for him here, anyway. Merline was his and the town would be his, only his place wasn't going to be handed to him. He'd have to fight for it.

He thought of Merline and looked around the room at the things that were hers. He remembered her eyes and her smile and the lithe strength of her body. Thinking of her, he knew what she would tell him if she could. Go on. You have come too far to go back now. Jeff Burle represents all the saloonkeepers in town. He controls the gamblers and prostitutes. Beat him and you've beat them all. Beat him now while you've got him on the run. From there, his thoughts flowed logically to the best way of accomplishing Burle's defeat. Wait. Give him time, all the time he wanted, for only by so doing could Merline's safety be assured. Plan for the onslaught of the cowmen, defeat them, and then get Burle. A simple plan that was not, however, as simple as it seemed. He blew out the lamp, went out, and closed the door behind him. He mounted the horse, rode back to the Cowman's Pride, and tied it where he had found it at the rail. Then he walked uptown slowly, thoughtfully, favoring his wounded leg now without even thinking of it.

He went into the office, lit the lamp, then looked at the huge gold watch he carried in his pocket. It was between 10:30 and 11:00. This would be a long night. He wondered how long the trail drivers would take to make up their minds. Burle's three men, the ones who had ambushed Sloan, would stir them up as much as they could. Maybe enough. Maybe enough to make them send their ultimatum in tomorrow. In the meantime, all he could do was wait. And hope that nothing panicked Burle, wherever he was.

Half an hour passed, during which Sloan walked to the door a dozen times and stared broodingly into the street. Most of the saloons had closed for lack of business. The street was quiet. A few of the saloonkeepers and their help sat on benches before their establishments, smoking, talking softly. There was a feeling in the town—of waiting. Like a charge of black powder with a long, smoldering fuse attached. Safe enough while the fuse was long . . .

Sloan sat down on the bench outside. His nerves were jumping, and his mind kept reviewing his decision to wait, searching it for flaws. He found none, but he hadn't expected to. Under the circumstances it was the only thing he could do.

At 11:30, three riders pounded into town, headed straight for the marshal's office, and drew their mounts to a halt. One of the mounted drovers spoke: "You the marshal?"

Sloan rose and nodded. It was here, he knew. Even before the mounted man spoke, he knew. The ultimatum.

The man said: "Got a message for you from Mister Towner."

"All right. What is it?"

"We're coming in tomorrow early. If you're gone, everything will be all right. If you're not, we'll kill you and tear your town to hell."

Sloan said: "Tell him not to come. Not that way."

The three laughed in arrogant unison. "That all?" the spokesman said.

Sloan replied: "That's all. Tell him not to come or he'll be the first to die."

"I'll tell him. But don't count on him being scared, Marshal." All three laughed again, whirled their horses, and pounded away in the direction they had come. A plume of dust followed their passage, spread, and began to settle slowly in the airless street.

So now the lines were drawn and by sunup tomorrow it would be over—finished. Either Sloan would be dead or Burle and Towner would. Either the town would be without law or it would be tamed. Wryly Sloan had to admit that the former was the most likely. One man couldn't meet and turn back a hundred Texas trail hands whose pride had been affronted.

He got up and crossed the street to the hotel, an idea stirring in his mind. He crossed the white-tiled lobby floor to the desk. "Tell me where Mister Dryden lives."

The sleepy clerk gave him directions. Sloan nodded his thanks and went on out. He walked the three blocks to Dryden's house and found it dark. He went up on the porch and turned the bell briskly.

After several moments a lamp went on upstairs. Its light flickered as someone carried it down-stairs. The door, whose pane was red-stained glass, opened, and Dryden stood there in a white nightshirt, his graying hair rumpled and his eyes dazed with sudden awakening.

"Hewitt. What the hell . . . ?"

"I want to talk to you."

"At this hour . . . ? All right. Come on in."

Dryden stood aside, and Sloan went in. Dryden led him along a wallpapered hall and into the parlor, luxuriously furnished and containing, among other treasures, several small marble statuettes. It reminded Sloan of some of the Southern mansions he had been in during the war. He sat down on the edge of a brocaded chair and said: "Mister Dryden, you've got your tail in a crack."

"Don't be flippant, Mister Hewitt. Just tell me what's happened."

"Well, among other things, Burle has kidnaped Merline Morris. He knows I'm fond of her and threatens to kill her if I hunt for him."

"God Almighty! What . . . ?"

Sloan interrupted him. "Secondly, I have an ultimatum from the trail drivers. They're coming to town early in the morning, and if I'm not gone, they're going to kill me and shoot up the town."

Dryden sat down abruptly. For a moment his face was extremely worried. Then he laughed nervously. "No problem there, Marshal. All you've got to do is leave. That way nobody will get hurt."

Sloan studied him, trying to remember all the things Dryden had said to him while he was trying to persuade him to take on the marshal's job. He said deliberately: "Just one thing wrong with that. I'm not going to leave."

"You can't mean that."

"I can and I do." Sloan stared at him inflexibly.

"Man, you're crazy. Do you know what a hundred of those wild Texas trail hands can do to a town?"

"I can imagine," Sloan said dryly. "Only they're not going to do it."

"You can't stop them. Nobody can stop them."

"We're going to try."

"We? Oh, no. Nothing doing."

Sloan played his ace. "I said you had your tail in a crack, Mister Dryden, and I meant just that. I won't leave. One man can't stop a hundred Texas trail drivers. You don't want your town shot up. What conclusion does that lead you to?"

Dryden's face lost color until it was almost gray. "No!"

"Yes, Mister Dryden. This is your town. Some of you are going to have to help."

"We won't do it! We're not lawmen. We're not equipped . . . most of us haven't even got guns. No!"

Sloan said: "Yes. Whether you like it or not, there comes a time when law is the business of every citizen. That time is now."

Dryden was completely unnerved. "They'll cut us to ribbons."

"Maybe. That's a chance you're going to have to take."

Dryden stared emptily at nothing. "The others . . ."

"Get dressed and we'll go see them now."

Dryden stared at him. His eyes mirrored stark fear. Sloan returned his gaze coldly. He was thinking of Sid, who was dead because of simple loyalty to Sloan. Sid hadn't cared whether this town had law or not. But he'd been a friend of Sloan's. Now this bunch—it was their town, their vital concern whether violence ruled it or whether it did not. Their own lives and those of their families were in jeopardy every time one of them walked the streets. Sid had gone into the fight without a protest. The protestations of Dryden and the others were therefore not likely to stir much sympathy in Sloan.

Dryden stumbled out of the room. He stopped just outside the door and looked back. Sloan's eyes remained inflexible, so he turned and clumped heavily up the stairs.

Sloan heard voices up there, those of Dryden and his wife, arguing. He wondered idly whether Dryden were frightened enough to run. He glanced around at the ornate, luxurious room. He thought of the bank, busy and very valuable. No. He doubted if Dryden were frightened enough to leave all that.

Time dragged. There was not much left before the deadline at dawn. And so much had to be done. The townspeople had to be aligned with him— some of them, at least. He had to formulate a plan, for without one he and those who helped him were doomed. Those trail hands were dangerous enough any time. But when they thought they had been wronged . . . He fidgeted in the chair, finally got up and began to pace the floor. The droning voices continued upstairs. If every townsman they tried to recruit took as much time as Dryden was taking, the cowmen would have the town before they even got organized.

He walked into the hall and yelled: "Come on! Come on! I haven't got all night!"

Dryden came clumping down the stairs, fully dressed, carrying an elaborately engraved and embossed double-barreled shotgun and a box of shells, a bird-shooting gun, probably made in Germany or Austria, probably costing $100 or more. But Sloan couldn't think of a better weapon for what they had to do. There is something about a shotgun that puts fear into any man. A single bullet can miss and most often does. Several ounces of lead can't miss.

He led the way to the door, followed by a Dryden who seemed to have aged ten years.

XVI

Outside, Sloan stopped. He said: "Gather the ones you want to help and bring them to the marshal's office. I'll wait there."

He watched Dryden scurry away, then turned and limped painfully toward Texas Street. Going with Dryden might have helped, he realized, but he also knew he wasn't going to do that much walking. Not with this injured leg. It would sap his strength, and come morning he was going to need all the strength he had. He wondered cynically how many Dryden would bring. He hoped for a dozen at least. Twenty would be better. But he'd probably be lucky if he got five or six.

He walked slowly along the street, turned the

corner past the bank, and entered the marshal's office. Wearily he lit the lamp. He was hungry and tired and scared. He hurt all the way to his shoulders from the wound, and wondered if it was becoming infected. He didn't want to go out and meet that bunch in the morning. All he wanted to do was to find Merline. What would Burle do if he was successful tomorrow? There would only be one thing he could do. Run. If he was pressed, he'd probably take Merline with him as a hostage. If he thought he had plenty of time, he'd probably turn her loose.

Sloan sank down on the couch and closed his eyes. He thought of Burle, and hatred for the man surged through his veins like a flood. There was a Burle in every town, a power-mad, tin-god type that thrived on vice and crime and had his fingers in everything that went on. If there was law, he tried to keep it bribed so that he could operate without interference. It took the people to defeat a Burle, but they had to want to defeat him before they had a chance. As long as they were willing to pocket profits and close their eyes, the Burles would remain and grow more powerful with every passing day.

Sloan must have dozed. He dreamed that he heard Merline screaming and woke up soaked with sweat. *To hell with the town,* he thought. *I've got to find her.*

He shook his head, got up, and splashed water

262

into his face. He was right back where he'd started—not knowing where to look, afraid to try for fear Burle would carry out his threat.

He walked to the door and stared up and down the street. It was dark and quiet. Most of the saloons had closed. Damn! There were a couple of dozen saloons in town, two or three hundred houses, several hotels besides the one across the street. There were thirty or forty shacks on the crib street. Burle might be keeping Merline in any one of the saloons, houses, hotels, or shacks. Or he might not even be in town. He might be out on the plain. He might be anywhere.

A group of men rounded the corner by the bank and marched along the street toward him. He stepped aside, and they marched inside. He grinned to himself at the expressions on their faces. Anger. Outrage. Whether at being wakened in the middle of the night or because they had been asked to help, he didn't know. There were more of them than he had expected. Forty or fifty, at least. He went inside and closed the door.

A big, hulking, red-faced man spoke: "Dryden says you've threatened us!"

"Threatened you? Dryden made a small mistake. It's the drovers that threatened you, not me."

"Same thing, ain't it?"

"Not exactly. I'm not going to tear up your town. I'm going to help you stop it."

"That's easy done. All you got to do is leave.

And by God we mean to see to it . . . that you do leave."

Sloan's face hardened. "Come on then, blacksmith. You start it off."

Dryden interrupted. "Now wait a minute, Ledbetter. Threats and bickering will get us nowhere."

Sloan said adamantly: "Talk will get us nowhere, either. There's nothing to talk about. I'm going to stay. I'm going out at dawn and stop that bunch. With help or without it. Only I'll tell you something. If I meet those trail hands out on the road, there are going to be some dead ones before they get past me, and Maverick Towner is going to be one of them. Think now, gentlemen. Think about what they're going to do to this town getting even for Towner. And for two or three others besides."

"You can't do that! There's women and children here!"

"So there are. And it's time you started thinking about them."

"We hired you to . . ."

"To do what I'm doing. If I can't cut it alone, then it's up to you to help."

He stared harshly around from face to face. They were cowed and uncertain and afraid, but no longer were they angry or hostile. Now they needed encouragement, assurance that what Sloan wanted them to do was possible.

He said: "With a dozen shotguns I can stop that bunch. I can straighten them out once and for all, but they've got to know that the town is back of me. If they don't accept that, we'll have this same battle to fight again and again. Until in the end we lose."

"There're too many . . ."

"I doubt that. If every one of you brought a shotgun and came along, we'd have it in the bag." Back at the rear of the room a man said: "Not me. I ain't paid three hundred a month to fight. That's your job. I'm goin' home an' get some sleep."

He was echoed by a couple of dozen others, who immediately began to inch their way toward the door.

Vast disgust flooded Sloan. He wouldn't beg them for help. He was finished. He wouldn't even plead. With a cold face and stony eyes, he watched them file from the room and into the street. Not one of those leaving would meet his eyes. They kept their heads averted and their eyes downcast.

Sloan made one more pitch. "There won't be much left of the business houses on Texas Street by the time the sun comes up."

That halted half a dozen of them. The others disappeared down the dark street, but the six remained. Sloan looked at them without approval. "You're in, then?"

They nodded almost sullenly. Dryden said:

265

"Have you got any plan? Or do we just go out and stand in the road?"

"I'll have a plan. Go on home, but be back here by three o'clock at the very latest. If you're tempted to change your minds or oversleep, just think what a hundred trail hands can do to a store or"—he stared at Dryden— "a bank."

The six edged toward the door. Dryden left his ornate shotgun leaning against the wall and put the box of shells on the floor beside it.

Sloan looked at a man named Ericson, who owned the hardware store. "I want two kegs of black powder and a hundred feet of fuse. Get them over here before you go home and give Mister Dryden the bill."

"What . . . ?"

"Never mind. Just get it here."

He waited until the six had gone. Then he went out and walked down an almost deserted Texas Street toward the livery barn.

He wakened the hostler rudely by kicking on the tack-room door. He said: "I want a buckboard and team."

"Hell of a . . ."

"Shut up and get it."

Surly, the man shuffled back into the stable. He led horses, one by one, to a buckboard and harnessed them. He hitched them up and led them out to Sloan. Sloan got up on the seat, picked up the reins, and drove outside. He drove to the marshal's office and stopped.

The black powder and fuse were inside, sitting beside Dryden's shotgun. Sloan carried out the kegs and fuse, then returned to blow out the lamp and close the door. A shovel. Damn it, he'd forgotten a shovel. But the light was still burning in Ericson's Hardware, so he drove over there, went in, and got one. Ericson never opened his mouth.

Sloan drove swiftly out of town, taking the road that began at the lower end of Texas Street. He had a plan that might work. It had been born suddenly back there in the office, when he'd realized he was going to have to stop the trail hands with six men or less. You don't pit force against force when you've only got six men against a hundred or more. You formulate a plan that will even the odds. A wartime trick—he was going to mine the road. Success of the plan, however, depended on a lot of imponderables. The trail drivers had to come in openly by the road—and by the southern road at that, or the plan would fail. But Sloan guessed they would come in openly, and they always used the southern road because it took them to the lower end of Texas Street. Yes. They would use the road. These damned Southerners had a monstrous pride. That pride would force them to enter the town openly and by the road.

Another imponderable was the charge of powder. Sloan had no experience with explosives, and didn't even know how long a given length of fuse would take to burn. And the blast had to be exactly on time or its effect would be wasted. What was not imponderable was the effect the blast would have. If they came in by the road and if he could explode the charge exactly when he wanted to, it would bring utter chaos to their ranks. He doubted if a single one of their horses had ever heard anything louder than a shotgun blast. This, blowing up right in their faces, would drive the horses wild. That was, of course, only the beginning. With the odds evened to where he and those with him had a chance, there was still a fight to be fought. But one he'd have some chance to win.

Now, just outside of town, he began to search for exactly the right spot. He found it where the road dipped down into a dry wash to cross. He stopped the buckboard and ground-tied the team with the cast-iron weight. He unloaded the powder and blindly, in darkness, began to dig. A hole at either side of the road. A hole deep enough to conceal a keg of black powder, but not deep enough to muffle its blast.

When he had finished that, he put the powder kegs in the holes and knocked out the tops with his shovel. Retreating now to the shelter of the wash, he got out his knife, matches, and the coil of fuse. He cut a foot-length piece, lit it, and timed its burning with his watch. He cut another length a little longer. Another and another. At last he had it as close as he thought was possible. He cut two equal lengths, inserted them in the powder carefully and covered all but the tips with loose dirt.

Now he got up in the buckboard. Shielding a match with his hands, he looked at his watch, then blew out the match and began to drive—not toward the town but away from it. He drove at a steady trot until he reached what he was looking for, a mound with a pile of scattered rocks on top. He struck another match and looked at his watch.

Satisfied, he turned the buckboard and returned along the road toward town. He knew it was a touchy thing, where seconds would count, where seconds could spell out the difference between success and failure. But he could reduce the risk —by openly halting the trail drivers and making talk. He could soak up a few seconds of the risk that way, dangerous though it might be to himself.

A consoling thought—if he failed in the morning, at least Merline would be safe. If he were dead, there would be no reason for Burle to hurt her. But if he won—that would be the difficult and dangerous thing, for then Burle would be both panicked and enraged and likely to do anything.

He drove toward town slowly, more weary, more near the point of exhaustion than he had ever been in his life before. Lack of sleep had told on him, and lack of proper food. The wound had bled him of strength and accentuated the effects of hunger and sleeplessness. But he didn't dare sleep now. If he closed his eyes, he'd sleep past the morning deadline and would arrive out here too late. He could eat, and would, if he could talk the clerk at the hotel into waking the cook. Thinking of that, he hurried the horse and drove across the tracks into town.

He returned the team and buckboard to the livery stable. He drove inside, unharnessed, and turned the horses loose in the corral behind the barn. Then he clumped wearily toward the hotel.

Fortunately, the cook was already up, starting his morning coffee. When he saw Sloan, he slung a skillet onto the enormous range and said: "Marshal, you look as beat as any man I ever saw. You sit down over there an' I'll have you a big thick steak before you know it."

Sloan sat down. His eyes kept closing and he'd doze, only to snap out of it when his senses began to fade. Half a dozen times, while the scrawny hotel cook was frying the steak, he dozed off and snapped awake again.

The cook put a plate in front of him laden with steak, potatoes, and beans. Sloan wanted sleep much more than he wanted food, but he forced himself to eat, and after he had taken half a dozen bites he began to feel better. He ate ravenously after that, even finishing a quarter of apple pie the cook slid to him. He got up, but, when he reached in his pocket for money, the cook said: "No pay, Marshal. It's on the damn' hotel. Least I can do, an' them, too."

Sloan grinned. "Thanks . . . ?"

"Willis. Jake Willis."

"Thanks, Jake."

He went out and crossed the street. Behind the marshal's office he found a pump, and he stuck his head under the cooling stream. Then he soaped and dried his face and went inside.

He didn't have a razor, and he'd probably cut himself if he tried to shave, but he felt a lot better for eating and washing up. Maybe good enough to do what he had to do when the sky got gray.

He looked at his watch. It was almost 2:00 a.m. Another hour and he'd have to leave. His face, right now, didn't show the confidence he had expressed to Dryden and the others a couple of hours ago. He didn't feel confident at all. Black powder or no, it was damned foolishness for half a dozen men to go out and face a hundred outraged trail hands who, while they might be overloaded with stiff-necked pride, were hard as nails, and tough. If they wanted to tree the town, they'd tree it, and nothing would stand in their way. Sloan cursed himself angrily. He was going out there at dawn and try, foolhardy or no. And there was no sense in hopeless thinking. It was too damned late for that.

XVII

It was scarcely past 2:00 when the door flung open and Sylvia Flint came in. She was fully dressed, and had obviously not been to bed. Sloan got up, snapping fully awake immediately. "Sylvia! What the devil . . . ?"

"Where's Jeff? He didn't come home and the Cowman's Pride is closed. Did you . . . ?"

Sloan shook his head.

She relaxed, but it was not with relief. Instead it seemed almost to be regret. "Where is he then?"

"I wish I knew. He grabbed Miss Morris as a hostage and disappeared. Left a note for me not to look for him or he'd kill her."

"He would, too." Her eyes were frightened. "Don't let worry for her get you killed, Sloan. No woman is worth that. I know." Sloan didn't reply, and after a moment she asked in a small voice: "What are you going to do?"

"Nothing right now. There's nothing I can do. I haven't the foggiest idea of where they might be, and until I do I'll just be endangering her by blundering around looking. Come morning, I've got to go out and meet Maverick Towner and his bunch. After that . . ."

"It's all over town. They're going to kill you and shoot up the town. Unless you leave. Why don't you leave, Sloan? This town isn't worth what you're giving it."

"I think you're wrong," he said gently. "I think . . ." He stopped. Then he said: "I think, for instance, that you're worth a great deal more than the value you put on yourself."

That brought a brief brightening of tears to her eyes. "Thank you, Sloan."

She watched him speculatively for several moments, unfathomed thoughts flickering across her expression. At last a calculating look appeared, and she said: "What if I told you where Jeff and Miss Morris are? What would you do?"

"I'd go there."

"Now? Right now?"

He frowned, but not for long. There was really no choice involved. Leaving Merline in Burle's hands endangered her because Burle was both scared and desperate. But leaving town—failing to appear on the road at dawn—that would hurt no one, immediately at least. The cowmen would simply assume that he had bowed to their ultimatum and could come in peacefully. The town would be no worse off than it had been several days ago before he accepted the marshal's badge. He nodded.

Sylvia said: "Then I'll tell you." There was relief visible in her now, and he understood that she had weighed the comparative danger to him—of an encounter with Burle against an encounter with the trail hands. She had decided his chances were better with Burle. He knew he ought to tell her that he might be able to do both, but he didn't open his mouth. She was not above withholding her information until a few minutes before dawn.

He said: "Where?"

"Jeff won a homestead out on Squaw Creek in a poker game a year or so ago. He has probably taken her there."

"How do you get there?"

"Go east out of town. Squaw Creek is about half a mile away. It runs north and south. Go south when you hit it, and you can't miss the homestead shack. It's less than two miles southeast of town."

Sloan picked up his hat off the desk and bent to blow out the lamp. Sylvia said: "I can lead you there."

There was a great deal of wistfulness in her voice, but there was something hard as well, and Sloan realized for the first time how deeply she hated Burle. He hesitated, on the point of saying no. Then abruptly he nodded his head. "All right. Come on."

As he did blow out the lamp, he turned his back

to her and looked at his watch. It was 2:15. Not much time to spare. But perhaps enough. If he happened to be extraordinarily lucky. He did not overlook the chance that Sylvia was lying to him—that she would lead him out across the prairie on a wild-goose chase that had no purpose other than to get him out of town and keep him out. But it was a chance he had to take.

He took her arm and hustled her toward the livery barn. Another ten minutes of precious time was consumed in saddling two horses. He tried to remember at what hour it got light as he boosted Sylvia to her saddle and swung astride his own. At 3:00, he remembered, the first faint line of gray appeared along the eastern horizon. But there was almost an hour after that before the sun came up. Perhaps the cowmen wouldn't arrive until sunup. He'd made his decision and could only hope.

The hoofs of their running horses echoed from the buildings they passed, and then they were out on the open plain and running hard. Sylvia, an excellent rider, kept pace in spite of the awkwardness of her skirts. She was riding astride in spite of them. She angled slightly south instead of heading straight east and by this Sloan realized that she thought the time was too short for him to return after his encounter with Burle. He hoped she was wrong.

They rode in silence and, about twenty minutes

after leaving town, Sylvia pulled over hard, rode into a clump of cottonwoods, and yanked her horse to a plunging halt. Sloan reined in beside her, and she said breathlessly: "It's over there. Just a little ways."

Sloan glanced toward the east. It was still black, and there was no hint of gray. He said: "Stay here with the horses." He started away, then turned and whispered: "You've been here before?"

"Yes."

"How many doors?"

"One. It's a sod shack. The only window is in the rear, but it's big enough to crawl through."

Sloan nodded, though it was doubtful that she could see him well enough to know he had. He moved away, as carefully as though he were stalking a herd of buffalo trying to get into position for a stand. Even now, he could not be sure he was not needlessly risking Merline's life. Yet he felt certain this would be what she would want. She would not want him to surrender that for which he had fought so hard. Nor would she believe, any more than he, that safety lay in surrender to force or the threat of force.

He could see the soddy now, so low it almost seemed to be a part of the grassy plain. Behind it a few cottonwoods rose, and through the cottonwoods flowed the trickle that was Squaw Creek. A buggy loomed beside the shack, shafts on the ground, and in the rickety corral stood the buggy horse. He raised his head and stared at Sloan, ears pricked forward. He snorted softly once. Sloan froze when he did. His gun was in his hand and now he muffled the sound of cocking it by holding the gun close to his body to deaden the sound.

Grass rustled faintly under his feet as he walked. In the utter silence of this place, the soft sounds seemed thunderous. The horse began to trot nervously around the corral, disturbed by Sloan's stealth.

Twenty feet to the door now. Twenty feet. Would Burle be waiting, shotgun cocked, inside the soddy's door? Would he shoot the instant the open door showed him a square of outside light? Sloan supposed he would. He counted on it, in fact, as he stepped up against the wall of the shack less than half a dozen feet from the sagging door.

He realized that his knees were shaking. He wished he had light, and knew he would have more chance if he could wait for it. But he was still conscious of the promise he had made to Dryden and the others. He was conscious of his obligation to the town he had agreed to tame. Would that door swing, or had it sagged enough to touch the ground? On that question depended his life—and maybe Merline's, too.

He kneeled and felt with his hands along the wall until he reached the door. There was a solid beam threshold beneath the door on which it rested. Chances were that if he hit it hard enough it would break clear and swing free. Carefully he eased out away from the wall until he was a dozen feet away. Then, surging into motion like a charging lion, he rushed toward the door. He hit it with his shoulder, felt it hold an instant, and then give way. He was falling, rolling, and the door banged savagely against the inside wall.

A shotgun roared, seemingly but inches from where Sloan was. The shot tore through the door opening and rattled viciously against the door itself. The flare of the gun momentarily blinded Sloan, but it gave him direction, and scarcely had it died away than he was scrambling to his feet, lunging toward the place where it had been. From the volume of sound, the amount of shot and the flare itself he guessed with lightning speed that both barrels had been fired at once. Plunging forward, he felt the hot muzzle of the gun with his hands, flung it impatiently aside, and clawed toward the man beyond.

Unthinking that Burle outweighed him, that Burle was strong and not weakened by a wound and loss of blood, he did not even remember that a gun was in his hand. He wanted the satisfaction of Burle's thick neck between his hands. He wanted the feel of his fist smashing into Burle's face. Burle had had Rose killed. He had bought Sid's murder. And he had kidnaped Merline.

Burle's knee came up, catching Sloan squarely on his wounded leg. The shock was tremendous. Lights flashed before Sloan's eyes, and his head reeled. He felt himself falling, blind, almost unconscious from the brutal pain. And Burle was rushing toward him, apparently able to see him now in the faint starlight filtering through the doorway. Was it starlight, or was the sky turning gray in the east? Something, some supreme effort of will, forced clarity into Sloan's thoughts, deadened the effects of that awful pain in his leg. He saw Burle coming, beyond him saw another shape rise from the rusted, creaking springs of the bed. Bound, her hands and feet both tied, she flung herself into Burle's path.

He slammed into her and flung her aside, knocking a cry of hurt from her lips. But he tripped on her as well, and fell sprawling just short of where Sloan lay. Now Sloan became conscious of the gun in his hand, which he had not released. He swung it, and with its muzzle raked a bloody furrow across the side of Jeff Burle's jaw. The gun discharged, but the shot went wild, thudding harmlessly into the beams and brush that supported the sod roof of the shack. Its thunder in Burle's ears, realization that the shotgun was empty, the unexpected fall—these things apparently combined to break Burle's nerve. When he scrambled on again, it was toward the door and away from Sloan.

Sloan muttered: "No! No, by God!" He lunged to his feet and threw himself after Burle. He could probably have used his gun, but not in this kind of light. His leg betrayed him. Hurt by Burle's savage knee, bleeding profusely again and mostly numb, it gave way beneath the weight he put upon it. He went crashing to the ground, half in and half outside the door.

He could hear Burle long after the man had disappeared around the corner of the shack in the direction of the corral. Behind him, Merline was struggling helplessly on the floor. He got up again and limped to the corner of the shack, cocking the hammer of his gun as he went. There was cold, smoldering anger in him, anger at himself and his own weakness, anger over the deaths of Rose and Sid, anger because of Merline lying helpless and tied on the dirt floor of the homestead shack. He rounded the corner, the gun half raised.

The flare did not, at first, surprise him, nor did the racket of noise that followed it. His mind assumed, without conscious thought, that Burle was shooting at him. But then he saw an answering flare across the corral from the first, and he realized that the first shot had come from a small-bore gun. Sylvia! God damn it, why hadn't she stayed put? Why . . . ? He began to run, hobbling, toward the corral. He prayed sound-lessly that he'd be able to see when he needed to see.

The corral gate swung open and a dark shadow came thundering toward him. He stopped, froze, and raised his gun. He squeezed down on the trigger, but even before the gun blasted he knew the shot was going wild. For Burle, seeing him there, swung his horse hard over just an instant before the gun discharged.

Sloan thumbed back the hammer for another shot, pivoting as he did. But Burle was gone, swallowed up in darkness, and there were only the sounds of his galloping horse's hoofs to mark the direction in which he had gone.

Sloan felt empty—sick. He roared: "Sylvia!"

She did not reply. He limped toward the corral. He heard it then—a faint, small sound that struck terror to his heart. Heavily he began to run.

XVIII

He found her lying in the dry manure just inside the corral. As he kneeled, he knew that here in this dark, abandoned place, he would lose all that remained of his earlier life. He started to slide his arms under her and pick her up, but she cried out sharply with pain. "No, Sloan . . . no! Don't move me."

He cradled her head in his arms, remembering now the other times he had held her, the delightful intimacy he had known with her. He was thinking, too, that she had run from him rather than deceive him. He was thinking that her only fault was that she was too generous and filled with too much love.

He asked softly: "Where are you hit?"

"Chest. I'm sorry, Sloan. I wanted to . . . kill him. I thought he'd . . ."—she paused, breathing heavily—". . . killed you."

He waited, full of terror and knowing there was nothing he could do. Her voice, when it came again, was very soft; he could scarcely hear it. "I love you, Sloan. I love you very much."

"And I love you." It was no lie to make her going easier. He did love her and perhaps always would even after she was gone. She held a place in his heart that would not interfere with the place he had reserved for Merline.

"Thank you, Sloan."

He thought: *Maybe I was wrong. Maybe she is wrong. Maybe the wound is not as bad . . .* He said: "I'll get some light and . . ."

"No. Stay with me. Hold me very close. I'm frightened now, Sloan. I'm scared."

He held her tightly against his chest. His throat closed until he could scarcely breathe. He felt his eyes burning with unshed tears. Her going was quiet, undramatic, almost unperceived in the vast, empty silence around her. One instant she was breathing and full of pain, the next she was still, relaxed, untroubled, and at peace.

Sloan brushed at his eyes, then picked her up and carried her toward the shack, limp as a sleeping child in his arms. He laid her down in the clean grass outside the door, then went inside and struck a match. There was a lamp, its chimney smoked and unwashed, which he lit before the match went out. He pulled out his pocket knife and cut Merline free at once, then rubbed her rope-chafed ankles and wrists to restore circulation.

"What is it, Sloan? You look . . ."

"Sylvia. Burle shot her."

"Is she . . . gone?"

He nodded.

A look of compassion touched Merline's face. She reached out and pulled his face against her breasts. "I'm sorry. I'm so terribly sorry."

He became conscious that there was grayish light in the room and pulled suddenly away. He glanced at the door, which faced the east, and saw a spreading line of gray out there, delineating the horizon.

Time, perhaps, to reach town. He got up and limped out the door. Merline followed. He walked swiftly to where he and Sylvia had left their horses. Mounting his own, he led the other back to the shack. Working swiftly, he unsaddled the horse Sylvia had ridden, then harnessed the animal and hitched him between the buggy shafts. He went over and picked Sylvia up gently. He carried her body to the buggy and laid it carefully inside.

He stared at Merline. "Would you mind . . . ?"

"Of course not. Are you going on ahead?"

He nodded. "I may be late but I've got to try."

"Jeff Burle . . ."

"Won't bother you now. He's gone to join the trail hands. He'll be with them when they ride into town."

He boosted her to the buggy seat and handed her the reins. He wanted to hold her in his arms, but, if he did, leaving would be that much harder for him. He said: "I'll come to your house as soon as it's over."

She didn't speak and he knew she was thinking that he'd come if he were still alive. She'd be praying for him, but the odds . . .

He swung to his horse, reined around, and rode away, digging his spurless heels savagely into the horse's sides. The line of gray had spread over the eastern sky until objects were visible at half a mile.

The horse was heavily lathered by the time Sloan reached town, for he had run him all the way. And the eastern sky was turning faintly pink. Dryden and five others were waiting at the marshal's office. Their faces were not particularly enthusiastic when they saw him coming. They obviously had been hoping that he wouldn't come at all.

He rode to them, dismounted, and limped inside. He got a shotgun and a box of shells, then limped out and mounted again. He said: "Come on."

He led the way down Texas Street, across the tracks, and out onto the wide, flat plain. He reached the spot where he had planted the powder without catching sight of the men he had to meet and stop. He led them into the wash and along it until he reached a place where the high bank would conceal the horses. He said curtly: "All right, gentlemen. Get down and leave your horses."

They dismounted, and he led them back to the road. He faced them, feeling his head beginning to reel, feeling more like sleeping than fighting. "Here's the plan. I've got black powder planted on both sides of the road. I've timed the fuses, and I've timed the ride from that mound out there."

"What good is an explosion going to do?" Dryden asked doubtfully.

Sloan grinned crookedly. "I was in the cavalry at the beginning of the war. Untrained horses . . . those that have never heard an explosion before . . . go wild when they hear their first. They rear and buck, and a good many of them bolt. When that powder goes off, there won't be a man in the bunch who won't be busy with his horse. That'll give you men a chance to climb out of the wash and put your shotguns on them. That'll reduce the chance of some damned fool snatching out a gun and getting off a shot."

The townsmen were silent, their faces doubtful. Sloan said: "Any questions?" Nobody replied. He said: "All right then. You stay hidden, and don't make a damned sound until that powder goes off. Understand? No matter what may happen to me."

Dryden nodded, and the others followed suit reluctantly.

Sloan stationed them along the wash where they could be hidden but where they would be instantly and strategically available. He returned up the wash and got his horse, thinking that seeing him alone and without a horse might make the drovers suspicious. Then he hunkered beside the road to wait. There was a crushed cigar in his pocket, and he got it out, repaired it painstakingly, and bit off the end. He lit it and puffed luxuriously. As he did, the sun poked its flaming rim above the plain.

He saw their dust a long time before he saw either men or horses. A big cloud of dust denoting a large group of men. His stomach muscles tightened, and he could feel the nerves in his arms and legs beginning to jump. Familiar symptoms that he'd known many times during the war. But when the action started he would be steady enough. He always had been before.

An eternity passed while he waited for them to pass the mound. He thought of Sylvia and of her daughter, both of whom were dead. He thought of Merline and of Sid and Rose. Merline was the only one left of those who had helped him or been close to him.

The group of horsemen reached the mound, but Sloan didn't stir. He waited a full two minutes before he got up and crossed the road to the first short length of exposed fuse. Kneeling, he lit a match and touched it to the fuse.

Several moments passed before it caught, but, immediately it did, he hurried across the road to the other fuse and lit it as well.

The fuses gave off a little smoke. Regretfully Sloan took a last puff on the dilapidated cigar and then tossed it deliberately into the middle of the road. The assumption upon seeing it there would be that both the others were also cigar butts, and he hoped no one would be quick enough to realize that he couldn't have smoked three that fast. Standing in plain sight, he waited with seeming equanimity, with apparently endless patience and no concern. But inside he was seething. He may have waited too long after the horsemen passed the mound to light the fuses. Maybe he couldn't stall them long enough. Maybe one of them would smell the peculiar odor of the burning fuses and realize . . . That was something he hadn't thought of, something he hadn't checked. Hastily he glanced at the smoke rising from the cigar in the road. He heaved an almost breathless sigh of relief. The smoke was drifting toward him—away from the approaching horsemen.

He checked his position and took a backward step. He wanted the charges between himself and the drovers. He wanted to be far enough back so that he wouldn't be blinded by flying dirt and dust, or stunned by concussion.

They came on at a steady, purposeful trot, neither stepping up the pace nor slowing it when they saw him standing in the road. Maverick Towner was easily recognizable because of his arrogant bearing and the sling supporting his arm. Beside Towner rode Jeff Burle, and to either side and behind Burle rode the three who had beaten Rose to death with their fists.

Three hundred yards. Two. Sloan glanced to right and left, noted that the fuses no longer were smoking. He knew they could be burning without smoke beneath the road, also knew they might have been snuffed out when the fire got below the level of the ground. The fortunes of war, he thought wryly. If his charges failed to blow, he didn't have a chance. Nor did the men with him if they showed themselves.

The group came on, at the same measured trot, like approaching doom. Sloan had never felt more alone; he knew he had never been closer to death before.

Three hundred yards. Two hundred. A hundred. He could see Jeff Burle's face very plainly now and felt a surge of implacable hatred and renewed determination at the expression it wore. Triumphant. Sneering.

They were now less than fifty feet away. But until they were less than twenty-five, Sloan kept his silence. Then he stepped sideways into the exact center of the road and said: "That's far enough."

Burle turned his head and roared: "Ride him down!" But Towner raised an arm, and the horsemen stopped.

Towner's face wore a look of reluctant admiration. He said: "You've got our terms, Marshal. Get out of the way or take the consequences."

Sloan thought of the two minutes he had delayed after they passed the mound. He knew he could be farther off than that. He said: "Don't do anything you're going to be sorry for, Mister Towner. You're welcome in town . . . we want you there. Just check your guns with me and ride on in."

"No." The man was inflexible now, and whatever had shown from his eyes before was gone. "We're going in, all right, but on our own terms. When we ride past this place, you're going to be dead, Marshal, and we're going to tear your town to hell."

Sloan's voice was very soft. "You won't ride

in Mister Towner. You'll be here in the dust with me. You're going to be the very first to die. You have my word for that. All the guns you've got won't keep me from getting off that shot."

How much time had passed since this group pulled to a halt before him? It seemed an eternity. But it could be less than a minute. Somehow, some way he had to prolong the delay. He said: "Know who you're riding with, Towner? A yellow skunk that hires men to beat women to death with their fists. A man that paid to have my deputy ambushed and shot in the back. A man that kidnaps decent women to guarantee his own safety. I thought you damned Southerners had some pride."

Towner's face flushed with anger. But his eyes switched sideways and glowered at Burle beside him.

Burle sneered: "He's a liar, Towner, and you know he is."

Sloan murmured softly: "Step down off your horse and call me that, Burle. Step down if you're not too yellow."

And it hung there in the still morning air, that challenge—hung there and gave Sloan the time he had to have.

XIX

Seconds ticked away, and a strange silence fell upon the whole group as they waited. Eyes were on Burle, but a few were watching Sloan. He knew that if Burle took up the challenge, his own men would back him. He saw Burle swing his head and stare at them one by one, and saw the unspoken message that passed back and forth. When Burle turned again, it was with more confidence than before. He grinned tightly at Sloan and moved to dismount.

Sloan's muscles tightened. He shifted his weight off the bad leg, using that leg now for balance and nothing more. His eyes narrowed and took on a strangely savage gleam. The time was here. He would have his revenge at last—for Sid, for Rose, for Sylvia, too. Die he might, but not until he had killed Jeff Burle. Now Sloan was hoping there would be time enough before the blasts went off to do this one last thing.

Never in his life had Burle met a challenge head-on if it could be avoided, and he did not do so now. Swinging off his horse, shielded momentarily by the animal's body, he drew his gun, dived beneath the horse's neck, and fired as he hit the ground. He missed, but the shot triggered the actions of Burle's three men.

Instantly they snatched guns from their holsters.

Sloan stood like a rock. Burle would be no menace until he stopped rolling, so he took the man on Burle's right first. His bullet caught the man in the throat, and blood instantly soaked the front of his shirt. He stayed upright in the saddle briefly, began to choke, and put both hands to his throat, releasing the gun as though it were hot. Then, still choking, he toppled sideways.

Sloan didn't see him because his eyes were on the second man, who had been immediately behind Burle's horse. This one had his gun up, and it fired as Sloan's did. The bullet seared the side of Sloan's neck but his own struck the horseman squarely in the chest.

Maverick Towner took the third, bringing his horse crowding sideways to jostle the other and upset his aim. And Sloan switched his attention back to Burle. The man was steady now, flat on his belly on the ground. His weight was on both elbows, and he held his gun with both hands, sighting it, steadying it.

Sloan stared into the gaping bore, waiting for it to burst with flame and smoke, but swinging his own cocked gun as he did. Burle's nerve broke. Sloan could see that in his eyes. It broke, even though Burle had his bead on Sloan and was ready to squeeze the trigger. But it broke too late, for Sloan could not stop the movement of his trigger finger in the small part of a second his mind willed it to stop. And perhaps he would not have stopped it even if he could. This was a thing he would never know. His gun bucked solidly against his palm. The bullet entered Burle's neck and coursed downward through his body. He glowered unbelievingly at Sloan for an instant before his eyes began to glaze.

No time to savor victory or revenge. No time. The powder on the left side of the road blew, followed closely by the blast on the right. Dirt and rock showered Sloan and the hundred horsemen, as well as Burle and his two men on the ground. It obscured them from Sloan's eyes, and then he was flung back as though by a giant hand. He landed on his back with an impact that drove the breath from him. His mind screamed at him to get up, that there wasn't time for being stunned. He, and those with him who had been hiding in the wash, must have the group under their guns before they recovered enough to realize what was going on.

Rubbing his eyes with the knuckles of one hand, Sloan got to his feet. He felt, rather than saw, the six townsmen leaping up out of the wash. But he heard the plainly audible, metallic sounds that were the cocking of their guns. And he heard the shrill screaming of the drovers' terrified horses, heard their plunging hoofs, the squeak of straining girth and stirrup leathers, the muffled thud of bodies striking the ground, the surprised, startled, angry cursing of the men.

Standing at last, he bawled: "Hold it! Don't a damned one of you draw a gun!"

Some of their horses bolted across the plain. Some bucked a circle around the group. Others were fought to a halt. Towner, his face gray with the pain of the horse's jolting his broken arm, screamed hysterically: "Yankee yellow-belly! You ain't got the guts to fight in the open like a man. You got to use a dirty Yankee trick!"

Sloan's voice was coldly vicious. "A hundred to one! Are those the odds a Southern gentleman has to have?"

The gray disappeared from Towner's face. It turned a shade that could only have been called purple. He opened his mouth to speak, but no words came out. Yet in spite of his monumental fury, there was something like guilt in his eyes, something that said he knew Sloan's accusation was true. Because it was true, his fury was greater. He found his voice at last and cursed Sloan bitterly, steadily. "You dirty Yankee coward, I'll show you what odds we need!" He flung himself from his horse, stumbled and nearly fell as he hit the ground. He rushed to Sloan and struck him solidly, with the flat of his hand, on the cheek. There was force in the blow, force enough to snap Sloan's head sideways with a crack that threatened to break his neck.

Towner roared: "There, suh! The choice of

weapons is yours! I'll show you the kind of odds we need!"

Rage leaped momentarily in Sloan, rage that he almost instantly controlled. Because he knew that he had succeeded, thus far at least. He had reduced this quarrel to its simplest form—that of man against man—instead of the way it had been, drovers against the town. On the point of speaking, he hesitated. Towner's arm was broken; he was in pain; he was twenty or thirty years older than Sloan. If Sloan fought with him and killed him, the Texas crowd was going to be hard to restrain. There had to be another way. . . .

He stared beyond Towner now at the others, still fighting their nervous mounts. He yelled: "I'll take that on! But I won't fight Towner!"

Towner bawled: "Look at me, suh, not at them!"

Sloan did, steadily and long. He said coldly: "I've not got much patience with your Southern code. If I fight a man, it's not for fun, it's for keeps and for a reason. Killing you won't solve a damned thing because your whole crowd knows as well as I do that it isn't fair. Your arm is broken, and you're at a disadvantage. If I killed you then, I'd still have to take on the whole damned bunch of them."

Dryden broke in, a grim-faced Dryden behind a shotgun that was none too steady. "What do you want, Hewitt? What are you getting at?"

Sloan didn't look at him, but he answered him. He said, looking straight at the dusty-faced crowd of trail hands: "Pick your best man and send him out. Let him proxy for Towner."

An instant of silence. Then clamor broke out in the cowmen's ranks—the clamor of men eager to pick up the challenge. Sloan roared: "Shut up! It's Towner's choice. Let him pick the man!"

That quieted them a little, but there were still those who shouted: "Me, Maverick. Pick me. I'll take that Yankee yellow-belly!"

Towner scowled. He plainly didn't like anyone doing his fighting for him, but he also plainly knew that Sloan would kill him if he didn't. Maybe he wasn't afraid to die, thought Sloan, but he wasn't exactly eager for it, either.

Towner said: "Denehy."

There was an instant's immobility, then the ranks of disappointed horsemen parted to let one of their number through. He was a small, scrawny man who, when he dismounted, displayed legs that were noticeably bowed. He had eyes as emotionless as those of a snake, and a thin, cruel mouth. His hair was uncut and long like most of the others, but there was an unkempt quality about him that the others did not possess, and his hair was the color of a mouse's fur.

"Bin wantin' to try you, Yankee yellow-belly," he said. "An' I bin hopin' you'd last that long."

Sloan said—"You're lucky then, aren't you?"—

in an even, steady voice. This one would be fast, he thought, perhaps faster than he. This one was professional. He could tell that by the gun rig he wore, by the easiness with which he waited now. Sloan stared at Towner. "I told you I only fight for a reason, and I want something understood." Towner frowned. "If I kill your man, that's an end to it. You shuck your guns right here and let Dryden haul them into town. Pick 'em up when you leave."

"What if he kills you?"

Sloan grinned wryly. "That won't concern me, will it? I won't be here to care."

Towner hesitated. Then he nodded a bit reluctantly. "You win, no matter whether you live or die. If you're dead, there ain't much point in treeing the town. We'll have it the way we want it anyhow."

Sloan grinned faintly. He looked at Denehy. "I'm ready."

Denehy side-stepped guardedly. His eyes were unblinking, steady on Sloan's face. Denehy was one who watched the eyes for a sign the man he faced was beginning to draw. That way, he got the signal a split second before his adversary's hand could move. It gave him an edge, one that had probably kept him alive through a dozen gunfights he might otherwise have lost. A cocky, prideful gunman who would not draw first. He didn't speak. Once he'd gotten himself set, he didn't move. He scarcely seemed to breathe.

Sloan waited, too, knowing the wait would be harder on Denehy than it was on him. He was thinking of Sid, of Rose, of Sylvia, who were now avenged. He was thinking of Merline. He had won every battle but the last. Something told him this one was a battle he couldn't win. He had a natural dexterity with his gun, but he hadn't the skill that Denehy had. He didn't spend hours practicing that lightning draw. He took a backward step—another. He narrowed his eyes until they were the mere slits. He'd draw in an instant now and he wondered how he would signal Denehy when he did—by a widening of his eyes? By a tightening of the muscles at the corners of his mouth? Suddenly his patience was gone. He couldn't beat Denehy to the draw, so there was only one other thing to do.

His hand moved, but Denehy moved faster. An instant after Sloan began to draw he abandoned it and flung his body forward and to one side. Denehy's gun blasted before he struck, but Sloan felt no bullet's shock. He was tumbling in the dust, hearing the repeated roar of Denehy's gun as he tried to follow Sloan's erratic course. Rolling, Sloan drew his gun and, when he faced Denehy, steadied himself with one outflung hand and squeezed off a shot with the other. It took Denehy in the left shoulder, spoiling his aim at Sloan's momentarily motionless form. Sloan snapped another shot just as he lost his balance, and this one missed. Denehy fought his way around again, but this time Sloan was ready for him. Crouched and steady, he squeezed off his shot and knew even before the roar of it reached his ears that it had gone where he willed it to go.

Denehy stumbled backward and sat down. His gun fell from his inert fingers.

Sloan got slowly, watchfully to his feet. He walked over and kicked Denehy's gun out of reach. He turned to face the shocked group of horsemen, who had been so sure he would die that they could not believe that he was still alive.

Sloan said: "Step down, gentlemen, and shuck your guns. Then you can ride on into town."

Towner stared at Denehy, and then at Sloan. "He was faster . . ."

"Maybe. But he's dead. Tell your men to shuck their guns, and bring that man of Burle's with you when you come into town. He's going to stand trial."

He looked at the still forms on the ground—at Burle and his two men, at Denehy, who looked small and helpless, lying there. Then he turned his back deliberately and mounted his horse. He sat astride, looking down, while the trail hands rode past the growing pile of armaments on the ground, dropping their guns upon it. Before they had finished, he turned and rode toward town, slowly at first but with increasing speed. Today it looked like a different town than it had before. Today it looked like home, and was home, because a girl was waiting for him in the dusty road just this side of the railroad tracks. There was nothing of self-possession or calmness about her now. She was crying hysterically and unashamedly, and when she saw him coming she began to run, holding up her skirts so that she would not fall.

And, when she could talk, through her tears and the rough material of his shirt, all she could say was: "Damn you. Damn you. If you ever put me through that again . . ."

Her hair was smooth under his callused hand, and her body warm against his own. He'd put her through the same torment again because he was a lawman now and couldn't help himself. But perhaps between times he could make it up to her. His arms tightened, and he held her very close.

About the Author

Lewis B. Patten wrote more than ninety Western novels in thirty years, and three of them won Spur Awards from the Western Writers of America, and the author received the Golden Saddleman Award. Indeed, this points up the most remarkable aspect of his work: not that there is so much of it, but that so much of it is so fine. Patten was born in Denver, Colorado, and served in the U.S. Navy, 1933-1937. He was educated at the University of Denver during the war years and became an auditor for the Colorado Department of Revenue during the 1940s. It was in this period that he began contributing significantly to Western pulp magazines, fiction that was from the beginning fresh and unique and revealed Patten's lifelong concern with the sociological and psychological effects of group psychology on the frontier. He became a professional writer at the time of his first novel, *Massacre at White River* (1952). The dominant theme in much of his fiction is the notion of justice, and its opposite, injustice. In his first novel it has to do with exploitation of the Ute Indians, but as he matured as a writer he explored this theme with significant and poignant detail in small towns throughout the early West. Crimes, such as rape or lynching, are often at the center of his stories. When the values embodied in these small towns are examined closely, they are found to be wanting. Conformity is always easier than taking a stand. Yet, in Patten's view of the American West, there is usually a man or a woman who refuses to conform. Among his finest titles, always a difficult choice, are surely *A Death in Indian Wells* (1970) and *The Law at Cottonwood* (1978). No less noteworthy are his more recent Westerns, *Tincup in the Storm Country* (1996), *Trail to Vicksburg* (1997), *Death Rides the Denver Stage* (1999), *The Woman at Ox-Yoke* (2000), and *Ride the Red Trail* (2001), now all available in trade paperback and e-book editions from Amazon Publishing.

Center Point Large Print
600 Brooks Road / PO Box 1
Thorndike, ME 04986-0001 USA

(207) 568-3717

US & Canada:
1 800 929-9108
www.centerpointlargeprint.com